"LISTEN, DAMN YOU,"
TIFFANY CRIED...

It had started as an angry speech, but then she paused and looked straight into his eyes and Bond saw that her lashes were wet. Suddenly she flung an arm around his neck and her face was against his and she was saying: "Take care of yourself, James. I don't want to lose you."

And then she kissed him once hard and long on the lips.

"Now get away from me," she said fiercely and slammed the door.

IAN FLEMING'S

DIAMONDS ARE FOREVER

CHARTER BOOKS, NEW YORK

This Charter book contains the complete
text of the original hardcover edition.
It has been completely reset in a typeface
designed for easy reading, and was printed
from new film.

DIAMONDS ARE FOREVER

A Charter Book / published by arrangement with
Macmillan Publishing Company, Inc.

PRINTING HISTORY
Macmillan edition published 1956
Jove edition / April 1980
Berkley edition / May 1982
Charter edition / July 1987

ISBN: 1-55773-215-9

Charter Books are published by The Berkley Publishing Group,
200 Madison Avenue, New York, New York 10016.
The name "CHARTER" and the "C" logo
are trademarks belonging to Charter Communications, Inc.

PRINTED IN THE UNITED STATES OF AMERICA

20   19   18   17   16   15   14   13   12   11

TO
j.f.c.b.
AND *e.l.c*
AND TO THE MEMORY OF *w.w., jr.*
at saratoga, 1954 and 1955

CONTENTS

CHAPTER 1

The Pipe Line Opens

With its two fighting claws held forward like a wrestler's arms the big *pandenus* scorpion emerged with a dry rustle from the finger-sized hole under the rock.

There was a small patch of hard flat earth outside the hole, and the scorpion stood in the centre of this on the tips of its four pairs of legs, its nerves and muscles braced for a quick retreat and its senses questing for the minute vibrations which would decide its next move.

The moonlight, glittering down through the great thornbush, threw sapphire highlights off the hard black polish of the six-inch body and glinted palely on the moist white sting which protruded from the last segment of the tail, now curved over parallel with the scorpion's flat back.

Slowly the sting slid home into its sheath and the nerves in the poison sac at its base relaxed. The scorpion had decided. Greed had won over fear.

Twelve inches away, at the bottom of a sharp slope of sand, the small beetle was concerned only with trudging on towards better pastures than he had found under the thornbush, and the swift rush of the scorpion down the slope gave him no time to open his wings. The beetle's legs waved in protest as the sharp claw snapped around his body, and then the sting lanced into him from over the scorpion's head and immediately he was dead.

After it had killed the beetle, the scorpion stood motionless for nearly five minutes. During this time it identified the nature of its prey and again tested the ground and the air for hostile vibrations. Reassured, its fighting claw withdrew from the half severed beetle and its two small feeding pincers reached out and into the beetle's flesh. Then for an hour, and with extreme fastidiousness, the scorpion ate its victim.

The great thornbush under which the scorpion killed the beetle was a landmark in the wide expanse of rolling veldt some forty miles south of Kissidougou in the southwestern corner of French Guinea. On all horizons there were hills and jungle, but here, over twenty square miles, there was flat rocky ground which was almost desert; and amongst the tropical scrub only this one thornbush, perhaps because there was water deep beneath its roots, had grown to the height of a house and could be seen many miles away.

The bush grew more or less at the junction of three African states. It was in French Guinea, but only about ten miles north of the northernmost tip of Liberia and five miles east of the frontier of Sierra Leone. Across this frontier are the great diamond mines around Sefadu. These are the property of Sierra International, which is part of the powerful mining empire of Afric International, which in turn is a rich capital asset of the British Commonwealth.

An hour earlier, in its hole among the roots of the great thornbush, the scorpion had been alerted by two sets of vibrations. First there had been the tiny scraping of the beetle's movements, and these belonged to the vibrations which the scorpion immediately recognised and diagnosed. Then there had been a series of incomprehensible thuds round the bush followed by a final heavy quake which had caved in part of the scorpion's hole. These were followed by a soft rhythmic trembling of the ground which was so regular that it soon became a background vibration of no urgency. After a pause the tiny scraping of the beetle had continued, and it was greed for the beetle that, after a day of sheltering from its deadliest enemy, the sun, finally got the upper hand against the scorpion's memory of the other noises and impelled it out of its lair into the filtering moonlight.

And now, as it slowly sucked the morsels of beetle flesh off its feeding pincers, the signal for the scorpion's own death sounded from far away on the eastern horizon, audible to a human, but made up of vibrations which were far outside the range of the scorpion's sensory system.

A few feet away, a heavy, blunt hand, with bitten fingernails, slowly raised a jagged piece of rock.

There was no noise, but the scorpion felt a tiny movement in the air above it. At once its fighting claws were up and groping and its sting was erect in the rigid tail, its near-sighted eyes staring up for a glimpse of the enemy.

The heavy stone came down.

"Black bastard."

The man watched as the broken insect whipped in its death agony.

The man yawned and got to his knees in the sandy depression against the trunk of the bush where he had been sitting for nearly two hours and, his arms bent protectingly over his head, scrambled out into the open.

The noise of the engine which the man had been waiting for and which had signed the scorpion's death warrant was louder. As the man stood and stared up the path of the moon, he could just make out a clumsy black shape coming fast towards him out of the east, and for a moment the moonlight glinted on whirling rotor blades.

The man rubbed his hands down the sides of his dirty khaki shorts and moved quickly around the bush to where the rear wheel of a battered motorcycle protruded from its hiding place. Below the pillion on either side were leather toolboxes. From one of these he extracted a small heavy package which he stowed inside his open shirt next to his skin. From the other he took four cheap flashlights. He then strode to an area fifty yards from the big thornbush where there was a clear patch of flat ground about the size of a tennis court. At three corners of the landing ground he screwed the butt end of a flashlight into the ground and switched it on. Then, the last one alight in his hand, he took up his position at the fourth corner and waited.

The helicopter was moving slowly towards him, not more than a hundred feet from the ground, the big rotor blades idling. It looked like a huge, badly constructed insect. To the man on the ground it seemed, as usual, to be making too much noise.

The helicopter paused, pitching slightly, directly over his head. An arm came out of the cockpit and a flashlight winked at him. It flashed dot-dash, the Morse for *A*.

The man on the ground flashed back a *B* and a *C*. He stuck the fourth torch into the ground and moved away, shielding his eyes against the coming whirl of dust. Above him the pitch of the rotor blades flattened imperceptibly and the helicopter settled smoothly into the space between the four flashlights. The clatter of the engines stopped with a final cough, the tail rotor spun briefly in neutral, and the main rotor blades completed a few awkward revolutions and then drooped to a halt.

In the echoing silence a cricket started to zing in the thornbush, and from somewhere nearby came the anxious chirrup of a nightbird.

After a pause to let the dust settle, the pilot banged open the door of the cockpit, pushed out a small aluminum ladder and climbed stiffly to the ground. He waited beside his machine while the other man walked around the four corners of the landing ground picking up and dowsing the flashlights. The pilot was half an hour late at the rendezvous and he was bored at the prospect of listening to the other man's inevitable com-

plaint. He despised all Afrikaners. This one in particular. To a Reichsdeutscher and a Luftwaffe pilot who
had fought under Galland in defense of the Reich they
were a bastard race—sly, stupid and ill-bred. Of course,
this brute had a tricky job, but it was nothing to
navigating a helicopter five hundred miles over jungle in
the middle of the night, and then taking it back again.

As the other man approached, the pilot half raised his
hand in greeting. "Everything all right?"

"I hope so. But you're late again. I shall only just
make it through the frontier by first light."

"Magneto trouble. We all have our worries. Thank
God there are only twelve full moons a year. Well, if
you've got the stuff let's have it and we'll tank her up
and I'll be off."

Without speaking the man from the diamond mines
reached into his shirt and handed over the neat, heavy
packet.

The pilot took it. It was damp with sweat from the
smuggler's ribs. The pilot dropped it into a side pocket
of his trim bushshirt, then wiped his fingers fastidiously
on the seat of his shorts.

"Good," he said. He moved towards his machine.

"Just a moment," said the diamond smuggler. There
was a sullen note in his voice.

The pilot turned back and faced him. He thought: It's
the voice of a servant who has screwed himself up to
complain about his food. "*Ja*. What is it?"

"Things are getting too hot. At the mines. I don't like
it at all. There's been a big intelligence man down from
London. You've read about him. This man Sillitoe.
They say he's been hired by the Diamond Corporation.
There've been a lot of new regulations, and all punish-
ments have been doubled. It's frightened out some of
my smaller men. I had to be ruthless and, well, one of
them somehow fell into the crusher. That tightened
things up a bit. But I've had to pay more. An extra 10
per cent. And they're still not satisfied. One of these
days those security people are going to get one of my
middlemen. And you know these black swine. They

can't stand a real beating." He looked swiftly into the pilot's eyes and then away again. "For the matter of that I doubt if anyone could stand the sjambok. Not even me."

"So?" said the pilot. He paused. "Do you want me to pass this threat back to A B C?"

"I'm not threatening anyone," said the other man hastily. "I just want them to know that it's getting tough. They must know it themselves. They must know about this man Sillitoe. And look what the chairman said in his annual report. He said that our mines were losing more than two million pounds a year through smuggling and I.D.B. and that it was up to the Government to stop it. And what does that mean? It means 'stop me'!"

"And me," said the pilot mildly. "So what do you want? More money?"

"Yes," said the other man stubbornly. "I want a bigger cut. Twenty per cent more or I'll have to quit." He tried to read some sympathy in the pilot's face.

"All right," said the pilot indifferently. "I'll pass the message on to Dakar, and if they're interested I expect they'll send it on to London. But it's nothing to do with me, and if I were you"—the pilot unbent for the first time—"I wouldn't put too much pressure on these people. They can be much tougher than this Sillitoe, or the company, or any government I've ever heard of. On just this end of the pipe line three men have died in the last twelve months—one for being yellow, two for stealing from the packet. And you know it. That was a nasty accident your predecessor had, wasn't it? Funny place to keep gelignite, under his bed. Unlike him. He was always so careful about everything."

For a moment they stood and looked at each other in the moonlight. The diamond smuggler shrugged his shoulders. "All right," he said. "Just tell them I'm hard up and need more money to pass down the line. They'll understand that, and if they've got any sense they'll add another 10 per cent on for me. If not . . ." He left the sentence unfinished and moved towards the helicopter. "Come on. I'll give you a hand with the gas."

Ten minutes later the pilot climbed up into the cockpit and pulled the ladder in after him. Before he shut the door he raised a hand. "So long," he said. "See you in a month."

The man on the ground suddenly felt lonely. "Tot siens," he said with a wave of the hand, almost the wave of a lover. "Alles van die beste." He stood back and again shielded his eyes against the dust.

The pilot settled into his seat and fastened the seatbelt, feeling for the rudder pedals with his feet. He made sure that the wheel brakes were on, pushed the pitch-control lever all the way down, turned on the fuel and pressed the starter. Satisfied with the beat of the engine, he released the rotor brake and softly twisted the throttle on the pitch control. Outside the cabin windows the long rotor blades slowly swung by, and the pilot glanced astern at the whirring tail rotor. He watched the rotor speed indicator creep up to 200 rpm. When the needle was just over 200 he released the wheel brakes and pulled up slowly and firmly on the pitch lever. Above him the blades of the rotor tilted and bit deeper into the air. More throttle, and the machine slowly rose clattering towards the sky until, at about 100 feet, the pilot simultaneously gave it left rudder and pushed forward the joystick between his knees.

The helicopter swung towards the east, gathering height and speed, and roared away back up the path of the moon.

The man on the ground watched it go and with it the £100,000 worth of diamonds his men had filched from the diggings during the past month and had casually held out on their pink tongues as he stood beside the dentist's chair and brusquely inquired where it hurt.

Still talking about their teeth, he would pick the stones out of their mouths and hold them up to the dentist's spotlight; then softly he would say 50, 75, 100, and they always nodded and took the notes and hid them in their clothes and went out of the surgery with a couple of aspirin in a twist of paper as an alibi. They had to accept his price. There was no hope of a native getting diamonds out. When the miners did get away, perhaps once a year to visit their tribe or to bury a relative, there was a whole routine of X-rays and castor oil to be gone through, and a grim future if they were caught stealing. It was so easy to go to the dental surgery and pick the day when "Him" was on duty. Paper money didn't show up on X-rays.

The man wheeled his motorcycle over the rough ground on to the narrow trail and started off towards the frontier hills of Sierra Leone. They were more distinct now. He would only just have time to get to Susie's hut before dawn. He grimaced at the thought of having to make love to her at the end of such an exhausting night. But it would have to be done. Money was not enough to pay for the alibi she gave him. It was his white body she wanted. And then another ten miles to the club for breakfast and the coarse jokes of his friends.

"Do a nice bit in inlay, Doc?" "I hear she has the best set of frontals in the Province." "Say, Doc, just what is it the full moon does to you?"

But each £100,000 worth meant £1,000 for him in a London safety deposit box. Nice crisp fivers. It was worth it. By God it was! But not for much longer. At £20,000 he would definitely quit. And then?

His mind full of lush dreams, the man on the motorcycle bumped his way as fast as he could across the plain and away from the great thornbush where the pipe line for the richest smuggling operation in the world started its devious route to where it would finally flow out onto soft bosoms five thousand miles away.

Gem Quality

"Don't push it in. *Screw* it in," said M impatiently.

James Bond, making a mental note to pass M's dictum on to the Chief of Staff, again picked up the jeweller's glass from the desk where it had fallen and this time managed to fix it securely into the socket of his right eye.

Although it was late July and the room was bright with sunshine, M had switched on his desk light and tilted it so that it shone straight at Bond. Bond picked the brilliant-cut stone up and held it to the light. As he turned it between his fingers, all the colours of the spectrum flashed back at him from its mesh of facets until his eyes stung with the dazzle.

He took out the jeweller's glass and tried to think of something appropriate to say.

M looked at him quizzically. "Fine stone?"

"Remarkable," said Bond. "It must be worth a lot of money."

"A few pounds for the cutting," said M drily. "It's a

bit of quartz. Now then, let's try again." He consulted a list on the desk in front of him and selected a fold of tissue paper, verified the number written on it, unfolded it and pushed it across to Bond.

Bond put the piece of quartz back into its own wrapping and picked up the second sample.

"It's easy for you, sir." He smiled at M. "You've got the crib." He screwed the glass back into his eye and held the stone, if it was a stone, up to the light.

This time, he thought, there could be no doubt about it. This stone also had the thirty-two facets above and the twenty-four below of the brilliant-cut, and it was also about twenty carats, but what he now held had a heart of blue-white flame, and the infinite colours reflected and refracted out of its depths lanced into his eye like needles. With his left hand he picked up the quartz dummy and held it beside the diamond in front of his glass. It was a lifeless chunk of matter, almost opaque beside the dazzling translucence of the diamond, and the rainbow colours he had seen a few minutes before were now coarse and muddy.

Bond put down the piece of quartz and gazed again into the heart of the diamond. Now he could understand the passion that diamonds had inspired down through the centuries, the almost sexual love they aroused among those who handled them and cut them and traded in them. It was domination by a beauty so pure that it held a kind of truth, a divine authority before which all other material things turned, like the bit of quartz, to clay. In these few minutes Bond understood the myth of diamonds, and he knew that he would never forget what he had suddenly seen inside the heart of this stone.

He put the diamond down on its slip of paper and dropped the jeweller's glass into the palm of his hand. He looked across in M's watchful eyes. "Yes," he said. "I see."

M sat back in his chair. "That's what Jacoby meant when I had lunch with him the other day at the

Diamond Corporation. He said that if I was going to get involved in the diamond business I ought to try to understand what was really at the bottom of it all. Not just the billions of money involved, or the value of diamonds as a hedge against inflation, or the sentimental fashions in diamonds for engagement rings, and so forth. He said one must understand the passion for diamonds. So he just showed me what I'm showing you. And''—M smiled thinly at Bond—"if it will give you any satisfaction, I was just as taken in by that bit of quartz as you were.''

Bond sat still and said nothing.

"And now let's run through the rest," said M. He gestured towards the pile of paper packets in front of him. "I said I'd like to borrow some samples. They didn't seem to mind. Sent this lot round to my house this morning." M consulted his list, opened a packet and pushed it across to Bond. "What you were looking at just now was the best—a 'Fine Blue-White.' " He gestured towards the big diamond in front of Bond. "Now this is a 'Top Crystal,' ten carats, baguette-cut. Very fine stone, but worth only about half the 'Blue-White.' You'll see there's the faintest trace of yellow in it. The 'Cape' I'm going to show you next has a slight brownish tinge according to Jacoby, but I'm damned if I can see it. I doubt if anyone can except the experts.''

Bond obediently picked up the "Top Crystal," and for the next quarter of an hour M led him through the whole range of diamonds down to a wonderful series of coloured stones, ruby red, blue, pink, yellow, green and violet. Finally M pushed over a packet of smaller stones, all flawed or marked or of poor colour. "Industrial diamonds. Not what they call 'gem quality.' Used in machine tools, and so forth. But don't despise them. America bought £5,000,000 worth of them last year, and that's only one of the markets. Bronsteen told me it was stones like these that were used for cutting the Saint-Gothard Tunnel. At the other end of the scale, dentists use them for drilling your teeth. They're the hardest substance in the world. Last forever." M pulled out his pipe and started to fill it. "And now you know as much about diamonds as I do."

Bond sat back in his chair and gazed vaguely at the bits of tissue paper and glittering stones that lay scattered across the red leather surface of M's desk. He wondered what it was all about.

There was the rasp of a match against a box, and Bond watched M tamp the burning tobacco down in the bowl of his pipe and then put the matchbox back in his pocket and tilt his chair in his favourite attitude for reflection.

Bond glanced down at his watch. It was 11:30. He thought with pleasure of the In-tray piled with Top Secret dockets he had gladly abandoned when the red telephone had summoned him an hour before. He felt fairly confident that now he wouldn't have to deal with them. "I guess it's a job," the Chief of Staff had said in answer to Bond's inquiry. "The Chief says he won't take any more calls before lunch and he's made an appointment for you at the Yard for two o'clock. Step on it." And Bond had reached for his coat and had gone into the outer office where he was pleased to see his secretary registering in another bulky file with a "Most Immediate" tab.

"M," said Bond as she looked up. "And Bill says it looks like a job. So don't think you're going to have the pleasure of shovelling that lot into my In-tray. You can post it off to the *Daily Express* for all I care." He grinned at her. "Isn't Sefton Delmer a boy friend of yours, Lil? Just the stuff for him, I expect."

She looked at him appraisingly. "Your tie's crooked," she said coldly. "I hardly know him." She bent over her registry, and Bond went out and along the corridor and thought how lucky he was to have a beautiful secretary.

There was a creak from M's chair, and Bond looked across the table at the man who held a great deal of his affection and all of his loyalty and obedience.

The grey eyes looked back at him thoughtfully. M took the pipe out of his mouth. "How long have you been back from that holiday in France?"

"Two weeks, sir."

"Have a good time?"

"Not bad, sir. Got a bit bored towards the end."

M made no comment. "I've been looking at your record sheet. Small-arms marks seem to be keeping well up in the top bracket. Unarmed combat's satisfactory, and your last medical shows you're in pretty good shape." M paused. "The point is," he went on unemotionally, "I've got rather a tough assignment for you. Wanted to make sure you'd be able to take care of yourself."

"Of course, sir." Bond was slightly nettled.

"Don't make any mistake about this job," said M sharply. "When I say it may be tough, I'm not being melodramatic. There are plenty of tricky people you haven't met yet, and there may be some of them mixed up in this business. Some of the most efficient. So don't be tetchy when I think twice before getting you involved in it."

"Sorry, sir."

"All right, then." M put his pipe down and leaned forward with his arms crossed on the desk. "I'll tell you the story and then you can decide whether you want to take it on. A week ago one of the high-ups in Treasury came to see me. Brought the Permanent Secretary to the Board of Trade with him. It had to do with diamonds. Seems that most of what they call 'gem' diamonds in the world are mined on British territory and that 90 per cent of all diamond sales are carried out in London. By the Diamond Corporation." M shrugged his shoulders. "Don't ask me why. The British got hold of the business at the beginning of the century and we've managed to hang on to it. Now it's a huge trade. Fifty million pounds a year. The biggest dollar-earner we've got. So when something goes wrong with it the Government gets worried. And that's what's happened." M looked

mildly across at Bond. "At least two million pounds'
worth of diamonds are being smuggled out of Africa
every year."

"That's a lot of money," said Bond. "Where are they
going to?"

"They say America," said M. "And I agree with
them. It's by far the biggest diamond market. And those
gangs of theirs are the only people who could run an
operation on this scale."

"Why don't the mining companies stop it?"

"They've done everything they can," said M. "You
probably saw in the papers that De Beers took on our
friend Sillitoe when he left MI5, and he's out there now,
working with the South African security people. I
gather he's put in a pretty drastic report and come up
with plenty of bright ideas for tightening things up, but
the Treasury and the Board of Trade aren't very impressed. They think the thing's too big to be handled by
a lot of separate mining companies, however efficient
they may be. And they've got one very good reason for
wanting to take official action on their own."

"What's that, sir?"

"There's a big packet of smuggled stones in London
at this very moment," said M, and his eyes glittered
across the desk at Bond. "Waiting to go to America.
And the Special Branch knows who the carrier is to be.
They also know who's to go out with him to keep an eye
on him. As soon as Ronnie Vallance came across the
story—it was leaked to one of his stool pigeons in
Soho—he went straight off with it to the Treasury. The
Treasury talked to the Board of Trade and then both
their Ministers formed up to the Prime Minister. And
the P.M. gave them authority to use the Service."

"Why not let the Special Branch or M15 handle it,
sir?" asked Bond, reflecting that M seemed to be going
through a bad phase of mixing in other people's
business.

"Of course, they could arrest the carriers as soon as
they took delivery and tried to get out of the country,"
said M impatiently. "But that won't stop the traffic.

These people aren't the sort that talk. Anyway, the carriers are only small fry. They probably just get the stuff from a man in a park and hand it over to another man in a park when they get to the other side. The only way to get to the bottom of the business is to follow the pipe line to America and see where it goes to there. And the F.B.I. won't be much help to us, I'm afraid. It's a very small part of their battle with the big-time crooks. And it's not doing any harm to the United States. Rather the reverse, if anything. It's only England that's the loser. Furthermore, America is outside the jurisdiction of the police and the MI5. Only the Service can handle the job."

"Yes, I see that," said Bond. "But have we got anything else to go on?"

"Ever heard of 'The House of Diamonds'?"

"Yes, of course, sir," said Bond. "The big American jewellers. On West Forty-sixth Street in New York and the Rue de Rivoli in Paris. I gather they rank almost as high as Cartier and Van Cleef and Boucheron nowadays. They've come up very quickly since the war."

"Yes," said M. "Those are the people. They've got a small place in London too. Hatton Garden. Used to be very big buyers at the monthly showings of the Diamond Corporation. But for the last three years they've bought less and less. Although, as you say, they seem to be selling more and more jewellery every year. Must be getting their diamonds from somewhere. It was the Treasury who brought their name up at our meeting the other day. But I can't uncover anything against them. They've got one of their biggest men in charge over here. Seems odd, as they do so little business. Man called Rufus B. Saye. Nothing much known about him. Lunches every day at the American Club in Piccadilly. Plays golf at Sunningdale. Doesn't drink or smoke. Lives at the Savoy. Model citizen." M shrugged his shoulders again. "But the diamond business is a nice, well regulated sort of family affair, and there's an impression that the House of Diamonds has an awkward look about it. Nothing more than that."

Bond decided it was time to put the jackpot question. "And where do I come in, sir?" he asked.

"You've got an appointment with Vallance at the Yard in"—M looked at his watch—"just over an hour. He's going to start you off. They're going to pull in this carrier tonight and put you into the pipe line instead of him."

Bond's fingers tightened slightly on the arms of his chair.

"And then?"

"And then," said M matter-of-factly, "you're going to smuggle those diamonds into America. At least that's the idea. What do you think of it?"

Hot Ice

James Bond shut the door of M's office behind him. He smiled into the warm brown eyes of Miss Moneypenny and walked across her office into the Chief of Staff's room.

The Chief of Staff, a lean relaxed man of about Bond's age, put down his pen and sat back in his chair. He watched as Bond automatically reached for the flat gunmetal cigarette case in his hip pocket and walked over to the open window and looked down into Regent's Park.

The thoughtful deliberation of Bond's movements answered the Chief of Staff's unspoken question.

"So you've bought it."

Bond turned around. "Yes," he said. He lit a cigarette. Through the smoke his eyes looked very directly at the Chief of Staff. "But just tell me this, Bill. Why's the old man got cold feet about this job? He's even looked up the results of my last medical. What's he so worried about? It's not as if this was Iron Curtain business. America's a civilised country. What's eating him?"

It was the Chief of Staff's duty to know most of what went on in M's mind. His own cigarette had gone out and he lit another and threw the spent match over his left shoulder. He looked around to see whether it had fallen in the wastepaper basket. It had. He smiled up at Bond. "Constant practice," he said. Then: "There aren't many things that worry M, James; you know that as well as anybody in the Service. SMERSH, of course. The German cypher-breakers. The Chinese opium ring—or at any rate the power they have all over the world. The authority of the Mafia. And—and he's got a damned healthy respect for them—American gangsters. The big ones. This diamond business looks as if it's pretty certain to bring you up against those gangsters. They're the last people he expected us to get mixed up with. He's got quite enough on his plate without them. That's what's giving him cold feet about this job. That's all."

"There's nothing so extraordinary about American gangsters," said Bond. "Anyway, they're not really Americans. Mostly a lot of Italian bums with mono-grammed shirts who spend the day eating spaghetti and meatballs and squirting scent all over themselves."

"That's what you think," said the Chief of Staff. "Those are only the ones you see. There are bigger ones behind them and still bigger ones behind those. Look at narcotics. Ten million addicts. Where do they get the stuff from? Look at gambling—legitimate gambling. Two hundred and fifty million dollars a year is the take at Las Vegas. Then there are the undercover games at Miami and Chicago, and so on. All owned and run by the underworld. A few years ago Buggsy Siegel got the back of his head blown off because he wanted too much of the take from the Las Vegas operation. And he was tough enough. These are big operations, James. Do you realize that gambling is the biggest single industry in America? Bigger than steel. Bigger than motor cars. And they take damned good care to keep it running smoothly. Get hold of the Kefauver Report if you don't believe me. Now these diamonds. Six million dollars a year is good money, and you can bet your life it'll be well protected." The Chief of Staff paused. He looked impatiently up at the tall figure in the dark blue single-breasted suit and into the obstinate eyes in the lean brown face. "Perhaps you haven't read the F.B.I. report on American crime for this year. Interesting. Just thirty-four murders every day. That's why M wanted to make sure you were fit before he put you into the pipe line. You're going to take these criminals on. And you'll be on your own. Satisfied?"

Bond's face relaxed. "Come on, Bill," he said. "If that's all there is to it, I'll buy you lunch. It's my turn, and I feel like celebrating. No more paperwork this summer. I'll take you to Scotts' and we'll have some of their dressed crab and a pint of black velvet. You've taken a load off my mind. I thought there might be something wrong with this job."

"All right, damn you." The Chief of Staff followed Bond out of the office, slamming the door with unnecessary force behind him.

Later, punctually at two o'clock, Bond was shaking hands with the dapper, level-eyed man in the old-fashioned office which hears more secrets than any other room in Scotland Yard. Bond had made friends with Assistant Commissioner Vallance over the Moonraker affair, and there was no need to waste time on preliminaries.

Vallance pushed a couple of C.I.D. identification photographs across the desk. They showed a dark-haired, rather good-looking young man with a clean-cut swashbuckling face.

"That's the chap," said Vallance. "Near enough like you to pass with someone who's only got his description. Peter Franks. Nice-looking fellow. Good family. Public school and all that. Then he went wrong and stayed wrong. Country-house burglaries are his line. May have been in on the Duke of Windsor job at Sunningdale a few years ago. We've pulled him in once or twice, but we could never get anything to stick. Now he's slipped up. They often do when they get into a racket they know nothing about. I've got two or three undercover girls in Soho, and he's keen on one of them. Funnily enough she's rather keen on him. Thinks she can make him go straight and all that sort of stuff. But she's got her job to do, and when he told her about this job, just casually, as if it was the hell of a lark, she passed the word back here."

Bond nodded. "Specialist crooks never take other people's lines seriously. I bet he wouldn't have talked to her about one of his country-house jobs."

"Not on your life," agreed Vallance. "Or we'd have had him inside years ago. Anyway, it seems he was contacted by a friend of a friend and agreed to do a smuggling job to America for $5,000. Payable on delivery. My girl asked him if it was drugs. And he laughed and said no—better still, 'hot ice.' Had he got the diamonds? No. His next job was to contact his 'guard.' Tomorrow evening at the Trafalgar Palace. Five o'clock in her room. A girl called Case. She would tell him what to do and go over with him." Vallance got up and paced to and fro in front of the framed forgeries of five-pound notes that lined the wall opposite the windows. "These smugglers generally go in pairs when big stuff is being moved. The carrier is never quite trusted, and the men at the other end like to have a witness in case anything goes wrong at the customs. Then the big men don't get caught napping if the carrier talks."

Big stuff being moved. Carriers. Customs. Guards. Bond killed his cigarette in the ashtray on Vallance's desk. How often in his early days in his own Service had he been part of this same routine—through Strasbourg into Germany, through Niegoreloye into Russia, over the Simplon, across the Pyrenees? The tension. The dry mouth. The nails ground into the palms of the hands. And now, having graduated away from all that, here he was going through it again.

"Yes, I see," said Bond, dodging his memories. "But what's the general picture? Got any ideas? What sort of operation was Franks going to fit into?"

"Well the diamonds certainly come from Africa."
Vallance's eyes were opaque. "Probably not the Union
mines. More likely the big leak out of Sierra Leone our
friend Sillitoe's been looking for. Then the stones may
get out through Liberia or more likely French Guinea.
Then perhaps into France. And since this packet's
turned up in London, presumably London's part of the
pipe line too."

Vallance stopped pacing and faced Bond. "And now
we know that this packet is on its way to America, and
what happens to it there is anybody's guess. The
operators wouldn't try and save money on the cutting—that's where half the price of a diamond goes—so
it looks as if the stones get funnelled into some
legitimate diamond business and then get cut and
marketed like any other stones." Vallance paused.
"You won't take it amiss if I give you a bit of advice?"

"Don't be ridiculous."

"Well," said Vallance, "in all these jobs the payoff
to subordinates is generally the weakest link. How was
this $5,000 to be paid to Peter Franks? Who by? And if
he did the job successfully, would he be taken on again?
If I were in your shoes I'd watch these points. Con-
centrate on getting through the cutout who does the
paying off and try to get further up the pipe line towards
the big men. If they like the look of you it shouldn't be
difficult. Good carriers aren't easy to come by, and even
the top men are going to be interested in the new
recruit."

"Yes," said Bond thoughtfully, "that makes sense.
The main thing will be to get past the first contact in
America. Let's hope the whole job doesn't blow up in
my face in the customs shed at Idlewild. I'll look pretty
silly if the Inspectoscope picks me up. But I expect this
Case woman will have some bright ideas about actually
carrying the stuff. And now what's the first step? How
are you going to substitute me for Peter Franks?"

Vallance started pacing again. "I think that ought to
be all right," he said. "We're going to take in Franks
this evening and hold him for conspiring to evade the

customs." He smiled briefly. "It'll break up a beautiful friendship with my girl, I'm afraid. But that's got to be faced. And then, the idea is for you to make the rendezvous with Miss Case."

"Does she know anything about Franks?"

"Just his description and his name," said Vallance. "At least that's what we guess. I doubt if she even knows the man who contacted him. Cutouts all along the line. Everybody does one job in a watertight compartment. Then if there's a hole in the sock it doesn't run."

"Know anything about the woman?"

"Passport details. American citizen. Twenty-seven. Born San Francisco. Blonde. Blue eyes. Height five foot six. Profession: single woman. Been over here a dozen times in the last three years. May have been more often under a different name. Always stays at the Trafalgar Palace. The hotel detective says she doesn't seem to go out much. Few visitors. Never stays more than two weeks. Never gives any trouble. That's all. Don't forget that when you meet her you'll have to have a good story yourself. Why you're doing the job, and so on."

"I'll see to that."

"Anything else we can help over?"

Bond reflected. The rest seemed to be up to him. Once he had got into the pipe it would just be a question of improvising. Then he remembered the jewellery firm. "What about this House of Diamonds lead the Treasury dreamed up? Seems a long shot. Any views?"

"Quite honestly I hadn't bothered with them." There was apology in Vallance's voice. "I checked on this man Saye, but again it's a blank except for his passport details. American. Forty-five. Diamond merchant. And so on. He goes to Paris a lot. Been going once a month for the last three years as a matter of fact. Probably got a girl there. Tell you what. Why not go along and have a look at the place and at him? You never can tell."

"How would I go about that?" asked Bond dubiously.

Vallance didn't answer. Instead he pressed a switch

on the big intercom on his desk.

"Yes, sir?" said a metallic voice.

"Send up Dankwaerts at the double, Sergeant. And Lobiniere. Then get me the House of Diamonds on the phone. Gem merchants in Hatton Garden. Ask for Mr. Saye."

Vallance went to the window and stood looking out at the river. He took a cigarette lighter out of his waistcoat pocket and flicked at it absent-mindedly. There was a knock on the door, and Vallance's staff secretary poked his head in. "Sergeant Dankwaerts, sir."

"Send him in," said Vallance. "Hold Lobiniere until I ring."

The secretary held open the door, and a nondescript man in plain-clothes came in. His hair was thinning, he wore spectacles and his complexion was pale. His expression was kindly and studious. He might have been any senior clerk in any respectable business.

"Afternoon, Sergeant," said Vallance. "This is Commander Bond of the Ministry of Defence." The sergeant smiled politely. "I want you to take Commander Bond to the House of Diamonds in Hatton Garden. He will be 'Sergeant James' of your staff. You think the diamonds from that Ascot job are on their way out to the Argentine through America. You will say so to Mr. Saye, the top man there. You will wonder if it is possible that Mr. Saye has heard any talk from the other side. His New York office may have heard something. You know, all very nice and polite. But just look him in the eye. Put as much pressure on as you can without giving any grounds for complaint. Then apologise and leave and forget all about it. All right? Any questions?"

"No, sir," said Sergeant Dankwaerts stolidly.

Vallance spoke into the intercom, and a moment later there appeared a sallow, rather obsequious man wearing extremely smart plain-clothes and carrying a small attaché case. He stood waiting just inside the door.

"Good afternoon, Sergeant. Come and have a look at this friend of mine."

The sergeant came and stood close to Bond and turned him politely towards the light. Two very keen dark eyes studied his face carefully for a full minute. Then the man stepped away.

"Can't guarantee the scar for more than six hours sir," he said. "Not in this heat. But the rest's all right. Who is he to be, sir?"

"He's to be Sergeant James, a member of Sergeant Dankwaerts' staff." Vallance looked at his watch. "Only for three hours. All right?"

"Certainly, sir. Shall I go ahead?" At Vallance's nod, he led Bond to a chair by the window, put his small attaché case on the floor beside the chair, knelt down on one knee and opened it. Then for ten minutes his deft fingers busied themselves over Bond's face and hair.

Bond resigned himself and listened to Vallance talking to the House of Diamonds. "Not until 3:30? In that case would you please tell Mr. Saye that two of my men will be calling on him at 3:30 sharp. Yes, I'm afraid it is rather important. Only a formality, of course. Routine inquiry. I don't expect it will take up more than ten minutes of Mr. Saye's time. Thank you so much. Yes. Assistant Commissioner Vallance. That's right. Scotland Yard. Yes. Thank you. Goodbye."

Vallance put back the receiver and turned towards Bond. "Secretary says Saye won't be back until 3:30. I suggest you get there at 3:15. Never does any harm to have a look round first. Always useful to get your man a bit off balance. How's it going?"

Sergeant Lobiniere held up a pocket mirror in front of Bond.

A touch of white at the temples. The scar gone. A hint of studiousness at the corners of the eyes and mouth. The faintest shadows under the cheekbones. Nothing you could put your finger on, but it all added up to someone who certainly wasn't James Bond.

"What's This All About?"

In the patrol car Sergeant Dankwaerts was occupied with his thoughts, and they drove in silence along the Strand and up Chancery Lane and into Holborn. At Gamages they turned left into Hatton Garden, and the car drew up near the neat white portals of the London Diamond Club.

Bond followed his companion across the pavement to a smart door in the centre of which was a well polished, engraved brass plate reading, "The House of Diamonds." And underneath, "Rufus B. Saye, Vice-President for Europe." Sergeant Dankwaerts rang the bell, and after a moment a smart-looking brunette opened the door and led them across a thickly carpeted entrance hall into a panelled waiting room.

"I am expecting Mr. Saye any minute now," she said indifferently, and went out, closing the door behind her.

The waiting room was luxurious and, thanks to an unseasonable log fire in the Adam fireplace, tropically hot. In the centre of the close-fitted dark red carpet were a circular Sheraton rosewood table and six matching armchairs that Bond guessed were worth at least a thousand pounds. On the table were the latest magazines and several copies of the Johannesburg *Diamond News*. Dankwaerts' eyes lit up when he saw these, and he sat down and started to leaf through the pages of the June issue.

On each of the four walls was a large flower painting in a golden frame. Something almost three-dimensional about the paintings caught Bond's attention, and he walked over to examine one of them. It was not a painting, but a stylised arrangement of freshly cut flowers set behind glass in niches lined with copper-coloured velvet. The others were the same, and the four Waterford vases in which the flowers stood were a perfect set.

The room was very quiet except for the hypnotic tick of a large sunburst wall clock and the soft murmur of voices from behind a door opposite the entrance. There was a click and the door opened a few inches and a voice with a thick foreign intonation expostulated volubly: "But, Mister Grunspan, why should you be so hard? A living we all have to make, yes? I am telling you this wonderful stone cost me ten tousant pounds. Ten tousant! You don't believe it? I'm telling you. My solemn word of honour." There was a negative pause and the voice made its final bid. "Bedder still! I bet you fife pounts!"

There was the sound of laughter. "Willy, you're a real card," said an American voice. "But it's no dice. Be glad to help you, but that stone isn't worth more than nine thousand and I'll give you a hundred on top of that for yourself. Now you go along and think about it. You won't get a better offer in The Street."

The door opened and a stage-American businessman with a paunch and a tightly buttoned mouth ushered out a small harassed-looking man with a large red rose in his lapel. They seemed surprised to find the waiting room occupied, and with a muttered "Pardon me" to no one in particular the American almost ran his companion across the room and out into the hall. The door closed behind them.

Dankwaerts winked at Bond and smiled. "That's the diamond business in a nutshell," he said. "That was Willy Behrens, one of the best known freelance brokers in The Street. I suppose the other man was Saye's buyer." He turned again to his paper, and Bond, resisting the impulse to light a cigarette, went back to his examination of the flower "pictures."

Suddenly the rich, carpeted, discreetly ticking silence of the room was broken. Simultaneously a log fell in the grate, the sunburst clock on the wall chimed the half-hour, the door was thrust open, and a big man took two quick steps into the room and stood looking sharply from one to the other.

"My name is Saye," he said harshly. "What's this all about?"

The door was open behind him. Sergeant Dankwaerts rose to his feet and walked politely but firmly around the man and closed it. Then he returned to the middle of the room.

"I am Sergeant Dankwaerts of the Special Branch of Scotland Yard," he said in a quiet, peaceable voice. "And this"—he nodded towards Bond—"is Sergeant James. I am making a routine inquiry about some stolen diamonds. It occurred to the Assistant Commissioner"—the voice was velvet—"that you might be able to help us."

"Yes?" said Mr. Saye. "Go ahead."

While Sergeant Dankwaerts spoke his piece in tones which to a lawbreaker would have sounded menacingly level, consulting from time to time a small black notebook, Bond made an unconcealed examination of Mr. Saye which appeared to affect Mr. Saye no more than the undertones of Sergeant Dankwaerts' recitation.

Mr. Saye was a large, compact man with the hardness of a chunk of quartz. He had a very square face whose sharp angles were accentuated by short, wiry black hair, cut *en brosse* and without sideburns. His eyebrows were

black and straight, and tucked in below them were two
extremely sharp and steady black eyes. He was clean-
shaven, and his lips were a thin and rather wide straight
line. The square chin was deeply cleft, and the muscles
bulged at the points of the jaw. He was dressed in a
roomy black single-breasted suit, a white shirt and an
almost bootlace-thin black tie held in place by a gold
tieclip representing a spear. His long arms hung relaxed
at his sides and terminated in two very large hands, now
slightly curled inwards, whose backs showed a
sprinkling of thick black hair. His feet, in expensive
black shoes, looked to be about size 12.

Bond summed him up as a tough and capable man
who had triumphed in a variety of hard schools and
looked as if he was still serving in one of them.

". . . and these are the stones we are particularly interested in," concluded Sergeant Dankwaerts. He
referred again to his black book. "One 20-carat
Wesselton. Two Fine Blue-Whites of about 10 carats
each. One 30-carat Yellow Premier. One 15-carat Top
Cape and two 15-carat Cape Unions." He paused. Then
he looked up from his book and very sharply into Mr.
Saye's hard black eyes. "Have any of those passed
through your hands Mr. Saye, or through your firm in
New York?" he asked softly.

"No," said Mr. Saye flatly. "They have not." He
turned to the door behind him and opened it. "And
now, good afternoon, gentlemen."

Without further ado he walked decisively out of the
room, and they heard his footsteps go rapidly up a few
stairs. A door opened and banged shut and there was
silence.

Undismayed, Sergeant Dankwaerts slipped his
notebook into his waistcoat pocket, picked up his hat
and walked into the hall and then out into the street.
Bond followed him.

They climbed into the patrol car and Bond gave the
address of his flat off the King's Road. When the car
was moving, Sergeant Dankwaerts relaxed his official
face. He turned to Bond. He looked amused. "I quite

enjoyed that," he said cheerfully. "Don't often meet a nut as tough as that one. Did you get what you wanted, sir?"

Bond shook his head. "Tell the truth, Sergeant, I didn't know exactly what I did want. But I was glad to get a good look at Mr. Rufus B. Saye. Quite a lad. Doesn't look much like my idea of a diamond merchant."

Sergeant Dankwaerts chuckled. "He's not a diamond merchant, sir," he said, "or I'll eat my credentials."

"How do you know?"

"When I read out that list of missing stones"—Sergeant Dankwaerts smiled happily—"I mentioned a Yellow Premier and Two Cape Unions."

"Yes?" said Bond.

"It just happens that there aren't such things, sir."

"Feuilles-Mortes"

Bond felt the elevator man watching him as he walked down the long quiet corridor to the end room, Room 350. Bond wasn't surprised. He knew there was more petty crime in this hotel than in any other large hotel in London. Vallance had once shown him the big monthly crime map of the city. He had pointed to the forest of little flags around the Trafalgar Palace. "That place annoys the map-room men," he had said. "Every month this corner gets so pitted with holes they have to paste fresh paper over it to hold the next month's pins."

As Bond neared the end of the corridor he could hear a piano swinging a rather sad tune. At the door of 350 he knew the music came from behind it. He recognised the tune: "Feuilles-Mortes." He knocked.

"Come in." The hall porter had telephoned up, and the occupant was waiting for him.

Bond walked into the small living-room and closed the door behind him.

"Lock it," said a woman's voice. It came from the bedroom.

Bond did as he was told and walked into the middle of the room until he was opposite the open bedroom door. As he passed the portable record player on the writing table the pianist began on "La Ronde."

She was sitting half naked, astride a chair in front of the dressing table, gazing across the back of the chair into the triple mirror. Her bare arms were folded along the tall back of the chair and her chin was resting on her arms. Her spine was arched and there was arrogance in the set of her head and shoulders. The thin black strap of her brassiere across the naked white back, the tight black lace pants and the angled thrust of her legs whipped at Bond's senses.

The girl raised her eyes from her own face and inspected Bond's in the mirror, briefly and coolly.

"So you're the new hired help," she said in a low, rather husky voice that made no commitment. "Have a chair. Relax. Enjoy the music."

Bond was amused. He obediently took the few steps to a deep armchair, moved it a little so that he could still see her through the doorway, and sat down.

"Mind if I smoke?" he said, taking out his case and putting a cigarette in his mouth.

"Not as long as it's tobacco."

Miss Case resumed the silent contemplation of her face in the mirror while the pianist played "J'attendrai."

When the record finished, she got up off the chair and turned indifferently toward Bond. The blond hair that fell heavily to her shoulders curved with the movement and caught the light.

"If you like it, turn it over," she said carelessly. "Be right with you." She moved slowly out of sight.

Bond walked over to the record player and picked up the record. It was George Feyer with rhythm accompaniment. He looked at the number and memorised it, thinking he would get it one day. It was Vox 500. He examined the other side and, skipping "La Vie en Rose" because it had memories for him, put the needle down at the beginning of "Avril au Portugal."

Before he left the phonograph he pulled the blotter from under it and held it up to the standard lamp beside the writing desk. He held it sideways under the light and glanced along it. It was unmarked. He shrugged his shoulders, slipped it back under the machine and returned to his chair.

He decided that the music was appropriate to the girl. It had her brazen sexiness, the insouciance of her manner and the melancholy that had been in her eyes as they had looked moodily back at him out of the mirror.

Bond had had no picture in his mind of the Miss Case who was to shadow him to America. He had taken for granted that she would be some tough, well used slattern with dead eyes, a hard, sullen woman who had gone the route and whose body was no longer of any interest to the men she worked for. This girl was tough, all right, in her self-containment; but whatever might be the history of her body, the skin had glowed with vitality under the light.

What was her first name? Bond got up again and walked over to the record player. There was a Pan-American Airways label attached to the handle that read, "Miss T. Case." T? Bond strolled back to his chair. Teresa? Tess? Thelma? Trudy? Tilly? None of them seemed to fit. Surely not Trixie or Toni or Tamara.

He was still toying with the problem when she appeared quietly in the doorway to the bedroom and stood with one elbow resting high up against the door-jamb, her head bent sideways on to her hand. She looked down at him reflectively.

Bond got unhurriedly to his feet and gazed back at her.

She was dressed for the street except for her hat, a small black affair that swung from her free hand. She wore a smart black tailor-made suit over an olive green shirt buttoned to the neck, golden-tan nylons and black square-toed crocodile shoes that looked extremely expensive. A slim gold wristwatch on a black strap adorned one wrist and a heavy gold chain bracelet the other. One large baguette-cut diamond flared on the third finger of her right hand, and a flat pearl earring in twisted gold showed on her right ear where the heavy pale gold hair swept away from it.

She was very beautiful in a casual sort of way, as if she kept her looks for herself and didn't care what men thought of them. There was an ironic tilt to the finely drawn eyebrows above the wide, level, rather scornful grey eyes that seemed to say: "Sure. Come ahead and try. But, brother, you'd better be good."

The eyes themselves had the rare quality of chatoyance. When jewels have chatoyance the colour in the lustre changes with movement in the light, and the colour of this girl's eyes seemed to vary between a light grey and a deep grey-blue.

Her skin was lightly tanned and without make-up except for a deep red on the lips, which were full and soft and rather sulky, giving the effect of what is called a "sinful mouth." But not, thought Bond, one that often sinned—if one was to judge by the level eyes and the hint of authority and independence that lay in their depths.

The eyes now looked impersonally into his.

"So you're Peter Franks," she said, and the voice was low and attractive, but with a touch of condescension.

"Yes," he said. "And I've been wondering what T. stands for."

She thought for a moment. "It stands for Tiffany." She walked over to the record player and stopped the record in the middle of "Je n'en connais pas la fin." She turned around. "But it's not in the public domain," she added coldly.

Bond moved over to the windowsill and leaned easily against it with his ankles crossed. His nonchalance seemed to irritate her. She sat down in front of the writing table. "Now then," she said, and her voice had an edge to it, "let's get down to business. In the first place, why did you take on this job?"

"Somebody died."

"Oh." She looked at him sharply. "They told me your line was theft." She paused. "Hot blood or cold blood?"

"Hot blood. A fight."

"So you want to get out?"

"That's about it. That and the money."

She changed the subject. "Got a wooden leg? False teeth?"

"No. Everything's real."

She frowned. "I keep telling them to find me a man with a wooden leg. Well, have you got any hobbies or anything? Any ideas about where you're going to carry the stones?"

"No," said Bond. "I play cards and golf. But I thought the handles of trunks and suitcases were good places for this sort of stuff."

"So do the customs men," she said drily. She sat silent for a moment, reflecting. Then she pulled a piece of paper and a pencil towards her. "What sort of golf balls do you use?" she asked unsmilingly.

"Dunlop 65's." He looked equally serious. "Maybe you've got something there."

She made no comment, but wrote the name on a slip of paper. She glanced up. "Got a passport?"

"Well, I have," admitted Bond. "But it's in my real name."

"Oh?" She was suspicious. "And what's your real name?"

"James Bond."

She looked disgusted. "Why not John Doe?" She shrugged one shoulder. "Who cares anyway. Can you get an American visa in two days? And a vaccination certificate?"

"Don't see why not," said Bond. (Q Branch would fix all that.) "There's nothing against me in America. Or at Criminal Records here, for that matter. Under Bond, that is."

"Okay," she said. "Now listen. Immigration will need this. You're going over to the States to stay with a man called Tree. Michael Tree. You'll be staying at the

Astor in New York. He's an American friend of yours. You met him in the war." She unbent slightly. "Just for the record, this man really exists. He'll back up your story. But he's not generally known as Michael. He's known as 'Shady' Tree to his friends. If any," she added sourly.

Bond smiled.

"He's not as funny as he sounds," said the girl shortly. She opened a drawer in the desk and took out a packet of five-pound notes secured with a rubber band. She riffled them through and detached about half their number and put these back in the drawer. She rolled up the rest, snapped the rubber band around them and tossed the packet across the room to Bond. Bond bent forward and caught it near the floor.

"There's about £500 there," she said. "Book yourself in at the Ritz and give that address to Immigration. Get a good used suitcase and pack it with what you'd take on a golfing holiday. Get your clubs. Keep out of sight. BOAC Monarch to New York. Thursday evening. Get a single ticket first thing tomorrow morning. The Embassy won't give you a visa without seeing your ticket. A car will pick you up at the Ritz at 6:30 Thursday evening. The driver will give you the golf balls. Put 'em in your bag. And"—she looked him straight in the eye—"don't think you can go into business for yourself with this stuff. The driver will be with you until your luggage has gone out to the 'plane. And I'll be at London Airport. So no monkey business. Got it?"

Bond nodded and smiled. "What would I do with this kind of merchandise? Too big for me. What happens at the other end?"

"Another driver will be waiting outside customs. He'll tell you what to do next. Now." Her voice was urgent. "If anything happens at customs, either end, you know nothing, see? You just don't know how the balls got into your bag. Whatever they ask you, just go on saying 'You've got me.' Act dumb. I'll be watching. And so will others, maybe. That I wouldn't know. If they lock you up in America, ask for the British consul and go on asking. You won't get any help from us. But that's what you're being paid for. Okay?''

"Fair enough," said Bond. "The only person I could get into trouble would be you." He looked appraisingly at her. "And I wouldn't want that to happen."

She smiled scornfully. "You've got nothing on me. Don't worry about me, friend. I can look after myself." She got up and walked over in front of him. "And don't 'little girl' me," she said sharply. "We're on a job. And I can take care of myself. You'd be surprised."

Bond smiled down into the flashing grey eyes that were now dark with impatience. " 'I can do anything better than you can,' that it? Don't worry. I'll be a credit to you. Now relax and stop being so business-like for a minute. I'd like to see you again. Could we meet in New York if everything goes all right?" Bond felt faintly treacherous as he said the words. He liked the girl. He wanted to make friends with her. But it would be a question of using their friendship to get further along the pipe line.

She looked thoughtfully at him for a moment and her eyes gradually lost their darkness. Her compressed lips relaxed and parted a little.

"Well, what the hell," she said, but the word sounded artificial. "I've got nothing on Friday night. I suppose we might have dinner. 21 on Fifty-second? All the cab drivers know it. Eight o'clock. If the job goes off all right. Suit you?" She turned back towards him and looked at his mouth, not his eyes.

"Fine," said Bond. He thought it was time to leave before he made a mistake. "Now," he said efficiently, "is there anything else?"

"No," she said. And then sharply, as if she had just remembered something, "What's the time?"

Bond looked at his watch. "Ten to six."

"I've got to get busy," she said. With a gesture of dismissal she walked towards the door. Bond followed her. With her hand on the key she turned. She looked at him, and there was confidence, almost warmth, in her eyes. "You'll be all right," she said. "Just keep away from me in the 'plane. Don't panic if anything goes wrong. If you work out''—the patronising note came back to her voice—"I'll try to get you more of this kind of work.''

"Thanks,'' said Bond. "I'd appreciate that. I'd enjoy working with you.''

She smiled ambiguously and then opened the door for him. Bond walked out into the corridor.

He turned. "See you on Friday,'' he said. He wanted to say more, to find an excuse to stay with this lonely girl who played records to herself while she sat in front of the mirror.

But now her expression was once more remote. He might have been a complete stranger. "Sure,'' she said indifferently. She looked at him without expression and then closed the door slowly but firmly in his face.

As Bond walked away down the long corridor to the elevator, the girl stood just inside the door and listened until his footsteps had vanished. Then she walked slowly over to the phonograph and switched it on. She picked up the Feyer record and searched for the groove she wanted. She put the record on the machine and found the place with the needle: "Je n'en connais pas la fin.'' She stood listening to it and wondering about the man who had just left. God, she thought to herself with sudden anger, another damn' crook. Couldn't she ever get away from them? But when the record stopped, her face was happy and she hummed the tune as she powdered her nose and got ready to go out.

On the street a few minutes later she paused and looked at her watch. Ten minutes past six. Five minutes to go. She walked across Trafalgar Square to Charing Cross Station, rehearsing in her mind what she was going to say. Then she went into the station and headed for one of the phone booths she always used.

It was just 6:15 when she dialled the Welbeck number. After the usual two rings she heard the click of the automatic recorder taking the call. For twenty seconds she heard nothing but the sharp hiss of a needle on wax. Then the neutral voice that was her unknown master said the one word "Speak," and then there was silence again except for the hiss of the recorder.

She had long got over being flustered by the abrupt, disembodied command. She spoke rapidly but distinctly into the black mouthpiece. "Case to A B C. I repeat, Case to A B C." She paused. "Carrier is satisfactory. Says real name is James Bond and will use that name on passport. Plays golf and will carry golf clubs. Suggest golf balls. Use Dunlop 65's. All other arrangements stand. Will call for confirmation at 1915 and 2015. That's all."

She listened for a moment to the hiss of the recorder, then put down the receiver and walked back to her hotel. She called room service for a double dry Martini, and when it came she sat and smoked and played more records and waited for 7:15.

Then, or perhaps not until she called again at 8:15, the neutral muffled voice would come back at her over the telephone wire: "A B C to Case. I repeat, A B C to Case. . . ." And then would follow her instructions.

And somewhere, in some rented room in London, the hiss of the recorder would stop as she put back the receiver. And then, perhaps, an unknown door would close and unknown footsteps would softly sound on some stairs and out into an unknown street and away.

CHAPTER 6

In Transit

At six o'clock on Thursday evening Bond was packing his suitcase in his bedroom at the Ritz. It was a battered but once expensive pigskin, and its contents were appropriate to his cover: evening clothes: his light-weight black and white hound's-tooth check for the country and for golf: Saxone golf shoes; a companion to the dark blue tropical worsted suit he was wearing; and some white silk and dark blue short-sleeved Sea Island cotton shirts. Socks and ties, some nylon underwear and two pairs of the long silk pajama coats he wore in place of two-piece pajamas.

None of these things bore, or had ever borne, any name tags or initials.

Bond completed his task and proceeded to fit his remaining possessions—his shaving gear, Tommy Armour on *How to Play Your Best Golf All the Time,* his tickets and passport—into a small attaché case, also of battered pigskin. This had been prepared for him by Q Branch, and there was a narrow compartment under the leather at the back which contained a silencer for his gun and thirty rounds of .25 ammunition.

The telephone rang. He assumed it was the car, early at the rendezvous, but it was the hall porter instead, saying that a representative of "Universal Export" was there with a letter to be delivered personally to Bond.

"Send him up," said Bond, wondering.

A few minutes later he opened the door to a man in plainclothes whom he recognised as one of the messengers from the pool at Headquarters.

"Good evening, sir," said the man. He took a large plain envelope out of his breast pocket and handed it to Bond. "I am to wait and take this back when you have read it, sir," he said.

Bond opened the white envelope and broke the seal of the blue envelope which it contained.

There was a page of blue typewritten foolscap paper with no address and no signature, but Bond recognised the extra-large type used in M's personal communications.

Bond waved the messenger to a chair and sat down at the writing desk opposite the window.

Washington [said the memorandum] reports that "Rufus B. Saye" is an alias for Jack Spang, a suspected gangster who was mentioned in the Kefauver Report but who has no criminal record. He is, however, twin brother to Seraffimo Spang and joint controller of the "Spangled Mob" which operates widely in the United States. The brothers Spang bought control of the House of Diamonds five years ago "as an investment," and nothing unfavourable is known about this business which appears to be perfectly legitimate.

The brothers also own a "wire service" which serves off-the-course bookmakers in Nevada and California, and is, therefore, illegal. The name of this is the "Sure-Fire Wire Service." They also own the Tiara Hotel in Las Vegas, and this is the headquarters of Seraffimo Spang and also, to benefit from the Nevada tax laws, the company offices of the House of Diamonds.

Washington adds that the Spangled Mob is interested in other illegal activities such as narcotics and organised prostitution, and these lines are handled from New York by Michael (Shady) Tree, who has five previous convictions for various offences. The gang has branch headquarters in Miami, Detroit and Chicago.

Washington describes the Spangled Mob as one of the most powerful syndicates in the United States with excellent "protection" in State and Federal governments and with the police. With the Cleveland outfit and the Detroit "Purple" gang, the Spangled Mob has top classification.

Our interest in these matters has not been divulged to Washington, but in the event that your inquiries lead you into dangerous contact with these criminals, you will report at once and be withdrawn from the case, which will then be handed over to the F.B.I.

This is an order.

The return of this document in a sealed envelope will acknowledge your receipt of this order.

Bond ran his eyes down the page again, folded it, and placed it in one of the Ritz envelopes and sealed it.

He got up and handed the envelope to the messenger.

"Thanks very much," he said. "Can you find your own way downstairs?"

"Yes, thank you, sir," said the messenger. He went to the door and opened it. "Good night, sir."

The door closed quietly.

Bond walked across the room to the window and looked out over Green Park.

For a moment he had a clear vision of the spare, elderly figure sitting back in his chair in the quiet office.

Give the case to the F.B.I.? Bond knew M meant it, but he also knew how bitter it would be for M to have to ask Edgar Hoover to take a case over from the Secret Service and pick Britain's chestnuts out of the fire.

The operative words in the memorandum were "dangerous contact." What constituted "dangerous contact" would be a matter for Bond to decide. Compared with some of the opposition he had been up against, these hoodlums surely wouldn't count for much. Or would they? He suddenly remembered the chunky, quartz-like face of "Rufus B. Saye." Well, at any rate it could do no harm to try to get a look at this brother with the exotic name. Seraffimo. The name of a night-club waiter or an ice-cream vendor. But these people were like that. Cheap and theatrical.

Bond glanced at his watch. 6:25. He looked around the room. Everything was ready. On an impulse he put his right hand under his coat and drew the .25 Beretta automatic with the skeleton grip out of the chamois leather holster that hung just below his left armpit. It was the new gun M had given him "as a memento" after his last assignment. With a note in M's green ink that said "You may need this."

Bond walked over to the bed, snapped out the magazine and pumped the single round in the chamber out on to the bedspread. He worked the action several times and tested the tension on the trigger-spring as he squeezed and fired the empty gun. He pulled back the breech and verified that there was no dust around the pin which he had spent so many hours filing to a point, and he ran his hand down the blue barrel from the tip of which he had personally sawn the blunt foresight. Then he snapped the spare round back into the magazine and the magazine into the taped butt of the thin gun, pumped the action for a last time, put up the safety and slipped the gun back under his coat.

The telephone rang. "Your car's here, sir."

Bond hung up and stood with his hand still on the receiver. So this was it. The jump-off. He walked thoughtfully over to the window and looked out again across the park. He felt a slight emptiness in the stomach, a sudden pang at leaving those green trees that were London in high summer, and a loneliness at the thought of the big building in Regent's Park, the fortress which would now be out of reach except for an SOS he knew it would not be in him to send.

There was a knock on the door and a page came in for

his bags. Bond followed him out of the room and along the corridor, his mind swept clean now of everything except what waited at the mouth of the pipe line that lay open for him on the other side of the swing doors of the Ritz Hotel.

It was a black Armstrong Siddeley Sapphire with red dealer plates. "You'd like to sit up front," said the uniformed chauffeur. It was not an invitation. Bond's two bags and his golf clubs were put in the back. He settled himself comfortably and, as they turned into Piccadilly, he examined the face of the driver. All he could see was a hard, anonymous profile under a peaked cap. The eyes were concealed behind black sun goggles. The hands that expertly used the wheel and the gears wore leather gloves.

"Just relax and enjoy the ride, mister." The accent was Brooklyn. "Don't bother with conversation. Makes me nervous."

Bond smiled and said nothing. He did as he was told. Forty, he thought. 170 pounds. Five feet ten. Expert driver. Very familiar with London traffic. No smell of tobacco. Expensive shoes. Neat dresser. No five o'clock shadow. Query: shaves twice a day with electric razor?

After the roundabout at the end of the Great West Road, the driver pulled over to the side. He opened the glove compartment and carefully removed six new Dunlop 65's in their black wrapping paper with the paper seals intact. Leaving the engine idling in neutral, he got out of the front seat and opened the rear door. Bond looked over his shoulder and watched the man unstrap the ball pocket on his golf bag and one by one carefully add the six new balls to the miscellaneous old and new ones the pocket already contained. Then without a word the man climbed back into the front seat and the drive continued.

At London Airport, Bond unconcernedly went through the luggage and ticket routine, bought himself an *Evening Standard*, allowing his arm, as he put down his pennies, to brush against an attractive blonde in a tan travelling suit who was idly turning the pages of a magazine and, accompanied by the driver, followed his luggage through to the customs.

"Just your personal effects, sir?"

"Yes."

"And how much English money have you, sir?"

"About three pounds and some silver."

"Thank you, sir." The blue chalk made a scribble on the three bags, and the porter picked up the suitcase and clubs and loaded them on a trolley. "Follow the yellow light to Immigration, sir," he said, and wheeled the trolley off towards the loading bay.

The driver gave Bond an ironic salute. "Good night, sir. Pleasant trip."

"Thank you, my man," said Bond cheerfully, and had the satisfaction of seeing the driver turn on his heel and walk quickly away.

Bond picked up his attaché case, showed his passport to a pleasant fresh-faced young man who ticked his name off the passenger list, and walked on into the departure lounge. Just behind him he heard Tiffany Case's low voice say, "Thank you," to the fresh-faced young man, and a moment later she also came into the lounge and chose a seat between him and the door. Bond smiled to himself. It was where he would have chosen to sit if he had been tailing someone who might have second thoughts.

He picked up his *Evening Standard* and casually examined the other passengers over the top of it.

The plane would be nearly full (Bond had been too late to get a sleeping berth), and he was relieved to see that among the forty people in the lounge there was not a face he recognised. Some miscellaneous English, two of the usual nuns who, Bond reflected, seemed always to be flying the Atlantic in the summer—Lourdes, perhaps—some nondescript Americans, mostly of the businessman type, two babies in arms to keep the passengers from sleeping, and a handful of indeterminate Europeans. A typical load, decided Bond, while admitting that if two of their number, himself and Tiffany Case, had their secrets, there was no reason why many of these seemingly dull people should not also be bound on strange missions.

Bond felt that he was being watched, but it was only the blank gaze of two of the passengers he had put down as American businessmen. Their eyes shifted away, and one of them, a man with a young face but prematurely white hair, said something to the other and they both got up, picked up their Stetsons, which, although it was summer, were encased in waterproof covers, and walked over to the bar. Bond heard them order double brandies and water, and the second man, who was pale and fat, took a bottle of pills out of his pocket and swallowed one down with his brandy. Dramamine, guessed Bond. The man would be a bad traveller.

The BOAC flight dispatcher was close to Bond. She picked up the telephone—to Flight Control, Bond supposed—and said, "I have forty passengers in the Final Lounge." She waited for the okay and then put the telephone back and picked up the microphone.

"Final Lounge?" Cheerful start to flying the Atlantic, reflected Bond, and then they were all walking across the tarmac and up into the big Boeing and with a burst of oil and metanol smoke the engines fired one by one. The chief steward announced over the loudspeaker that the next stop would be Shannon, where they would dine, and that the flying time would be one hour and fifty minutes, and the great doubledecked Stratocruiser rolled slowly out to the east-west runway. The aircraft trembled against its brakes as the captain revved the four engines one at a time up to take-off speed, and through his window Bond watched the wing flaps being tested. Then the great plane turned slowly towards the setting sun, there was a jerk as the brakes were released, and the grass on either side of the runway flattened as, gathering speed, the Monarch hurtled down the two miles of stressed concrete and rose into the west, aiming ultimately for another little strip of concrete carpet on the other side of the world.

Bond lit a cigarette and was settling himself with his book when the back of the reclining seat on the left of

the pair in front of him was lowered sharply towards
him. It was one of the two American businessmen, the
fat one, lying slumped down with his safety belt still
fastened around his stomach. His face was green and
sweating. He held a briefcase clutched across his chest
and Bond could read the name on the visiting card in-
serted in the leather label tag. It said "Mr. W. Winter,"
and below in neat red ink capitals was written "MY
BLOOD GROUP IS F."

Poor wretch, thought Bond. He's terrified. He knows
the plane is going to crash. He just hopes the men who
pull him out of the wreckage will give him the right
blood transfusion. To him this plane is nothing but a
giant tube full of anonymous deadweight, supported in
the air by a handful of sparking plugs and guided to its
destination by a scrap of electricity. He has no faith in it
and no faith in safety statistics. He is suffering the same
fears he had as a small child—the fear of noise and the
fear of falling. He won't even dare to go to the lavatory
for fear he'll put his foot through the floor of the plane
when he stands up.

A silhouette broke the rays of the evening sun that
filled the cabin, and Bond glanced away from the man.
It was Tiffany Case. She walked past him to the stairs
leading down to the cocktail lounge on the lower deck,
and disappeared. Bond would have liked to follow her,
but instead he waited for the steward to wheel around
the tray of Martinis and the caviar and smoked salmon
canapés. He turned again to his book and read a page
without a single word registering. He put the girl out of
his mind and started the page again.

He had read a quarter of the book when he felt his
ears begin to block as the plane started its fifty-mile
descent towards the western coast line of Ireland.
"Fasten your seat-belts. No smoking," and there was
the green and white searchlight of Shannon and the red
and gold of the flare path rushing towards them, and
then the brilliant blue of the ground-lights between
which the Stratocruiser trundled towards the unloading
bay. Steak and champagne for dinner and the wonder-

ful goblet of hot coffee laced with Irish whiskey and topped with half an inch of thick cream. A glance at the junk in the airport shops: the "Irish Horn Rosaries," the "Bog Oak Irish Harp," and the "Brass Leprechauns," all at $1.50; the ghastly "Irish Musical Cottage" at $4.00; the furry, unwearable tweeds and the dainty Irish linen doilies and cocktail napkins. And then the Irish rigmarole coming over the loudspeaker in which only the words "BOAC" and "New York" were comprehensible, the translation into English, the last look at Europe, and they were climbing to 15,000 feet and heading for their next contact with the surface of the earth, the radio beacons on the weather ships *Jig* and *Charlie* marking time around their compass points somewhere in the middle of the Atlantic.

Bond slept well and awoke only as they were approaching the southern shores of Nova Scotia. He went forward to the washroom and shaved, and gargled away the taste of a night of pressurised air, and then went back to his seat between the lines of crumpled, stirring passengers and had his usual moment of exhilaration as the sun came up over the rim of the world and bathed the cabin in blood.

Slowly, with the dawn, the plane came alive. Twenty thousand feet below, the houses began to show like grains of sugar spilt across a brown carpet. Nothing moved on the earth's surface except a thin worm of smoke from a train, the straight white feather of a fishing boat's wake across an inlet, and the glint of chromium from a toy motor car caught in the sun; but Bond could almost see the sleeping humps under the bedclothes beginning to stir and, where there was a wisp of smoke rising into the still morning air, he could smell the coffee brewing in the kitchens.

Breakfast came, that inappropriate assortment of foods that BOAC advertises as "an English country-house breakfast," and the chief steward came around with the U.S. customs forms—Form No. 6063 of the Treasury Department—and Bond read the small print: "Failure to declare any article or any wilfully false

statement . . . fine or imprisonment or both,'' and wrote
''Personal effects'' and cheerfully signed the lie.

And then there were three hours when the plane hung
dead steady in the middle of the universe and only the
patches of bright sunshine slowly rising and falling a
few inches on the walls of the cabin gave a sense of
motion. But at last there was the great sprawl of Boston
below them, and then, shortly thereafter, the bold pattern of a clover-leaf on the New Jersey Turnpike and
Bond's ears began to block again with the slow descent
towards the pall of haze that was Greater New York.
There was the hiss and sickly smell of the insecticide
bomb, the shrill hydraulic whine of the air brakes and
the landing wheels being lowered, the dip of the plane's
nose, the tearing bump of the tires on the runway, the
ugly roar as the screws were reversed to slow the plane
for the entrance bay, the rumbling progress over the
tired grass plain towards the tarmac apron, the clang of
the hatch being opened, and they were there.

"Shady" Tree

The customs officer, a paunchy good-living man with dark sweat marks at the armpits of his grey uniform shirt, sauntered over from the Supervisor's desk to where Bond stood, his three pieces of luggage in front of him, under the letter B. Next door, under C, the girl took a pack of filter-tip cigarettes out of her bag and put one between her lips. Bond heard several impatient clicks of her lighter and the sharper snap as she put it back in her bag and closed the fastening. Bond felt aware of her watchfulness. He wished that her name began with a Z. Zarathustra? Zacharias? Zophany?

"Mr. Bond?"

"Yes."

"Is this your signature?"

"Yes."

"Just your personal effects?"

"Yes, that's all."

"Okay, Mr. Bond." The man tore a customs stamp out of his book and pasted it on the suitcase. He did the same for the attaché case. He came to the golf clubs. He paused with the stamp book in his hand. He looked up at Bond.

"What d'ya shoot?"

Bond had a moment of blackout.

"They're golf clubs," he said.

"Sure," said the man patiently. "But what d'ya shoot? What d'ya go around in?"

Bond could have kicked himself for forgetting the Americanism. "Oh, high eighties, that's all."

"Never broken a hundred in my life," said the customs officer. He gummed a blessed stamp on the side of the bag a few inches away from the richest haul of contraband that had ever been missed at Idlewild. "Have a good vacation, Mr. Bond."

"Thanks," said Bond, grateful that the ordeal, so unexpectedly easy, was over. He beckoned a porter and followed his bags across to the last hurdle, the Inspector at the door. There was no hitch. The man bent over, searched for the stamps, overstamped them and waved him through.

"Bond?"

It was a tall hatchet-faced man with mud-coloured hair and mean eyes. He was wearing dark brown slacks and a coffee-coloured shirt.

"I have a car for you." As he turned and led the way out into the hot early-morning sun Bond noticed a square bulge in his hip-pocket, about the shape of a small-caliber automatic. Typical, thought Bond. Mike Hammer routine. These American gangsters were too obvious. They had read too many horror-comics and seen too many movies.

The car was a black Oldsmobile Sedan. Not waiting to be told, Bond climbed into the front seat, leaving the disposal of his luggage in the back and the tipping of the porter to the man in brown. When they had left the arid prairie of Idlewild and had merged into the stream of commuter traffic on the Van Wyck Parkway he felt he ought to say something.

"How's the weather been over here?"

The driver didn't take his eyes off the road. "Damn' near a hundred."

"That's pretty hot," said Bond. "We haven't had it much over seventy-five in London."

"That so?"

"What's the program now?" asked Bond after a pause.

The man glanced in his rear-view mirror and pulled into the centre lane. For a quarter of a mile he busied himself with passing a bunch of slow-moving cars on the inside lanes. When they came to an empty stretch of road Bond repeated his question. "I said, what's the program?"

The driver gave him a quick glance. "Shady wants you."

"Does he?" said Bond. He was suddenly impatient with these people. He wondered how soon he would be able to throw some weight around. The prospect didn't look good. His job was to stay in the pipe line and follow it further. Any sign of independence or non-cooperation and he would be discarded. He would have to make himself small and stay that way. He would just have to get used to the idea.

They swept into uptown Manhattan and followed the river as far as the forties. Then they cut across town and pulled up between Fifth and Sixth avenues on west Forty-sixth Street, the Hatton Garden of New York. The driver double-parked outside an inconspicuous doorway sandwiched between a grubby-looking shop selling costume jewellery and an elegant shopfront faced with black marble. The silver italic lettering above the black marble entrance of the elegant shopfront was so discreet that if the name had not been in the back of Bond's mind he would not have been able to decipher it from where he sat. It said, "The House of Diamonds, Inc."

As the car stopped a man stepped off the pavement and sauntered around the car. "Everything okay?" he said to the driver.

"Sure. Boss in?"

"Yeah. Want me to park the heap?"

"Do that." The driver turned to Bond. "This is it, Jack. Let's get the bags out."

Bond got out and opened the rear door. He picked up his small attaché case and reached for the golf clubs.

"I'll take the sticks," said the driver behind him. Obediently Bond hauled out his suitcase. The driver reached in for the clubs and slammed the door of the car. The other man was already in the driver's seat and the car moved off into the traffic as Bond followed the driver across the sidewalk and through the inconspicuous door.

There was a man in a small receiving room in the narrow hallway. As they came in, he looked up from the sports section of the *News*. "Hi," he said to the driver. He looked sharply at Bond.

"Hi," said the driver. "Mind if we leave the bags with you?"

"Go ahead," said the man. "Be okay in here." He jerked his head back.

The driver, with Bond's clubs over his shoulder, waited for Bond beside the doors of an elevator across the hall. When they were both inside, he pressed the button for the fourth floor and they rode up in silence. They emerged into another small hallway. It contained two chairs, a table, a large brass spittoon and a smell of stale heat.

They crossed the frayed carpet to a glass-fronted door and the driver knocked and walked through without waiting for an answer. Bond went in behind him and shut the door.

A man with very bright red hair and a big peaceful moon-shaped face was sitting at a desk. There was a glass of milk in front of him. He stood up as they came in, and Bond saw that he was a hunchback.

The hunchback moved slowly from the desk over to where Bond was standing. He circled Bond, making a show of examining him minutely from head to foot, and then came and stood close in front of Bond and looked up into his face. Bond looked impassively back into a pair of china eyes that were so empty and motionless that they might have been hired from a taxidermist. He had the feeling that he was being subjected to some sort of test. Casually he inspected the hunchback, noting the big ears with their exaggerated lobes, the dry red lips of the big half open mouth, the almost complete absence of a neck, and the short powerful arms in the expensive yellow silk shirt cut to make room for the barrel-like chest and its sharp hump.

"I like to have a good look at the people we employ, Mr. Bond." The voice was sharp and pitched high.

Bond smiled politely.

"London tells me you've killed a man. I believe them. I can see you are capable of it. Would you like to do more work for us?"

"Depends what it is," said Bond. "Or rather"—he hoped he was not being too theatrical—"how much you pay."

The hunchback gave a short squeal of laughter. He turned abruptly to the driver. "Rocky, get those balls out of the bag and cut them open. Here." He gave a quick shake of his right arm and held his open hand out to the driver. On it lay a double-bladed knife with a flat handle bound with adhesive tape. Bond recognised it as a throwing knife. He had to admit that the bit of leger-demain had been neatly executed.

"Right," said the driver, and Bond noticed the alacrity with which he took the knife and knelt on the floor to unstrap the ball pocket of the golf bag.

The hunchback walked away from Bond and back to his chair. He sat down and picked up the glass of milk. He looked at it with distaste and swallowed the contents in two huge gulps. He looked at Bond as if for comment.

"Ulcers?" asked Bond sympathetically.

"What's it to you?" said the hunchback angrily. His anger was transferred to the driver. "What are you waiting for? Put those balls on the table where I can see what you're doing. The number on the ball is the centre of the plug. Dig 'em out.''

"Coming, boss," said the driver. He stood up and put the six new balls on the desk. Five of them were still in their black wrappings. He took the sixth and turned it around in his fingers. Then he picked up the knife, dug its point into the cover of the ball and levered. A half-inch circular section of the ball came away on the tip of the blade and he passed the ball across the desk to the hunchback, who tipped the contents, three uncut stones of ten to fifteen carats, onto the leather surface of the desk.

The hunchback moodily poked the stones with his finger.

The driver went on with his work until Bond counted eighteen stones on the table. They were unimpressive in their rough state, but if they were of top quality Bond could easily believe they might be worth $300,000 after cutting.

"Okay, Rocky," said the hunchback. "Eighteen. That's the lot. Now get those God-damn' golfsticks out of here and send the boy to the Astor with them and this guy's bags. He's registered there. Have them sent up to his room. Okay?"

"Okay, boss." The driver left the knife and the empty golf balls on the table, strapped up the ball pocket on Bond's bag, hoisted the bag on his shoulder and left the room without a backward glance.

Bond went over to a chair against the wall, pulled it around to face the hunchback across the desk, and sat down. He took a cigarette and lit it. He looked across at the hunchback and said, "And now, if you're happy, I'd like that $5,000."

The hunchback, who had been carefully watching Bond's movements, lowered his gaze to the untidy pile of diamonds in front of him. He poked them into a circle. Then he looked up at Bond.

"You will be paid in full, Mr. Bond." The high voice was precise and businesslike. "And you may get more than $5,000, but the method of payment will be devised as much for your protection as for ours. There will be no direct payment. You understand why, Mr. Bond, having made payoffs during your career of burglary. It is very dangerous for a man suddenly to be flush. He talks about it. He throws it around. And if the cops catch up with him and ask him where it all came from he hasn't got an answer. Agree?"

"Yes," said Bond, surprised by the sanity and authority of what the man was saying. "That makes sense."

"So," said the hunchback, "I and my friends pay only very seldom and in small amounts for services rendered. Instead, we arrange for the buy to make the money on his own. Take yourself. How much money have you got in your pocket?"

"About three pounds and some silver," said Bond.

"All right," said the hunchback. "Today you met your friend Mr. Tree." He pointed a finger at his chest. "Which is me. A perfectly respectable citizen whom you knew in England in 1945 when he was concerned with the disposal of army surplus goods. Remember?"

"Yes."

"I owed you $500 for a bridge game we had at the Savoy. Remember?"

Bond nodded.

"When we meet today I toss you double or nothing for it. And you win. Okay? So you now have $1,000 and I, a taxpaying citizen, will support your story. Here's the money." The hunchback took a wallet out of his hip pocket and pushed ten $100 bills across the table.

Bond picked them up and put them in the breast pocket of his coat.

"And then," continued the hunchback, "you say you'd like to see some horse racing while you're over here. So I say to you, 'Why not go take a look at Saratoga? The track opens on Monday.' And you say okay, and you do in fact go up to Saratoga, with your thousand bucks in your pocket. Okay?"

"Fine," said Bond.

"And you back a horse there. And it pays off at least fives. So you have your $5,000, and if anybody asks where it came from, you earned it and you can prove it."

"What if the horse loses?"

"It won't."

Bond made no comment. So he was getting somewhere already—into the underworld with a bang. The racing end of it. He looked across into the pale china eyes. It was impossible to read an expression in them. They stared blankly back at him. But now for the big step through the cutout.

"Well, that's fine," he said, hoping that flattery was the key. "You people certainly seem to think things through. I like working for careful people."

There was no encouragement in the china eyes.

"I'd like to stay away from England for a bit. I suppose you people couldn't do with an extra hand?"

The china eyes shifted away from his and inched reflectively over Bond's face and shoulders as if the hunchback were judging horseflesh. Then the man looked down at the circle of diamonds in front of him and carefully, thoughtfully, poked it into a rough square.

There was silence in the room. Bond looked at his fingernails.

At last the hunchback looked up at him again. "Could be," he said thoughtfully. "Could be there'd be something else for you. You made no mistakes so far. You go on that way and keep your nose clean. Call me up after the race, and I'll tell you what the word is. But, like I said, just take it easy and do what you're told. Okay?"

Bond's muscles relaxed. He shrugged his shoulders. "Why should I get out of line? I'm looking for a job. And you can tell your outfit that I'm not particular so long as the pay's good."

For the first time the china eyes showed emotion. They looked hurt and angry, and Bond wondered if he had overplayed his hand.

"Who d'you think we are?" The hunchback's voice rose to an indignant squeal. "Some sort of cheap crook outfit? Well, hell." He sighed resignedly. "Can't expect a Limey to understand the way things are over here nowadays." The eyes went dull again. "Here's a pencil. This is my number. Write it down. Wisconsin 7-3697. And write this down too. But keep it to yourself or you may get your tongue split." Shady Tree's short, shrill laugh was not merry. "Third race on Tuesday. The Perpetuity Stakes. Mile and a quarter for three-year-olds. And put your money on just before the windows close. You'll shift the odds with that grand of yours. Okay?"

"Okay," said Bond, writing obediently in his notebook.

"Right," said the hunchback. "Shy Smile—a big horse with a blaze face and four white stockings. And play him to win."

CHAPTER 8

The Eye That Never Sleeps

It was 12:30 when Bond went down in the elevator and out onto the roasting street.

He turned right and walked slowly towards Times Square. As he passed the handsome black-marble frontage of the House of Diamonds he stopped to examine the two discreet show windows lined with dark blue velvet. In the centre of each was just one piece of jewellery, an earring consisting of a big pear-shaped diamond hanging from another perfect stone, circular and brilliant-cut. Below each earring was a thin plate of yellow gold in the shape of a visiting card with one edge turned down. On each plate were engraved the words "Diamonds Are Forever."

Bond smiled to himself. He wondered which of his predecessors had smuggled those four diamonds into America. He sauntered on in search of an air-conditioned bar where he could get out of the heat and do some thinking. He was pleased with his interview. At least it hadn't been the brush-off he had more than half expected. He was amused by the hunchback. There was something splendidly theatrical about him, and his vanity was oddly appealing. But he wasn't at all funny.

Bond had walked for only a few minutes when it suddenly occurred to him that he was being followed. There was no evidence for it except a slight tingling of the scalp and an extra awareness of the people near him, but he had faith in his sixth sense and he immediately stopped in front of the shop window he was passing and looked casually back along Forty-sixth Street. Nothing but a lot of miscellaneous people moving slowly on the sidewalks, mostly on the same side as himself, the side that was shaded from the sun. There was no sudden movement into the shelter of a doorway, nobody idly wiping his face with a handkerchief to avoid recognition, nobody bending down to tie a shoelace.

Bond examined the Swiss watches in his shop window and then turned and sauntered on. After a few yards he stopped again. Still nothing. He went on and turned right onto the Avenue of the Americas, stopping in the first doorway, the entrance to a lingerie shop where a man in a tan suit with his back to him was examining the black lace pants on a particularly realistic dummy. Bond turned and leaned against a pillar and gazed lazily but watchfully out into the street.

And then something gripped his pistol arm and a voice rasped: "All right, Limey. Take it easy unless you want lead for lunch," and he felt something press into his back just above the kidneys.

What was so familiar about that voice? Bond glanced down to see what was holding his right arm. It was a steel hook. Well, if the man had only one arm! Like lightning he swivelled, bending sideways and bringing his left fist around in a flailing blow, low down.

There was a smack as his fist was caught in the other man's left hand, and at the same time the contact telegraphed to Bond's mind the message that there could have been no gun, there came a well remembered laugh and a lazy voice saying, "Not so good, James. You must be getting old."

Bond straightened himself slowly and for a moment

he could only stare with blank disbelief into the grinning, hawklike face of Felix Leiter.

"So you were doing a front tail, you bastard," he finally said. He looked with delight at the friend he had last seen as a cocoon of dirty bandages on a blood-stained bed in a Florida hotel, the American secret agent with whom he had worked so often in the past. "What the hell are you doing here?" Bond took out a handkerchief and wiped his face. "For a moment you almost had me feeling a little nervous."

"Nervous!" Leiter laughed scornfully. "You were saying your prayers. Your conscience is so bad you didn't even know if you were going to get it from the cops or the robbers. Am I right?"

Bond laughed and dodged the question. "Come on, you crooked spy," he said. "You can buy me a drink and tell me all about it. I just don't believe in odds as long as this. In fact, you can buy me lunch. You Texans are lousy with money."

"Sure," said Leiter. He slipped his steel hook into the right-hand pocket of his coat and took Bond's arm with his left hand. They moved out onto the street, and Bond noticed that Leiter walked with a decided limp. "In Texas even the fleas are so rich they can hire themselves dogs. Come on. Sardi's is just over the way."

Leiter avoided the fashionable main room of the famous actors' and writers' eatinghouse and led Bond upstairs. His limp was more noticeable and he held on to the banisters. Bond made no comment, but when he left his friend at a corner table and went off to the washroom he added up his impressions. The right arm had gone, and the left leg, and there were imperceptible scars below the hairline above the right eye that suggested a good deal of grafting, but otherwise Leiter looked in reasonable shape. The steady eyes were undefeated, the shock of straw-coloured hair had no hint of grey in it and there was none of the bitterness of a cripple around the mouth. But in their short walk there had been a hint of reticence in Leiter's manner, and Bond felt this had something to do with him, Bond, and perhaps with Leiter's present activities. Certainly not, he thought as he walked across the room to join his friend, with Leiter's injuries.

There was a medium-dry Martini with a twist of lemon peel waiting for him. Bond smiled at Leiter's memory and tasted his drink. It was excellent but he didn't recognise the vermouth.

"Domestic stuff," explained Leiter. "New brand from California. Like it?"

"Best vermouth I ever tasted," admitted Bond.

"And I've taken a chance and ordered you smoked salmon and Brizzola," said Leiter. "This is one of the best places in town for beef, and Brizzola's the best cut of that, straight cut across the bone. Roasted and then broiled. Suit you?"

"Anything you say," said Bond.

"I told them not to hurry," said Leiter. He rapped on the table with his hook. "We'll have another Martini first, and while you drink it you'd better come clean." There was warmth in his smile but his eyes were watchful. "Just tell me one thing. What business have you got with my old friend Shady Tree?" He gave his order to the waiter and leaned forward in his chair and waited.

Bond finished his Martini and lit a cigarette. He glanced briefly at the tables near them. They were empty. He turned back and faced the American.

"You tell me something first, Felix," he said softly. "Who are you working for these days? Still the CIA?"

"Nix," said Leiter. "With my gun hand gone they could only offer me desk work. Very nice about it, and paid me off handsomely when I said I wanted an open-air job. Then Pinkertons made me a good offer. You know, 'The Eye That Never Sleeps' people. So now I'm just a 'door-basher'—private detective, 'put-on-some-clothes-and-open-up' routine. But it's fun. They're a nice crowd to work for, and someday I'll be able to retire with a pension and a presentation gold watch that goes green in the summer. As a matter of fact I'm in charge of their Race Gang squad—doping, crooked running, nightguards at the stables, that sort of thing.

Good job, and it takes you all over the country.''

"Sounds all right," said Bond. "But I didn't know you knew anything about horses.''

"Never used to be able to recognise a horse unless a milkwagon was tied on behind," admitted Leiter. "But you soon pick it up, and it's mostly the people you have to know about, not the horses. What about you?" He lowered his voice. "Still with the old firm?''

"That's right," said Bond.

"On a job for them now?''

"Yes.''

"Undercover?''

"Yes.''

Leiter sighed. He sipped his Martini reflectively. "Well," he said finally, "you're a damn' fool to be operating alone if it's got anything to do with the Spangled boys. In fact, you're such a bad risk I'm crazy even to be having lunch with you. But I'll tell you why I was gunshoeing around Shady's neck of the woods this morning, and maybe we can help each other out. Without involving our outfits, of course. Okay?''

"You know I'd like to work with you, Felix," said Bond seriously. "But I'm still working for the Government, while you're probably in competition with yours. But if it turns out our target's the same there's no sense in getting wires crossed. If we're chasing the same hare I'll be happy to run with you. Now"—Bond looked quizzically at the Texan—"am I right in thinking you're interested in someone with a blaze face and four white stockings? Called Shy Smile?''

"That's right," said Leiter, not particularly surprised. "Running at Saratoga Tuesday. And what might the running of this horse have to do with the security of the British Empire?''

"I've been told to back him," said Bond. "One thousand dollars to win. Payoff for another job. I brought £100,000 worth of uncut diamonds in by plane this morning for Mr. Spang and his friends.''

Leiter's eyes narrowed. He gave a low whistle of surprise. "Man!" he said respectfully. "You're certainly in a bigger league than I am. I'm only interested because Shy Smile is a ringer. The horse that's due to win on Tuesday won't be Shy Smile at all. Shy Smile didn't even place the last three times he ran. It'll be a very fast steed called Pickapepper. Just by chance he's got a blaze face and four white stockings too. Big chestnut, and they've done a good job with his hooves and various other small points of difference. They've been getting this job ready for over a year. Out in the desert in Nevada, where the Spangs have got some sort of ranch. And are they going to clean up! It's a big race, with $25,000 added, and you can bet they'll plaster the country with their money just before the off. Can't fail to be better than fives. More like ten or fifteen. They'll make a packet."

"But I thought all horses in America had to have their lips tattooed," said Bond. "How have they got around that?"

"Grafted new skin on to Pickapepper's mouth. Copied Shy Smile's marks on it. But this tattoo gimmick is getting old fashioned. The word in Pinkerton's is that the Jockey Club is going to change to photos of the night eyes."

"What are night eyes?"

"They're those calluses on the inside of a horse's knees. The English call them 'chestnuts.' Seems they're different on every horse. Like a man's fingerprints. But it'll be the same old story. They'll photo the night eyes on every racehorse in America and then find the gangs have dreamed up a way of altering them with acid. The cops never catch up with the robbers."

"How do you know all this about Shy Smile?"

"Blackmail," said Leiter cheerfully. "I had a drugging rap all lined up on one of the Spang stableboys. I let him buy his way out of it with the details of this little caper."

"What are you going to do about it?"

"Remains to be seen. Going up to Saratoga on Sunday." Leiter's face lit up. "Hell, why don't you come along with me? I'm driving up, and I'll get you in at my dump. The Sagamore. Swanky motel. You've got to sleep somewhere. Better not be seen together too much, but we'll be able to meet up in the evenings. What do you say?''

''Wonderful,'' said Bond. ''Couldn't be better. And now let's have some lunch and I'll tell you my end of the story.''

The smoked salmon was from Nova Scotia, and a poor substitute for the product of Scotland, but the Brizzola was all that Leiter had said, so tender that Bond could cut it with a fork. He finished his lunch with half an avocado with French dressing and then dawdled over his Espresso.

''And that's the long and short of it,'' said Bond, concluding the story he had been telling between mouthfuls. ''And my guess is that the Spangs are doing the smuggling and the House of Diamonds, which they own, is doing the merchandising. Any views?''

Leiter tapped a cigarette out onto the table with his left hand and lit it with Bond's lighter.

''Sounds possible,'' he agreed after a pause. ''But I don't know much about this brother of Seraffimo's, Jack Spang. If Saye is Jack Spang it's the first I've heard of him for a long while. We've got records on all the rest of the mob, and I've run across Tiffany Case. Nice kid but she's been on the fringe of the gangs for years. Didn't have much chance from the cradle up. Her mother ran the snazziest cathouse in San Francisco. Doing fine until she made one hell of a mistake. Decided one day not to pay the local outfit's protection money. She was paying the police so much I guess she reckoned they'd look after her. Crazy. One night the mob turned up in force and wrecked the joint. Left the girls alone but had themselves a gangbang with Tiffany. She was only sixteen at the time. Not surprising she hasn't had anything to do with men since then. Next day she got hold of her mother's cash box, busted it open, and took to the hills. Then the usual round—hatcheck girl, taxi-dancer, studio extra, waitress—until she was about twenty. Then she took to liquor. Settled in a rooming

house down on one of the Florida keys and started
drinking herself to death. Got so she was known as
'The Pickled Relish' down there. Then a kid fell in the
sea and she jumped in and saved him. Got her name in
the papers, and some rich woman took a fancy to her
and practically kidnapped her. Got her to join
Alcoholics Anonymous and then took her around the
world as her companion. But she skipped when they got
to Frisco and went and lived with her old ma, who had
retired from the girl game by then. But she never would
settle down and I guess she found life a bit quiet, so she
took off again and ended up in Reno. Worked at
Harold's Club for a bit. Came across our friend Seraffimo and got him all excited because she wouldn't sleep
with him. Offered her some sort of job at the Tiara at
Las Vegas, and she's been there for the last year or two.
Doing these trips to Europe in between, I suppose. But
she's a good kid. Just never had a chance after what the
gang did to her.''

Bond saw again the eyes gazing sullenly at him out of
the mirror and he heard the record playing ''Feuilles-
Mortes'' in the lonely room. ''I like her,'' he said
briefly. He felt Leiter's eyes watching him speculatively.
He looked at his watch. ''Well, Felix,'' he said, ''it
looks as if we've both got hold of the same tiger. But by
different tails. It's going to be fun pulling at them both
at the same time. Now I'm going to go and get some
sleep. Got a room at the Astor. Where shall we meet on
Sunday?''

''Better keep away from this part of town,'' said
Leiter. ''Meet you outside the Plaza. Early, so we can
avoid the traffic on the Parkway. Let's say nine
o'clock? Fifty-ninth Street entrance. You know, where
the horse cabs are. Then if I'm late you can get to
recognise a horse. Useful up at Saratoga.''

He paid the check and they walked down and out
onto the grilling street. He took Bond affectionately by
the arm.

''Just one thing, James,'' he said, and his voice was
serious. ''You may not have a very high opinion of

American gangsters. Compared with SMERSH, for instance, and some of the other people you've been up against. But I can tell you these Spangled boys are tops. They've got a good machine, even if they do have funny names. And they've got protection. That's how it works in America. But don't misunderstand me. They really stink. And this job of yours stinks too." He let go of Bond's arm. Then he said, "And do you know what your job stinks of, you poor dumb Limey?" He smiled grimly. "Formaldehyde and lilies!"

Bitter Champagne

"I'm not going to sleep with you," said Tiffany Case in a matter-of-fact voice, "so don't waste your money getting me tight. But I'll have another and probably another one after that. I just don't want to drink your vodka Martinis under false pretences."

Bond laughed. He gave the order and turned back to her. "We haven't ordered dinner yet," he said. "I was going to suggest shellfish and hock. That might have changed your mind. The combination's supposed to have quite an effect."

"Listen, Bond," said Tiffany, "it'd take more than Crabmeat Ravigotte to get me into bed. In any case since it's your check, I'm going to have caviar and what you English call cutlets and some pink champagne. I don't often date a good-looking Englishman, and the dinner's going to live up to the occasion." Suddenly she leaned towards him and reached out a hand and put it over his. "Sorry," she said abruptly. "I didn't mean that about the check. The dinner's on me. But I did mean it about the occasion."

Bond smiled into her eyes. "Don't be a goose, Tiffany," he said using her name for the first time. "I've been longing for this evening. And I'm going to have just the same as you. I've got plenty of money for the check. Mr Tree tossed me double or nothing for $500 this morning and I won."

At the mention of Shady Tree, the girl's manner changed. "That ought to cover it," she said coldly. "Just. You know what they say about this place? 'All you can eat for three hundred bucks.'"

The waiter brought the Martinis, shaken and not stirred, as Bond had stipulated, and some slivers of lemon peel in a shot glass. Bond twisted two of them and let them sink to the bottom of his drink. He picked up his glass and looked at the girl over the rim. "We haven't drunk to the success of our mission," he said.

The girl's mouth turned down sarcastically at the corners. She drank half the Martini and put the glass down firmly on the table. "Or to the heart-failure I only just survived," she said drily. "You and your damn' golf. I thought you were going to tell that man all about the chip shot you holed in oughty-ought. A little encouragement and you'd have taken out a club and one of those balls and shown him your swing."

"You made me nervous. Clicking away with that damn' lighter trying to get it to work. I bet you put the wrong end of that cigarette in your mouth and lit the filter."

She gave a short laugh. "I nearly did just that. Okay. We'll call it quits." She finished her Martini. "Come on, you're not much of a spender. I want another of these. I'm beginning to enjoy myself. And how about ordering dinner. Or d'you hope I'll pass out before you get around to it?"

Bond beckoned to the captain. He gave the order, and the wine waiter, who wore a striped jacket and a green apron and had a silver chain with a tasting-cup around his neck, went off for the Clicquot Rosé.

"If I have a son," said Bond, "I'll give him just one piece of advice when he comes of age. I'll say 'spend your money how you like, but don't buy yourself anything that eats.' "

"Well," said the girl, "I must say this really is life with a small *l*. Can't you say something nice about my dress or something instead of grumbling the whole time about how expensive I am?"

"As for the dress," Bond said, "it's a dream, and you know it is. I love black velvet, especially against a sunburnt skin, and I'm glad you don't wear too much jewellery and I'm glad you don't paint your nails. Altogether, I daresay you're the prettiest smuggler in New York tonight. Who are you smuggling with tomorrow?"

She picked up her third Martini and peered into it. Then, very slowly, she drank it down. She put down the glass and took a cigarette out of the box beside her plate and bent towards Bond's lighter. The valley between her breasts deepened. She looked up at him through the smoke of her cigarette, and suddenly her eyes widened and then slowly narrowed again. "I like you," they said. "Anything can happen. But don't be impatient. And be kind."

Then the waiter came with the caviar, and suddenly the noise of the restaurant burst into the warm silent room-within-a-room which they had built for themselves and the spell was broken.

"What am I doing tomorrow?" echoed Tiffany Case in the voice one puts on in front of waiters. "Why I'm going to Las Vegas. Going to Chicago on the Twentieth Century and then taking the Superchief to Los Angeles. It's a long way around, but I've had enough flying for a few days. What about you?"

The waiter had gone. For a while they ate their caviar in silence. There was no need to answer the question immediately. Bond suddenly felt they had all the time in the world. They both knew the answer to the big question. For the answers to the small ones there was no hurry.

Bond sat back. The wine waiter brought the champagne, and Bond sampled it. It was ice cold and seemed to have a faint taste of strawberries.

"I'm going up to Saratoga," he said, "I'm to back a horse that's supposed to make me some money."

"I assume it's a fix," said Tiffany sourly. She drank some of her champagne. Her mood had changed again. She shrugged. "You seem to have made quite a hit with Shady this morning," she said coolly. "He wants to put you to work for the mob."

Bond looked down into the pink pool of champagne. Again he could feel the fog of treachery creeping up between him and this girl he liked. He closed his mind to it. He must get on with his job, whatever it involved.

"That's fine," he said easily. "I'd like that. But who is 'the mob'?" He busied himself with lighting a cigarette, conjuring up the professional to keep the human being quiet.

Her sharp glance put him on his mettle. The secret agent took over, and his mind began to work coldly, watching for clues, for lies, for hesitations.

He looked up and his eyes were candid.

She seemed satisfied. "It's called the Spangled Mob. Two brothers called Spang. I work for one of them in Las Vegas. Nobody seems to know where the other one is. Some say he's in Europe. And then there's somebody called A B C. When I'm on this diamond racket, all the orders come from him. The other one, Seraffimo, he's the brother I work for. He's more interested in gambling and horses. Runs a wire service and the Tiara at Vegas."

"What do you do there?"

"I just work there," she said, closing the subject.

"Do you like it?"

She ignored the question as being too stupid to answer. "And then there's Shady," she went on. "He's not a bad guy, really. He looks after the cathouses and the dope and the rest of the stuff. There are plenty of others—hoodlums of one sort and another. Rough operators." She looked at him and her eyes hardened. "You'll get to know them. You'll like them. Just your type."

"Hell," said Bond indignantly, "it's just another job. It's a living."

"There are plenty of other ways."

"Well, these are the people you've chosen to work for."

"You've got something there." She laughed wryly and the ice was broken again. "But believe me, you're getting into the big league when you sign up with the Spangles. If I were you I'd think a hell of a long time before joining our little group. Don't go and get in wrong with the mob. If you're planning anything cosy you'd better start taking harp lessons."

They were interrupted by the arrival of the cutlets accompanied by asparagus with mousseline sauce, and by one of the famous Kriendler brothers who have owned 21 ever since it was the best speakeasy in New York.

"Hullo, Miss Tiffany," he said. "Long time no see. How are things out at Vegas?"

"Hello, Mac." The girl smiled up at him. "Tiara's going along okay." She glanced around the packed room. "Seems your little hot-dog stand isn't doing too badly."

"Can't complain," said the tall young man. "You ought to come in more often. Never enough pretty girls around." He smiled at Bond. "Everything all right?"

"Couldn't be better."

"Come again." He snapped a finger at the wine waiter. "Sam, ask my friends what they'd like to have with their coffee." And with a final smile which included them both he moved off to another table.

Tiffany ordered a stinger and Bond ordered the same.

When the liqueurs and the coffee came, Bond took up the conversation where they had left it. "But, Tiffany," he said, "this diamond racket looks easy enough. Why shouldn't we just go on doing it together? Two or three trips a year will get us good money and that won't be often enough to make immigration or customs ask any awkward questions."

Tiffany was not impressed. "Try putting it up to A B C," she said. "I keep telling you that these people aren't fools. They're running a big operation with this stuff. I've never had the same carrier twice, and I'm not the only guard doing the run. What's more, I'm pretty certain we weren't alone on that plane. I bet they had someone else watching us both. They check and double check on every damn' thing they do." She was irritated with his lack of respect for the quality of her employers. "Why, I've never even seen A B C," she said. "I just call up a number in London and get my orders on a wire-recorder. Anything I've got to say I send back to A B C the same way. I tell you all this is way over your head. You and your country-house burglaries." She was crushing. "Brother!"

"I see," said Bond respectfully, wondering how the hell he could get the A B C telephone number out of her. "They certainly seem to think of everything."

"Bet your life," said the girl flatly. The subject was now boring. Moodily, she drank her stinger down.

Bond sensed the beginning of a *vin triste*. "Care to go somewhere else?" he said, knowing that it was he who had killed the evening.

"Hell, no," she said dully. "Take me home. I'm getting tight. Why couldn't you dream up something else to talk about except these God-damn' crooks?"

Bond paid the check and in silence they went down and out of the cool envelope of the restaurant into the sultry night that stank of exhaust fumes and hot asphalt.

"I'm staying at the Astor, too," she said as they got into a cab. She pressed into the far corner of the seat and sat hunched up with her chin in her hand, looking out at the hideous deadly nightshade of the neon.

Bond said nothing. He looked out of the other window and cursed his job. All he wanted to say to this girl was, "Listen: come with me. I like you. Don't be afraid." But if she said yes he would have been smart. And he didn't want to be smart with this girl. It was his job to use her; but whatever the job dictated, there was one way he would never "use" this particular girl: through the heart.

In front of the Astor he helped her out onto the sidewalk, and she stood with her back to him while he paid the driver. They walked up the steps in the stiff silence of a married couple after a bad evening ending in a row.

They got their keys at the desk and she said "Five" to the boy on the elevator. She stood with her face to the door as they rode up. Bond saw that the knuckles of the hand that held her evening bag were white. At the fifth she walked quickly out and made no protest when Bond followed her. They walked around several corners until they came to her door. She bent down and fitted the key into the lock and pushed the door open. Then she turned in the entrance and faced him.

"Listen, damn you—"

It had started as the beginning of an angry speech, but then she paused and looked straight into his eyes and Bond saw that her lashes were wet. Suddenly she flung an arm around his neck and her face was against his and she was saying: "Take care of yourself, James. I don't want to lose you." And then she pulled his face against hers and kissed him once hard and long on the lips, with a fierce tenderness that was almost without sex.

But, as Bond's arms went around her and he started to return her kiss, she suddenly stiffened and fought her way free and the moment was over.

With her hand on the knob of the open door she turned and gazed back at him, and the bitter look was back in her eyes.

"Now get away from me," she said fiercely, and slammed the door and locked it.

Studillac to Saratoga

James Bond spent most of Saturday in his air-conditioned room at the Astor, avoiding the heat, sleeping, and composing a hundred-group cable addressed to the Chairman, Universal Export, London. He used a simple transposition code based on the fact that it was the sixth day of the week and that the date was the fourth of the eighth month.

The report concluded that the diamond pipe line began somewhere near Jack Spang, in the shape of Rufus B. Saye, and ended with Seraffimo Spang and that the main junction in the pipe was the office of Shady Tree from which, presumably, the stones were fed into the House of Diamonds for cutting and marketing.

Bond requested London to put a close tail on Rufus B. Saye, but he warned that an individual known as "A B C" seemed to be in direct command of the actual smuggling on behalf of the Spangled Mob and that Bond had no clue to this indiviual's identity except that he appeared to be located in London. Presumably only this man would provide a lead back to the actual source of the smuggled diamonds somewhere on the continent of Africa.

Bond reported that his own intention was to continue working up the pipe line in the direction of Seraffimo Spang, using as an unconscious agent Tiffany Case, whose background he briefly reported.

Bond sent the cable collect via Western Union, had his fourth shower of the day and went to Voisin where he had two vodka Martinis, Eggs Benedict and strawberries. Over dinner he read the dope sheets for the Saratoga meeting and noted that the joint favourites for the Perpetuities Stakes were Mr. C. V. Whitney's Come Again and Mr. William Woodward, Jr.,'s Pray Action. Shy Smile was not mentioned.

Then he walked back to his hotel and went to bed.

Punctually at nine on Sunday morning a black Studebaker convertible drew up to the sidewalk where Bond was standing beside his suitcase.

When Bond had thrown his case onto the back seat and climbed in, Leiter reached up to the roof and pulled back a lever. Then he pressed a button on the dash and, with a thin hydraulic whine, the canvas roof slowly raised itself up into the air and folded itself down and back into a recess between the rear seat and the boot. Then, manipulating the steering-wheel gearshift with easy movements of his steel hook, he took the car fast across Central Park.

"It's about two hundred miles," said Leiter when they were on the Henry Hudson Parkway. "Almost due north up the Hudson. Just south of the Adirondacks on the way to the Canadian border. We'll take the Taconic State Parkway. There's no hurry, so we'll go easy. And I don't want to get a ticket. There's a fifty-mile speed limit in most of New York State, and the cops are fierce. I can generally get away from them if I'm in a hurry. They don't book you if they can't catch you. Too ashamed to turn up in court and admit something is faster than they are."

"But I thought those Indians could do well over

ninety," said Bond. "I didn't know these Studebakers had it in them."

There was a straight stretch of empty road in front of them. Leiter gave a brief glance in his rear-view mirror and suddenly rammed the gear lever into second and thrust his foot to the floor boards. Bond's head jerked back on his shoulders and he felt his spine being pressed into the back of the bucket seat. Incredulously, he watched the hooded speedometer. Eighty. With a clang Leiter's hook moved the gear lever into high and the car went on gathering speed. Ninety, ninety-five, six, seven—and then there was a bridge and a converging road and Leiter's foot was on the brake and the deep roar of the engine gave way to a steady thrumming as they settled down into the fifties again and swept easily through the graded curves.

Leiter glanced sideways at Bond and grinned. "Nearly another thirty on top of that," he said proudly. "Not long ago I paid five dollars and put her through the measured mile at Daytona. She clocked 127, and that beach surface isn't any too hot."

"Well, I'll be damned," said Bond admiringly. "But what sort of car is this anyway? Isn't it a Studebaker?"

"Studillac," said Leiter. "Studebaker with a Cadillac engine. Special transmission and brakes and rear axle. Conversion job. A small firm near New York turns them out. Only a few, but they're a damn' sight better sports car than those Corvettes and Thunderbirds. And you couldn't have anything better than this body. Designed by that Frenchman Raymond Loewy. Naturalised now. One of the best designers in the world, but it's a bit too advanced for the American market. Studebakers never got enough credit for this body. Too unconventional. Like the car? Bet I could give your old Bentley a licking." Leiter chuckled and reached in his left-hand pocket for a dime as they came to the toll.

"Until one of your wheels came off," said Bond caustically as they accelerated away again. "This sort of hotrod job's all right for kids who can't afford a real car."

They wrangled cheerfully over the respective merits of English and American sports cars until they came to the Taconic State Parkway, that snaked northwards through more than a hundred miles of meadows and woodlands, and Bond settled back and silently enjoyed one of the most beautifully landscaped highways in the world and wondered idly what the girl was doing and how, after Saratoga, he was to get to see her again.

At 12:30 they stopped for lunch at a "Chicken in the Basket," a log-built "frontier-style" roadhouse with standard equipment—a tall counter covered with the best known name-brands of chocolates and candies, cigarettes and cigars, a juke box blazing with chromium and coloured lights that looked like something out of science-fiction, a dozen or more polished pine tables in the centre of the raftered room and as many low booths along the walls, a menu featuring fried chicken and "fresh mountain trout" which had spent months in some distant deep-freeze, a variety of short-order dishes, and a couple of waitresses who couldn't care less.

But the scrambled eggs and sausages and hot buttered rye toast came quickly and were good and so was the iced coffee that followed it, and with their second glass they got away from "shop" and their private lives and got on to Saratoga.

"Eleven months of the year," explained Leiter, "the place is just dead. People drift up to take the waters and the mud baths for their troubles, rheumatism and such like, and it's just like any other off-season spa anywhere in the world. Everybody's in bed by nine, and the only signs of life in the daytime are when two old gentlemen in Panama hats get to arguing about the surrender of Burgoyne at Schuylerville just down the road, or about whether the marble floor of the old Union Hotel was black or white. And then for one month—August—the place goes hogwild. It's probably the smartest race-meeting in America, and the place crawls with Vanderbilts and Whitneys. The rooming houses all multiply their prices by ten, and the race-track committee lick the old grandstand up with paint and somehow find swans for the pond in the centre of the track and anchor the old Indian canoe in the middle of it and turn on the fountain. Nobody can remember where the canoe came from, and an American racing writer who tried to find out got as far as the fact that it was something to do with an Indian legend. He said that when he heard that he didn't bother any more. He said that when he was in the fourth grade he could tell a better lie than any Indian legend he ever heard."

Bond laughed. "What else?"

"You ought to know about it yourself," said Leiter. "Used to be a great place for the English—the belted ones, that is. The Jersey Lily used to be around there a lot, your Lily Langtry. About the time Novelty beat Iron Mask in the Hopeful Stakes. But it's changed a bit since the Mauve Decade. Here." He pulled a clipping out of his pocket. "This'll bring you up to date. Cut it out of the *Post* this morning. This Jimmy Cannon is their sports columnist. Good writer. Knows what he's talking about. Read it in the car. We ought to be moving."

Leiter left some money on the check and they went out, and while the Studillac throbbed along the long winding road towards Troy, Bond made the acquaintance of Jimmy Cannon's muscular, craftsmanlike prose. As he read, the Saratoga of the Jersey Lily's day vanished into the sweet dusty past and the twentieth century leered out at him from the piece of newsprint and bared its teeth.

"The village of Saratoga Springs," he read beneath the photograph of an attractive man with wide straight eyes and a rather thin-lipped smile, "was the Coney Island of the underworld until the Kefauvers put their show on the television. It frightened the hicks and chased the hoodlums to Las Vegas. But the mobs exercised dominion over Saratoga for a long time. It was a colony of the national gangs and they ran it with pistols and baseball bats.

"Saratoga seceded from the union as did the other gambling hamlets that placed their municipal governments in the custody of the racket corporations. It is still a place where the decent inheritors of old fortunes and famous names come to run their stables under racing conditions that are primitive and suggest a country fair meeting for quarter horses.

"Before Saratoga closed down, hitchhikers were thrown into the can by a constabulary that banked its pay checks and lived off the tips of murderers and panderers. Impoverishment was a serious violation of the law in Saratoga. Drunks, who got loaded at the bars of dice joints, were also considered menaces when they tapped out.

"But the killer was extended the liberty of the place as long as he paid off and held an interest in a local institution. It could be a house of prostitution or a backroom crap game where the busted could shoot two bits.

"Professional curiosity compels me to read the literature of the scratch sheets. The racing journalists call back the tranquil years as though Saratoga was always a town of frivolous innocence. What a rotten burg it used to be.

"It is possible that there are bust-out gaffs sneaking in farm houses on back roads. Such action is insignificant and the player must be prepared to be knocked out as rapidly as the dealer can switch the dice. But the gambling casinos of Saratoga were never square and anyone who caught a hot hand was measured for a trimming.

"The road-houses ran through the night on the shores of the lake. The big entertainers shilled for the games which were not financed to be beaten. The stick men and the wheel turners were the nomadic hustlers who were paid by the day and travelled the gambling circuit from Newport, Ky., down to Miami in the winter and back up to Saratoga for August. Most of them were educated in Steubenville, O., where the penny-ante games were trade schools for the industry.

"They were drifters and most of them had no talent for mussing up a welsher. They were clerks of the underworld and they picked up and left as soon as any heat was turned their way. Host of them have settled down in Las Vegas and Reno where their old bosses have taken charge with licenses hanging on the walls.

"Their employers were not gamblers in the tradition of old Col. E. R. Bradley who was a stately man of courteous deportment. But there are those who tell me that his gambling bazaar in Palm Beach would go along with a mark until his score piled up too high.

"Then, according to those who have gone against Bradley's games, mechanics took over and used any device that would keep the house solvent. It delights those who recollect Bradley when they read his canonization as a philanthropist whose hobby was giving the rich a little divertissement denied them by the state of Florida. But, compared to the lice who controlled Saratoga, Col. Bradley is entitled to all the praise he gets in the remembrances of the sentimentalists.

"The track at Saratoga is a ramshackle pile of kindling wood and the climate is hot and humid. There are some, such as Al Vanderbilt and Jock Whitney, who are sportsmen in the obsolete sense of the identification. Horse-racing is their game and they are too good for it. So are such trainers as Bill Winfrey who sent Native Dancer to the races. There are jockeys who would bust you in the nose if you propositioned them to pull a horse.

"They enjoy Saratoga and they must be glad that the likes of Lucky Luciano are gone from the rube town that flourished because it allowed tough guys to fleece the dropins. The bookmakers were yegged as they left the track in the era of the handbooks. There was one called Kid Tatters who was relieved of $50,000 in the parking lot. The heist guys told them they intended to kidnap him if he didn't come up with more.

"Kid Tatters knew Lucky had a piece of most of the gambling spots and appealed to him to settle his trouble. Lucky said it was a simple matter. No one would bother the bookie if he did as he was told. Kid Tatters had a permit to book at the track and his reputation was clean but there was only one way he could protect himself.

" 'Make me your partner,' Lucky informed him and the conversation was repeated for me by a man who was present. 'No one would stick up a partner of Lucky's.'

"Kid Tatters thought of himself as an honorable guy in business sanctioned by the state, but he gave in and Lucky was his partner until he died. I asked a guy if Lucky put up any money or worked for his end of the bookmaker's profit.

" 'All Lucky did was collect,' the fellow said. 'But in those days, Kid Tatters made himself a good bargain. He was never bothered again.'

"It was a stinking town but all gambling towns are."

Bond folded the clipping and put it in his pocket. "It certainly sounds a long way from Lily Langtry," he said after a pause.

"Yeah," said Leiter indifferently. "And Jimmy Cannon doesn't let on he knows the big boys are back again, or their successors. But nowadays they're owners, like our friends the Spangs, running their horses against the Whitneys and the Vanderbilts and the Woodwards and now and then putting over a fast fix like Shy Smile. They aim to net fifty grand on that job, and that's better than knocking off a bookie for a few C's. Sure, some of the names have changed around Saratoga. So's the mud in the mud baths there.''

A big road sign loomed up on the right. It said: STOP AT THE SAGAMORE. AIR-CONDITIONED. SLUMBERITE BEDS. TELEVISION. FIVE MILES TO SARATOGA SPRINGS AND THE SAGAMORE—FOR GRACIOUS LIVING.

''That means we get our bathroom glasses wrapped in cellophane and the lavatory seat sealed with a strip of sanitised paper,'' commented Leiter sourly. ''And don't think you can steal those Slumberite beds. Motels used to lose about one a week. Now they screw 'em down.''

CHAPTER 11

Shy Smile

The first thing that struck Bond about Saratoga was the green majesty of the elms, which gave the discreet avenues of colonial-type clapboard houses some of the peace and serenity of a European watering place. There were horses everywhere, being walked across the streets while a policeman held up traffic, being coaxed out of horseboxes around the sprawling groups of stables, cantering along the cinder borders of the roads and being led to work on the exercise track alongside the race course near the centre of the town. Stableboys and jockeys, white, Negro and Mexican, hung about at the street corners, and the whinny and the occasional trumpeting snort of horses were in the air.

It was a mixture of Newmarket and Vichy, and it suddenly occurred to Bond that although he wasn't in the least interested in horses he rather liked the life that went with them.

Leiter dropped him at the Sagamore, which was on the edge of town and only half a mile from the racetrack, and went off about his business. They agreed to contact each other only at night or casually in the crowds at the races but decided to pay a dawn visit to the exercise track if Shy Smile was being given a last workout at sunrise the next day. Leiter said he would know about this, and much more, after an evening around the stables and at the Tether, the all-night restaurant and bar that was the home of the racing underworld when they came up for the August meeting.

Bond checked himself in at the central office of the Sagamore, signed "James Bond, Hotel Astor, New York," in front of a shark-mouthed woman whose steel-rimmed regard conveyed that Bond, like most of her other seekers after "gracious living," probably intended to steal the towels and possibly the sheets. He paid sixty dollars for three days and was given a key to Room 49.

He carried his bag across the parched lawn between the beds of Beauty Bush and forced gladioli and let himself into the neat, sparsely furnished double room with the armchair, the bedside table, the Currier and Ives print, the chest of drawers and the brown plastic ashtray that are standard motel equipment all over America. The lavatory and shower were immaculate and neatly designed and, as Leiter had prophesied, the bathroom glasses were contained in cellophane "for your protection" and the lavatory seat was barred by a strip of paper which said "Sanitised."

Bond took a shower and changed and walked down the road and had two Bourbon old-fashioneds and the chicken dinner for $4.50 in the air-conditioned restaurant on the corner that was as typical as the motel. Then he returned to his room and lay on his bed with the *Saratogian* from which he learned that a certain T. Bell would be riding Shy Smile in the Perpetuities.

Soon after ten, Felix Leiter knocked softly on the door and limped in He smelled of liquor and cheap cigar smoke and looked pleased with himself.

"Made some progress," he said. He hooked the armchair up to the foot of the bed on which Bond was lying. He sat down and shook out a cigarette. "Means getting up damned early in the morning. Five o'clock. The word is they'll be timing Shy Smile over four furlongs at 5:30. I'd like to see who's around when they're doing that. The owner's given as 'Pissaro.' One of the directors of the Tiara happens to be called that. He's another one with a joke name: 'Lame-Brain' Pissaro. Used to be in charge of their dope racket. Ran the stuff over the Mexican border and then broke it down and parcelled it out to middlemen on the coast. The F.B.I. got onto him and he did a term in San Quentin. Then he came out and Spang gave him the job at the Tiara in exchange for the rap he'd taken. And now he's a race-horse owner, just like the Vanderbilts. I'll be interested to see what sort of shape he's in these days. He was almost a mainliner in the days he was dealing in coke. They gave him the cure in San Q. but it's left him a bit soft in the head. Hence 'Lame-Brain.' Then there's the jock, 'Tingaling' Bell. Good rider but not above this sort of caper if the money's right and he's in the clear. I want to have a word with Tingaling if I can get him alone. I've got a little proposition for him. The trainer's another hoodlum, name of Budd, 'Rosy' Budd. They all sound pretty cute, these names. But you don't want to be taken in by it. Budd's from Kentucky, so he knows all about horses. He's been in trouble all over the South, what they call a 'little habitch' as opposed to a 'big habitch'—habitual criminal. Larceny, mugging, rape—nothing big. But enough to give him quite a bulky packet in police records. For the last few years, though, he's been straight, if you care to call it that, as a trainer for Spang."

Leiter flicked his cigarette accurately into the waste basket, and Bond thought fleetingly of his Chief of Staff. Leiter got up and stretched. "Those are the actors in the order of their appearance," he said. "Distinguished cast. I look forward to lighting a fire under them."

Bond was mystified. "But why don't you just turn them over to the Stewards? Who are your principals in all this? Who pays the bills?"

"Retained by the leading owners," said Leiter.
"They pay us a retainer and extra by results. And I
wouldn't get far with the Stewards. Wouldn't be fair to
put the stableboy in the box. Be the death sentence for
him. The veterinary has passed the horse, and the real
Shy Smile was shot and burned months ago. No. I've
got my own ideas, and they're going to hurt the
Spangled boys far more than a disbarment from the
tracks. You'll see. Anyway, five o'clock and I'll come
and hammer on the door just in case."

"Don't worry," said Bond. "I'll be on the doorstep
with my boots and saddle while the coyotes are still
baying at the moon."

Bond woke on time, and there was a wonderful
freshness in the air as he followed the limping figure of
Leiter through the half-light that filtered through the
elms among the waking stables. In the east the sky was
pearly grey and iridescent, like a toy balloon filled with
cigarette smoke, and among the shrubs the mocking
birds were beginning their first song. Blue smoke rose
straight up in the air from the fires in the camps behind
the stables, and there was a smell of coffee and wood
smoke and dew. There were the clank of pails and the
other small noises of men and horses in the early morning, and as Bond and Leiter moved out from under the
trees to the white wooden rail that bordered the track a
file of blanketed horses came by, a boy at each head,
holding the leading ring up close to the bit and talking
with soft roughness to their charges: 'Hey lazybones,
pick yo' feet up. You sho ain't no Man-o-War dis
mornin'."

"They'll be getting ready for the morning works,"
said Leiter. "The gallops. This is the time the trainers
hate most. When the owners come."

They leaned against the rail, and the sun suddenly
caught the trees half a mile away on the other side of the
track and brushed the topmost branches with pale gold,
and in minutes the last shadows had gone and it was
day.

As if they had been waiting for the sign, three men ap-

peared, one of them leading a big chestnut with a blaze
face and four white stockings.

"Don't look at them," said Leiter softly. "Turn your
back on the track and watch that file of horses coming
up. That old bent man with them is Sunny Jim Fitz-
simmons, greatest trainer in America. And those are the
Woodward horses. Most of them will be winners this
meeting. Just look nonchalant and I'll keep an eye on
our friends. Wouldn't do to seem too interested, Now
let's see. There's a stable boy leading Shy Smile and
that's Budd all right and my old friend Lame-Brain in a
beautiful lavender shirt. Always was a dresser. Nice-
looking horse. Powerful shoulders. They've taken the
blanket off him and he doesn't like the cold. Bucking
around like mad with the stableboy hanging on. Sure
hope he doesn't kick Mr. Pissaro in the face. Now
Budd's got him and he's quieted down. Budd's given the
boy a leg up. Leading him onto the track. Now he's cantering slowly up the far side of the track to one of the
furlong posts. The boys have got their watches out;
they're looking around. They've spotted us. Just look
casual, James. Once the horse gets going they won't be
interested in us. Shy Smile's on the far side of the track,
and they've got their glasses on her to be ready for the
off. It will be four furlongs. Pissaro's just by the fifth
post. Okay. You can turn around now."

Bond turned and looked along the rail to his left at
the two stocky, intent figures with the sun glinting on
their glasses and on the watches in their hands and,
although he didn't believe in these people, the murk of
the underworld seemed to seep out around them under
the elms.

"He's off." Far away Bond could see a flying brown
horse rounding the top end of the track and turning into
the long stretch towards them. At that distance not a
sound came to them, but quickly there was a soft drumming on the tan track that grew until with a swift
thunder of hooves the horse rounded the bend in front
of them, right up against the far rails, and hurtled on
the last furlong towards the watching men.

A tingle of excitement ran down Bond's spine as the chestnut flashed by, its teeth bared and its eyes wild with the effort, its gleaming quarters pounding and the breath snorting out of its wide nostrils, the boy on its back arched like a cat in the stirrups, his face down close, almost touching the horse's neck. And then they had gone in a spray of sound and upflung earth and Bond's eyes moved to the two watching men, now crouching, and he saw the two arms jerk downwards as they thumbed the stop on their watches.

Leiter touched him on the arm and they moved away and back under the trees towards the car.

"Moving damn' well," commented Leiter. "Better than the real Shy Smile ever did. No idea what the time was, but he certainly was burning up the track. If he can do that for a mile and a quarter he'll get home. And he'll have an allowance of six pounds, seeing as how he hasn't won a race this year. That'll give him the extra edge. Now let's go and have one hell of a breakfast. It's given me an appetite, seeing those crooks so early in the morning." And then he added softly, almost to himself: "And then I'm going to see how much Master Bell will take to ride foul and get himself disqualified."

After breakfast, and after hearing some more of Leiter's plans, Bond idled away the morning and then had lunch at the track and watched the indifferent racing that Leiter had warned him he would see on the first afternoon of the meeting.

But it was a beautiful day and Bond enjoyed absorbing the Saratoga scene: the milling crowds, the elegance of the owners and their friends in the tree-shaded paddock, the efficient mechanics of the pari-mutuel and the big board with its flashing lights recording the odds and the money invested, the trouble-free starts through the tractor-drawn starting gate, the toy lake with its six swans and the anchored canoe and everywhere the Negroes who, except as jockeys, are so much a part of American racing.

The organization looked better than in England.

There seemed less chance of crookedness where so much crookedness had been ensured against, but behind it all Bond knew that the illegal wire services were relaying the results of each race throughout the States, cutting the odds to a maximum of 20-8-4, twentys for a win, eights for first or second, and fours for a place, and that millions of dollars every year were going straight into the pockets of gangsters to whom racing was merely a source of revenue, like prostitution or drugs.

Bond tried out the system made famous by "Chicago" O'Brien. He backed every firm favourite for "place" or "show," as his first ticket window told him to call it, and he had somehow made fifteen dollars and some cents by the end of the eighth race and the day's meeting. He walked home with the crowds, had a shower and some sleep and then found his way to a restaurant near the sales ring and spent an hour drinking bourbon and branch water. Then he walked over to the sales ring which Leiter had fixed as a rendezvous.

It was a white painted wooden enclosure, roofed but without walls, in which tiered benches descended to a circle of mock-greensward enclosed with silver painted ropes in front of the auctioneer's platform. As each horse was led in under the glare of the neon lighting, the auctioneer, the redoubtable Swinebroad from Tennessee would give the history of the horse and start the bidding at what he thought a likely figure and run it up through the hundreds in a kind of rhythmic chant, catching, with the help of two dinner-jacketed men in the aisles, every nod or raised pencil among the tiers of smartly dressed owners and agents.

Bond sat down behind a scrawny woman in evening dress and mink whose wrists clanked and glittered with jewellery every time she bid. Beside her sat a bored man in a white dinner jacket and a dark red evening tie who might have been her husband or her trainer.

A nervous bay came chasséing into the ring with the number 201 pasted carelessly on his rump. The nasal chant began. "I'm bid six thousand now seven thousand will yer? I'm bid seven thousand and three and four and five only seven and a half for this good-looking colt by Tehran eight thousand thank you sir and nine will yer do it? Eight thousand five hundred I am bid will yer give me nine eight five will yer give me nine and six and seven and who'll bid the big figure?"

A pause, a bang of the hammer, a look of sincere reproach towards the ringside seats where the big money sat. "Folks, this two-year-old is too cheap. I'm selling more winning colt for this amount of money than I've sold all summer long. Now, eight thousand seven hundred and who'll give me nine? Where's nine, nine, nine?" (The mummified hand in the rings and bracelets took the gold and bamboo pencil out of the bag and scribbled a calculation on the program which Bond could see said "34th Annual Saratoga Yearling Sales. No. 201. A Bay Colt." Then the leaden eyes of the woman looked across the silver ropes into the electric eyes of the horse and she raised the gold pencil.) "And nine thousand is bid nine will yer give me ten will yer do it? Any increase on nine thousand do I hear nine one nine one nine one?" (A pause and a last questing look around the crammed white seats and then a bang of the hammer.) "Sold for nine thousand dollars. Thank you, ma'am."

And the heads turned around and craned and the woman looked bored and said something to the man beside her who shrugged his shoulders. And 201, "A Bay Colt," was led from the ring and 202 came sidling in to stand for a moment trembling with the shock of the lights and the wall of unknown faces and the fog of strange smells.

There was a movement in the row of seats behind Bond, and Leiter's head came forward and his voice whispered into Bond's ear: "It's done. Cost three thousand bucks but he'll work the double-cross. Foul riding in the last furlong just as he's due to make his winning sprint. See you in the morning." Bond didn't look around, but went on watching the sales for a while and then slowly strolled home under the elms, feeling sorry for a jockey called Tingaling Bell who was playing such a desperately dangerous game, and for the big chestnut called Shy Smile who was now not only a ringer but was going to be ridden foul into the bargain.

CHAPTER 12

The Perpetuities

Bond sat high up in the grandstand and through rented glasses watched Shy Smile's owner eating soft-shell crabs.

The gangster was sitting in the restaurant enclosure four rows below Bond. Opposite him sat Rosy Budd forking down frankfurters and sauerkraut and drinking beer out of a stein. Although most of the other tables were occupied there were two waiters hovering around this one and the maître d'hôtel made frequent visits to see that all was going well.

Pissaro looked like a villain in a horror-comic. He had a round bladder-like head in the middle of which the features were crowded together—two pin-point eyes, two black nostrils, a pursed wet pink mouth above the hint of a chin—and a fat body in a brown suit and a white shirt with a long-pointed collar and a figured chocolate bow tie. He paid no attention to the preparations for the first race but concentrated on his food, occasionally glancing across at his companion's

plate as if he might reach across and fork something off
it for himself.

Rosy Budd was broad and hard-looking with a
square, immobile poker player's face in which pale eyes
were buried deep under thin fair eyebrows. He was
wearing a striped seersucker suit and a dark blue tie. He
ate slowly and rarely looked up from his plate. When he
had finished he picked up a race program and studied it,
turning over the pages carefully. Without looking up he
gave a curt shake of the head when the maître d'hôtel
offered him the menu.

Pissaro picked his teeth. Then his ice cream arrived,
and he bent his head again and started spooning it
rapidly into his small mouth.

What did these people amount to? Bond remembered
cold, dedicated, chess-playing Russians; brilliant, neu-
rotic Germans; silent, deadly, anonymous men from
Central Europe; the people in his own Service, the
double-firsts, the gay soldiers of fortune, the men who
counted life well lost for a thousand a year. Compared
to such men, Bond decided, these people were just teen-
age pillow-fantasies.

The results went up for the first race, and now there
was only half an hour to go before the Perpetuities.
Bond put down his glasses and picked up his program,
waiting for the big board on the other side of the track
to start flickering as the money went on the tote and the
odds began to move.

He took a final look at the details. "Second Day.
August 4," read the program. "The Perpetuities Stakes.
$25,000 added. 52nd Running. For Three-Year-Olds.
By subscription of $50 each, to accompany the
nomination. Starters to pay $250 additional. With the
$25,000 added of which $5,000 to second, $2,500 to
third and $1,250 to fourth. A trophy to be presented to
the owner of the winner. One Mile and a Quarter." And
then the list of twelve horses with owners, trainers and
jockeys and the *Morning Line* forecast of the odds.

The joint favourites, No. 1, Mr. C. V. Whitney's
Come Again and No. 3, Mr. William Woodward's Pray

Action, were both forecast at six to four on. Mr. P. Pissaro's Shy Smile, Trainer R. Budd, Jockey T. Bell, was forecast at 15 to 1, the bottom horse in the betting. His number was 10.

Bond turned his glasses on the restaurant enclosure. The two men had gone. Bond's eyes followed on across the track to where the lights were flashing on the big board. The favourite was now No. 3, at 2 to 1 on. Come Again had gone out to evens. Shy Smile was quoted at 20 to 1, but he went down to 18's as Bond watched the board.

Another quarter of an hour to go. Bond sat back and lit a cigarette, going over again in his mind what Leiter had told him, wondering if it was going to work.

Leiter had tracked the jockey down to his rooming house and had flashed his private detective's license at him. And then he had quite calmly blackmailed him into throwing the race. If Shy Smile won, Leiter would go to the Stewards, expose the ringer, and Tingaling Bell would never ride again. But there was one chance for the jockey to save himself. If he took it, Leiter promised to say nothing about the ringer. Shy Smile must win the race but be disqualified. This could be achieved if, in the final sprint, the jockey interfered with the running of the horse closest to him so that it could be shown that he had prevented this other horse from being the winner. Then there would be an objection, which had to be upheld. It would be easy for Bell, at the last corner before the home stretch, to do this in such a way that he could argue to his employers that it had just been over-zealous riding, that another horse had crowded him over to the left, that his own horse had stumbled. There was no conceivable reason why he shouldn't want to win (Pissaro had promised him an extra thousand dollars if he did) and it was just one of those strokes of bad luck that happen in racing. And Leiter would now give Tingaling $1,000 and there would be another $2,000 for him if he did what he was told.

And Bell had bought it. Without any hesitation. He had asked that the $2,000 be passed to him after the day's racing in the Acme Mud and Sulphur Baths, where he went every evening to take a mud bath to keep his weight down. Six o'clock. Leiter had promised that this would be done. Bond now had the $2,000 and he had reluctantly agreed to help Leiter out by going to the Acme Baths and make the payoff if Shy Smile failed to win the race.

Would it work? Bond picked up his glasses and swept them around the course. There were the four thick posts at the quarter miles that held the automatic cameras that recorded the whole race and whose film was available to the Stewards within minutes of each finish. It was this last one near the winning post whose eye would see and record all that happened at the final turn. Bond felt a shiver of excitement. Five minutes to go, and the starting gate was being pulled into position a hundred yards up to his left. Once around the course plus an extra furlong and the winning post was just below him. He put his glasses on the big board. No change in the favourites or in Shy Smile's odds. And now here came the horses, cantering easily down to the barrier. First came No. 1, Come Again, the second favourite. A big black horse carrying the light blue and brown colors of the Whitney Stable. And there was a cheer for the favourite Pray Action, a fast-looking grey carrying the Woodward white with the red spots of the famous Belair Stud, and at the tail of the field was the big chestnut with the blaze face and four white stockings and the pale-faced jockey wearing a jacket of lavender silk with a big black diamond on chest and back.

The horse moved so well that Bond glanced across at the board and was not surprised to see his price come quickly back to 17's, then 16's. Bond went on watching the board. In a minute the big money would go on (all except the remains of Bond's thousand dollars, which would stay in his pocket) and the price would plummet. The loudspeaker was announcing the race. Off to the left the horses were being marshalled behind the starting gate. Ping, ping, ping, the lights opposite No. 10 on the board started to wink and flash—15, 14, 12, 11 and finally 9 to 1. Then the lights stopped talking and the tote was closed. And how many more thousands had gone away by Western Union to harmless telegraphic addresses in Detroit, Chicago, New York, Miami, San Francisco, and a dozen more off-the-course books throughout the States?

A handbell clanged sharply and there was an electric smell in the air and a muting of the noise of the crowds, then down thundered the ragged charging line towards the grandstand and past and away in a scud of hooves and flying earth and tanbark. Bond caught a glimpse of sharp, pinched faces half hidden by goggles, a stream of pounding shoulders and hindquarters, a flash of wild white eyes and a confusion of numbers amongst which Bond caught only the vital No. 10 well to the fore and close to the rails. And then the dust was settling and the brown-black mass was at the first corner and slowly streaming around the bottom straight, and Bond felt the glasses slip in the sweat round his eyes.

No. 5, a black outsider, was leading by a length. Was this some unknown horse that was going to steal the whole show? But then there was No. 1 level with him and then No. 3. And No. 10 half a length behind the leaders. Just these four out in front and the rest bunched three lengths behind. Round the corner, and now No. 1 was in the lead. The Whitney black. And No. 10 was fourth. Down the long straight opposite, and No. 3 was moving up with Tingaling Bell on the chestnut at his heels. They both passed No. 5 and were well up with No. 1, who was still leading by half a length. And then the first top bend and the top straight and No. 3 was leading with Shy Smile second and No. 1 a length behind. And Shy Smile was coming up level with the leader. He was level and they were coming into the final corner. Bond held his breath. Now. Now. He could almost hear the whirr of the concealed camera in the big white post. No. 10 was ahead, right on the band, but No. 3 was inside on the rails. And the crowd was howling for the favourite. Now Bell was inching towards the grey, his head well down on his horse's neck on the outside so that he could pretend that he couldn't see the grey horse on the rails. Inch by inch the horses drew closer, and suddenly Shy Smile's head hid No. 3's head and his quarters were in front and, yes, Pray Action's boy suddenly stood right up in his stirrups, forced to take-up by the foul, and at once Shy Smile was a length ahead.

There was a roar from the crowd. Bond lowered his glasses and sat back and watched as the foam-flecked chestnut thundered past the post below him with Pray Action five lengths behind and Come Again just failing to beat him into second place.

Not bad, thought Bond, as the crowd howled around him. Not bad at all.

And how brilliantly the jockey had done it! His head so well down that even Pissaro would have to admit Bell couldn't have seen the other horse. The natural curve in for the final straight. The head still well down as he passed the post and the whip flailing for the last few lengths as if Tingaling still thought himself only half a length ahead of No. 3.

Bond watched for the results to be posted. There was a scattering of groans. No. 10. Shy Smile five lengths. No. 3. Pray Action one-half length. No. 1. Come Again three lengths. No. 7. Pirandello three lengths.

The horses came cantering back for the weighing in and Tingaling Bell, grinning hugely, threw his whip to the valet and slipped off the sweating chestnut and carried his saddle to the scales.

Then there was a great burst of cheering. Opposite the name of Shy Smile the word OBJECTION, white on black, had been slipped in and the loudspeaker was saying: "Attention please. In this race there has been an objection lodged by Jockey T. Lucky on No. 3, Pray Action, against the riding of Jockey T. Bell on No. 10, Shy Smile. Do not destroy your tickets. I repeat, Do not destroy your tickets."

Bond took out his handkerchief and wiped his hands. He could imagine the scene in the projection room behind the judge's box. Now they would be examining the film. Bell would be standing there looking injured and beside him No. 3's jockey, looking still more injured. Would the owners be there? Would the sweat be running down Pissaro's fat jowls into his collar? Would some of the other owners be there, pale and angry?

And then came the loudspeaker again and the voice saying: "Attention please. In this race, No. 10, Shy Smile has been disqualified and No. 3, Pray Action, has been declared the winner. The result is now official."

Amidst the thunder of the crowd, Bond got stiffly up from his seat and walked off in the direction of the bar. And now for the payoff. Perhaps a bourbon and water would give him some ideas about getting the money to Tingaling Bell. He was uneasy about it. And yet the Acme Baths sounded safe enough. Nobody knew him in Saratoga. But after that he would have to stop working for Pinkertons. And call up Shady Tree and complain about not getting his five thousand. It had been fun watching Leiter push these people around. Now it was his turn. He shouldered his way into the crowded bar.

CHAPTER 13

Acme Mud and Sulphur

In the small red bus there was only a Negro woman with a withered arm and, beside the driver, a girl who kept her sick hands out of sight and whose head was completely shrouded in a thick black veil which fell to her shoulders like a beekeeper's hat without touching the skin of her face.

The bus, which said "Acme Mud and Sulphur Baths" on its sides and "Every Hour on the Hour" above the windshield, went through the town without picking up any more customers and turned off the main road down a badly maintained gravel track through a plantation of young firs. After half a mile it rounded a corner and went down a short hill towards a cluster of dingy grey clapboard buildings. A tall yellow brick chimney stuck up out of the centre of the buildings and from it a thin wisp of black smoke rose straight up into the still air.

There was no sign of life in front of the Baths, but as the bus pulled up on the weedy gravel patch near what seemed to be the entrance, two old men and a limping coloured woman emerged through the screen doors at the top of the steps and waited for the passengers to alight.

Outside the bus the smell of sulphur hit Bond with sickening force. It was a nauseous smell from somewhere down in the moiling stomach of the world. He moved away from the entrance and sat down on a rough bench under a group of dead-looking firs. He remained there for a few minutes, steeling himself for what was going to happen to him through the screen doors and trying to shake off his sense of oppression and disgust. It was partly, he decided, the reaction of a healthy body to contact with disease, and it was partly the tall grim Belsen-like chimney with its plume of innocent smoke. But most of all it was the prospect of going in through those doors, buying the tickets and then stripping his clean body and giving it over to the somehow obscene things they did in this grisly ramshackle establishment.

The bus rattled off and he was alone. It was absolutely quiet. Bond noticed that the two side windows and the front door made two eyes and a mouth. The place seemed to be watching him, waiting for him. Would he come in? Would they have him?

Bond jerked his head impatiently. He got to his feet and walked straight across the gravel and up the wooden steps, and the frame doors banged to behind him.

He found himself in a dingy reception room. The sulphur fumes were stronger. There was a reception desk behind an iron grille. Many framed testimonials adorned the walls, some of them with red paper seals below the signature, and there was a glass-fronted showcase full of cellophane-wrapped packages. Above it a notice said in badly handwritten capitals: "Take Home an Acme-Pak. Treat Yourself in Privacy," and gave a list of prices.

A faded woman with a screw of orange hair above a face like a sad creampuff raised her head slowly and looked at him through the bars, keeping one finger at her place in *True Love Stories*.

"Can I help you?" It was the voice reserved for

strangers, people who didn't know the ropes.

Bond looked through the bars with the uncertain smile she had expected. "I'd like a bath."

"Mud or sulphur?" She reached for the tickets with her free hand.

"Mud."

"Would you care for a book of tickets? They're cheaper."

"Just one, please."

"Dollar fifty." She pushed through a mauve ticket and kept a finger on it until Bond had put his money down.

"Which way do I go?"

"Right," she said. "Follow the passage. Better leave your valuables." She slipped a large white envelope under the grille. "Write your name on it." She watched sideways as Bond put his watch and the contents of his pockets into the envelope and scribbled his name on it.

The twenty hundred-dollar bills were inside Bond's shirt. He wondered about them. He pushed the envelope back. "Thank you."

"You're welcome."

There was a low wicket at the back of the room and two white painted wooden hands whose drooping index fingers pointed right and left. On one hand was written "MUD" and on the other "SULPHUR." Bond went through the wicket and turned to the right along a dank corridor with a cement floor which sloped downwards. He followed it and pushed through a swing door at the end and found himself in a long high room with a skylight in the roof and wooden stalls along the walls.

It was hot and steamy and sulphurous in the room. Two youngish, soft-looking men, naked except for grey towels around their waists, were playing gin rummy at a deal table near the entrance. On the table were two ashtrays full of cigarette butts and a kitchen plate piled with keys. The men looked up as Bond entered and one of them picked up a key from the plate and held it out. Bond walked over and took it.

"Twelve," said the man. "Got ya ticket?"

Bond handed it over and the man made a gesture towards the stalls behind him. Then he jerked his head towards a door at the end of the room. "Baths through there." The two men went back to their game.

There was nothing in the frowzy stall but a folded towel from which constant washing had removed all the nap. Bond undressed and tied the towel around his waist. He folded the bulky packet of notes and stuffed them into the breast pocket of his coat under his handkerchief. He hoped it would be the last place that a petty thief would look in a quick search. He hung up his gun in the shoulder holster on a prominent hook and walked out and locked the door behind him.

Bond had no idea what he would see through the door at the end of the room. His first reaction was that he had walked into a morgue. Before he could sort out his impressions a fat bald Negro with a down-turned straggling moustache came over and looked him up and down. "What's wrong with you, mister?" he asked.

"Nothing," said Bond shortly. "Just want to try a mud bath."

"Okay," said the Negro. "Any heart trouble?"

"No," said Bond.

"Okay. Over here." Bond followed the Negro across a slippery concrete floor to a wooden bench alongside a pair of dilapidated shower cubicles in one of which a naked body plastered with mud was being hosed down by a man with a cauliflower ear.

"Be right with you," said the Negro pleasantly, his big feet slapping against the wet floor as he sauntered off about his business.

Bond looked about him. It was a square grey concrete room. From the ceiling four naked electric light bulbs, spotted with fly droppings, threw an ugly glare on the dripping walls and floor. Against the walls were trestle tables. Bond automatically counted them. There were twenty. On each table was a heavy wooden coffin with a three-quarter lid. In most of the coffins the profile of a sweating face showed above the wooden sides and pointed up at the ceiling. A few eyes were rolled inquisitively towards Bond, but most of the congested red faces looked asleep.

One coffin stood open, its lid up against the wall and its side hinged down. This seemed to be the one destined for Bond. The Negro was draping a heavy, unclean-looking sheet over it and smoothing it down to form a lining for the box. When he had finished he went to the middle of the room and chose two from a line of pails filled to the top with steaming dark brown mud and dropped them with a thud beside the open box. Then he dug his huge hand into one of them and smeared the thick viscous stuff along the bottom of the shroud and went on doing this until the sheet was two inches thick with mud. He then left it—to cool, Bond supposed—and went to a dented hipbath full of ice blocks, groped around and extracted several dripping hand towels. He put these over his arm and made a round of the occupied coffins, stopping every now and then to wrap a cool towel around the sweating forehead of one of the occupants.

Nothing else was happening, and the room was silent except for the hiss of the hose close to Bond. This stopped and a voice said, "All right, Mr. Weiss. That should fix you for today," and a fat naked man with a great deal of black body-hair tottered weakly out of the shower cubicle and waited while the man with the cauliflower ear helped him into a terrycloth bathrobe, gave him a quick rubdown inside it and led him to the door through which Bond had come.

Then the man with the cauliflower ear walked over to a door in the far corner of the room and went out. For a few moments light streamed through the door and Bond saw grass outside and a blessed glimpse of blue sky, and then the man came back with two more steaming buckets of mud. He kicked the door shut behind him and added them to the line of buckets in the middle of the room.

The Negro went over to Bond's coffin and touched the mud with the flat of his hand. He turned and beckoned to Bond. "Okay, mister," he said.

Bond walked over and the man took his towel and hung his key on a hook above the box.

Bond stood naked in front of him.

"You ever had one of these before?"

"No."

"Thought maybe not, so I'm giving you the mud at 110. If you're acclimated you can take 120 or even 130. Lie down there."

Bond gingerly climbed into the box and lay down, his skin smarting at its first contact with the hot mud. He slowly stretched himself out full length and lowered his head on to the clean towel that had been placed over the kapok pillow.

When he was settled the Negro dug both hands into one of the buckets of fresh mud and proceeded to slap it all over Bond's body.

The mud was a deep chocolate brown and it felt smooth and heavy and slimy. A smell of hot peat filled Bond's nostrils. He watched the shining blubbery arms of the Negro working over the obscene black mound that had once been his body. Had Felix Leiter known what this was going to be like? Bond grinned savagely at the ceiling. If this was one of Felix's jokes . . .

At last the Negro had finished and Bond was loaded with hot mud. Only his face and an area round his heart were still white. He felt stifled, and the sweat began to pour down his forehead.

With a deft movement the Negro bent down and picked up the edges of the sheet and wrapped them tightly around Bond's body and arms. Then he reached up for the other half of the dirty shroud and bound this also around him. Bond could just move his fingers and his head, but otherwise he had less freedom of movement than in a strait jacket. Then the man closed the open side of the coffin, lowered the heavy wooden lid, and that was that.

The Negro took a slate down from the wall above Bond's head and glanced at a clock high up on the far wall and scribbled the time down. It was just six o'clock.

"Twenty minutes," he said. "Feel good?"

Bond gave a neutral grunt.

The Negro moved away, and Bond stared dumbly up at the ceiling. He felt the sweat running down from his hair into his eyes. He cursed Felix Leiter.

At three minutes past six the door opened to admit the scrawny figure of Tingaling Bell. He had a sharp, weasly face and a miserably thin, almost skeletal, body. He walked cockily into the middle of the room.

"Hi, Tingaling," said the man with the cauliflower ear. "Heard you had some trouble today. Too bad."

"Them Stewards is a pile of obscenity," said Tingaling sourly. "Why would I want to ride across Tommy Lucky? One of my best pals. And why would I need to? The race was sewed up. Hey, you black bastard." He put out his foot to trip up the Negro who was passing with a pail of mud. "You got to get six ounces off me. Just had me a plate of French fries. On top of that they've given me a ton of lead to carry in the Oakridge tomorrow."

The Negro stepped over the outstretched foot and chuckled fatly. "Don't worry, baby," he said affectionately. "Ah kin always break yo' arm off. Be right with you."

The door opened again and one of the card players put his head in.

"Hey, Boxer," he said to the man with the cauliflower ear, "Mabel says she can't get through to the delicatessen to order your chow. Phone's busted. Line down or sumpn."

"Aw, Jesus," said the other. "Tell Jack to bring it on his next trip."

"Okay."

The door closed. Since a telephone breakdown in America is a rare thing, this was the moment when a small danger signal might have shrilled in Bond's mind. But it didn't. Instead he looked at the clock. Another ten minutes to go. The Negro sauntered across with the cold towels over his arm and wrapped one around Bond's forehead. It was a delicious relief, and Bond had a moment of thinking that perhaps the whole business was just supportable.

The seconds ticked by. The jockey, with a monotonous string of obscenities, lowered himself into the box directly in front of Bond, and Bond guessed that he was being given the mud at 130 degrees. He was wound up in the shroud and the lid was banged shut over him.

The Negro wrote 6:15 on the jockey's slate.

Bond closed his eyes and wondered how he was going to slip the man his money. In the rub-down room after the bath? There was presumably somewhere one went to lie down after all this. Or in the passage on the way out? Or in the bus? No. Not in the bus. Better not be seen with him.

"All right. Nobody move now. Just take it easy and nobody'll get hurt."

It was a hard, deadly voice that meant business.

Bond's eyes snapped open and his body tautened at the sudden presence of danger in the room.

The outside door, the door through which the mud came, was wide open. A man stood in the opening and another, shorter man was advancing into the middle of the room. They both had guns in their hands and both had black hoods over their heads with holes cut for the eyes and mouth.

There was silence in the room except for the sound of water in the shower cubicles. Several wet faces peered out into the room through the veil of water, their mouths gulping for air and the hair streaming into their eyes. The man with the cauliflower ear was a motionless pillar. His eyes shifted whitely and the hose in his hand poured water over his feet.

The shorter man was now in the middle of the floor by the steaming pails of mud. He stopped in front of the Negro, who was standing with a full bucket in each hand. The Negro quivered slightly so that the handle on one of the buckets gave a slight rattle.

The man's eyes bored into the Negro's, and Bond saw him turn the gun around in his hand so that he was holding it by the barrel. Suddenly, with a back-handed blow that had all his shoulder behind it, he lashed the butt of the revolver into the centre of the Negro's huge belly.

There was only a sharp wet slap from the blow, but the buckets crashed to the floor as the Negro's hands jerked up and clutched his stomach. He let out a soft moan and sagged forward onto his knees, his glistening shaven head bowing down almost to the man's shoes, as though in worship.

The man drew back a foot. "Where's the jock?" he said menacingly. "Bell. Which box?"

The Negro's right arm shot out.

The man turned on his heel and walked across to where Bond was lying toe to head with Tingaling Bell.

He came up and looked first down at Bond's face. He seemed to stiffen. Two glittering eyes showed through the slits in the black hood, and then the man moved to the left and stood over the jockey.

For a moment he stood motionless, then with a quick heave he hoisted himself up so that he was sitting on the lid of Tingaling's box looking down into his eyes.

"Well, well. If it ain't Tingaling Bell." There was a ghastly friendliness in his voice.

"Whatsamatter?" The jockey's voice was shrill and terrified.

"Why, Tingaling." The man was reasonable. "What would be the matter? Got anything on your mind?"

The jockey shook his head, his mouth open and eyes wide with fear.

"Maybe you never heard of a horse called Shy Smile, Tingaling. Maybe you weren't there when he was rode foul at around 2:30 this afternoon." The voice took on a hard edge.

The jockey started to whimper softly. "Jesus, boss, that weren't my fault. Happen to anybody." It was the whine of a child about to be punished. Bond winced.

"My friends figure it could've been a double cross." The man was bending close over the jockey, and his voice was harsher. "My friends figure a jock like you could only of done something like that intentional. My friends looked over your room and found a G plugged away in a lamp socket. My friends wish me to inquire where that lettuce come from.''

The sharp slap and shrill cry were simultaneous.

"Give, you bastard, or I'll blow your brains out." Bond heard the click of the hammer going back.

A stammering scream came out of the box. "My wad. All I got. Hid it away in the lamp. My wad. I swear it. Christ, you gotta believe me. You gotta!''

The man gave a disgusted grunt and lifted his gun into Bond's line of vision. A thumb with a big angry wart on the first joint eased the hammer forward. The man slipped down off the box. He looked into the jockey's face and his voice went slimy.

"You been riding too much lately, Tingaling," he almost whispered. "You're in bad shape. You need a rest. Plenty of quiet. Like in a sanitarium." The man slowly moved back across the floor. He went on talking quietly and solicitously. Now he was out of the jockey's line of vision. Bond saw him reach down and pick up one of the steaming buckets of mud. He came back, holding the bucket low, still talking, his tone still reassuring.

He came back to the jockey's box and looked down.

Bond stiffened and felt the mud stir heavily on his skin.

"Like I said, Tingaling. Plenty of quiet. Nothing to eat for a while. Nice dark room with the curtains drawn to keep out the light.''

The soft voice droned on and on in the dead silence. Slowly the arm came up. Higher . . . higher.

And then the jockey could see the bucket and he knew what was going to happen and he started to moan.

"No, no, no, no, no.''

Although it was hot in the room the black stuff steamed as it poured sluggishly out of the bucket upon the jockey's unprotected face. His scream tore at the walls of the room.

The man stepped swiftly aside and hurled the empty

bucket at the man with the cauliflower ear, who stood still and let it hit him. Then he moved fast across the room to where the other man with the gun stood near the door.

He turned. "No funny business. No cops. Phone's busted." He gave a harsh laugh. "Better dig the boy out before his eyeballs fry."

The door banged, and there was silence except for a bubbling sound and the noise of the water still gushing in the showers.

"We Don't Like Mistakes"

"Then what happened?"

Leiter was sitting in Bond's chair in the motel, and Bond was pacing up and down the room, stopping every now and then to take a drink from the glass of whiskey and water by the bed.

"Bloody chaos," said Bond. "Everybody yammering to be let out of his box and the man with the cauliflower ear hosing the stuff off Tingaling's face and shouting for help to the two card players in the next room. The Negro moaning on the floor and the naked men from the showers teetering about like extras out of Doré. Then the card players came busting in and they took the lid off Tingaling's box and unwrapped him and carried him under the shower. I guess he was nearly gone. Half suffocated. Whole face puffed up with the burns. Ghastly sight. Then one of the naked men pulled himself together and went around opening the boxes and letting the people out and there we were, twenty men with mud overcoats on and only one shower to spare. Well, it gradually got sorted out. One of the help went off for an ambulance. Someone doused the Negro with a bucket of water and he gradually came to life. Without pushing it too hard, I tried to find out if anyone had an idea who the two gunmen were. No one had a clue. It was thought they were from an out-of-town mob. Nobody cared now that no one had got hurt except the jockey. All they wanted to do was get dressed and get the hell out of there.'' Bond took another swallow of whiskey and lit a cigarette.

"Was there anything in particular that struck you about these two guys,'' asked Leiter. "Height, clothes, anything else?''

"I couldn't see much of the man by the door,'' said Bond. "He was smaller than the other, and thinner. Dark trousers and a grey shirt with no tie. Gun looked like a .45. Might have been a Colt. The other man, the one who did the job, was a big fattish buy. Quick moving but deliberate. Black trousers. Brown shirt with white stripes. No coat or tie. Black shoes, neat, expensive. .38 Police Positive. No wrist watch. Oh, yes.'' Bond suddenly remembered. "He had a wart on the top joint of his right thumb. Red-looking, as if he sucked it.''

"Wint,'' said Leiter flatly. "And the other guy was Kidd. Always work together. They're the top torpedoes for the Spangs. Wint is a mean bastard. A real sadist. Likes it. He's always sucking at that wart on his thumb. He's called 'Windy.' Not to his face, that is. Wint can't bear to travel. Gets sick in cars and trains and thinks planes are death traps. Has to be paid a special bonus if there's a job that means moving around the country. But he's cool enough when his feet are on the ground. Kidd's a pretty boy. His friends call him 'Boofy.' Probable shacks up with Wint. Some of these homos make the worst killers. Kidd's got white hair though he's only thirty. That's one of the reasons they like to work in hoods. But one day Wint is going to be sorry he didn't have that removed. I thought of him as soon as you mentioned it. Guess I'll get along to the cops and tip them off. Won't mention you, of course. But I'll give them the lowdown on Shy Smile, and they can work it out for themselves. Wint and his friend'll be taking a train out of Albany by now. But no harm in getting some heat on." Leiter turned at the door. "Take it easy, James. Be back in an hour and we'll go and get ourselves a good dinner. I'll find out where they've taken Tingaling and we'll mail the dough to him there. Might cheer him up a bit, poor little bastard. Be seeing you."

Bond stripped and spent ten minutes under the shower, lathering himself all over and washing his hair to get rid of the last filthy taint of the Acme Baths. Then he dressed in trousers and shirt and went over to the telephone booth in the reception hall and put in a call to Shady Tree.

"The line is busy, sir," chanted the operator.

"Keep trying," said Bond, relieved that the hunchback was still in his office and that now he would be able to say truthfully that he had tried to get through earlier. He had an impression that people might be wondering why he hadn't called sooner to complain about Shy Smile. After seeing what had happened to the jockey he was more inclined to treat the Spangled Mob with circumspection.

The telephone gave a dry muted burr.

"Did you want Wisconsin 7-3697?"

"Yes."

"I have your party now, sir. Go ahead, New York," and then the high, thin voice of the hunchback. "Yes? Who's calling?"

"Bond. I tried to reach you earlier."

"Yes?"

"Shy Smile didn't pay off."

"I know. The jock bitched it. So what?"

"Money," said Bond.

There was silence at the other end. Then, "Okay, we start from scratch. I'll wire you a grand, the grand you won off me. Remember?"

"Yes."

"Stand by the phone. I'll call you back in a few

minutes and tell you what to do with it. Where you staying?"

Bond told him. "Okay. You'll get the money in the morning. Be calling you in a few minutes." The phone went dead. Bond strolled over to the reception counter and glanced over the rack of paper-backs. He was amused and rather impressed by the meticulous accounting of these gangsters and the lengths to which they went to have each step of their operations protected by a legitimate cover plan. They were right, of course. Where would he, an Englishman, be able to get $5,000 except by gambling? And what would the next gamble be?

The telephone crooked a mechanical finger at him and he went back into the booth.

"That you, Bond? All right, now listen carefully. You'll get it at Las Vegas. Come back to New York and pick up a plane. Charge the ticket to me. I'll okay it. Non-stop to Los Angeles and there's a local plane every half-hour from there to Vegas. You'll have a reservation at the Tiara. Find your way around and—now listen to this carefully—at just five minutes past ten on Thursday night you go to the centre of the three blackjack tables at the Tiara on the side of the room near the bar. Got that?"

"Yes."

"Sit down and play the maximum—that's a grand—five times. Then quit. And don't gamble any more. D'you hear me?"

"Yes."

"Your bill at the Tiara will be taken care of. After the game, hang around and wait for further instructions. Got that? Repeat."

Bond did so.

"Check," said the hunchback. "Don't talk and don't make any mistakes. We don't like mistakes. You'll find that out when you read tomorrow's papers."

There was a soft click. Bond put down the receiver and walked thoughtfully across the lawn to his room.

Blackjack! The old 21 of his childhood days. It brought back memories of big teas in other children's playrooms; of grownups counting out the coloured bone counters in piles so that each child had a shilling's worth; the excitement of turning up a ten and an ace and being paid double; the thrill of that fifth card when one already had seventeen and wanted a four or less for "Five and Under." And now he was going to play the nursery game again. Only this time the dealer would be a crook and the chips would be worth $1,000 apiece.

Bond lay down on his bed and stared at the ceiling. As he waited for Felix Leiter his imagination was already dwelling on the famous gambling town of Las Vegas, wondering what it was going to be like, wondering how much he would be able to see of Tiffany Case.

Five cigarette ends had piled up in the plastic ash tray before he heard Leiter's limping step on the gravel path outside. They drove off in the Studillac, and Leiter brought him up to date.

The Spangled boys had all checked out—Pissaro, Budd, Wint, Kidd—and even Shy Smile was already off on the first leg of his long journey by horsebox right across the continent to the ranch in Nevada.

"The F.B.I. are on the case now," said Leiter, "but it will only be one more short story in their collected works of Spang. Without you as a witness, nobody's going to have any idea who the two gunmen were, and I'd be surprised if the F.B.I. get very worked up about Pissaro and his horse. They'll leave that to me and my outfit. I've talked to my head office, and they've told me to get out to Vegas and find out where the remains of the real Shy Smile are buried. I've got to get my hands on his teeth. How d'ya like that?"

Before Bond had time to comment they had drawn up outside a restaurant called the Pavilion. They got out, leaving the car to be parked by the doorman.

It was late and most of the diners had finished their meal and gone off to the sales ring. They had a corner table to themselves, and Leiter told the head waiter not to hurry with the lobsters but to bring two very dry Martinis made with domestic vermouth.

"So you're going to Las Vegas," said Bond. "Funny coincidence department." He told Leiter about his conversation with Shady Tree.

Leiter smiled. "No coincidence about it. We're both travelling bad roads and all bad roads lead to bad towns. I've got some cleaning up to do here in Saratoga first. And a pile of reports to write. That's half my life with Pinkertons, writing reports. But I'll be in Vegas before the end of the week, sniffing around. Won't be able to see much of you right under the Spang nose, but maybe we could meet up from time to time and exchange notes. Tell you what," he added. "We've got a good man there. Undercover, of course. Cab driver by the name of Cureo, Ernie Cureo. Good guy. I'll pass the word along to him you're coming and he'll look after you. He knows all the dirt, where the big fixes are, who's in town from the outside mobs, everything. He even knows where you can find the one-arm bandits that pay the best percentages. And the slots that pay best are the most valuable secret on the whole Strip. And boy, you ain't seen nothing 'till you've seen that Strip. Five solid miles of gambling joints. Neon lighting that makes Broadway look like a kid's Christmas tree. Monte Carlo!" Leiter snorted. "Steam-age stuff."

Bond smiled. "How many zeros have they got on the roulette?"

"Two, I guess."

"There's your answer. At least we play against the right percentage in Europe. You can have your neon lighting. The other zero's what pays the electric-light bills."

"Maybe. But the craps only pay 2½ per cent to the House. And that's our national game."

"I know," said Bond. " 'Baby needs a new pair of shoes.' Kid stuff. I'd like to hear the banker for the Greek Syndicate whining 'Baby needs a new pair of shoes' when he's got two nines against him at the high table and there are ten million francs on each tableau."

Leiter laughed. "Hell," he said. "You've got it easy

with this crooked playoff at the blackjack table. You'll be able to swank around back in London and tell the story of how you took 'em at Vegas.'' Leiter took a pull at his whiskey and sat back in his chair. "But I better give you some of the background to the games just in case you get it into your head to stake your pennies against their pot of gold.''

"Go ahead.''

"And I mean pot of gold,'' continued Leiter. "You see, James, the whole State of Nevada, which, so far as the public cares, consists solely of Reno and Las Vegas, is the proverbial pot of gold at the end of the rainbow. The answer to the universal dream of 'something for nothing' is to be picked up for the price of your plane fare on the Strip at Las Vegas or on the Main Stem at Reno. And it really *is* there. Not so long ago, when the stars and the dice were right, a young G.I. made twenty-eight straight passes at a crap table at the Desert Inn. Twenty-eight! If he'd started with a dollar and been allowed to let it ride over the house limits, which, knowing the management at the Inn, I guess he might not have been, he would have made $250,000! Of course, he didn't let it ride. Side-betters made $150,000. The G.I. made $750 and took to his heels as if the devil was after him. They never even got his name. Today that pair of red dice is on a satin pillow in a glass case in the Desert Inn Casino.''

"Must have been good publicity.''

"Bet your life!'' said Leiter. "All the ad men in the world couldn't have dreamed it up. It made the wishing-well dream come true—and wait till you see them wishing in those casinos. In just one of them, they use up eight pairs of dice every twenty-four hours and 120 packs of plastic cards. Fifty slot machines go to the garage every day at dawn. And wait till you see the little old ladies in gloves and chokers working those slots. They have shopping baskets to carry away their loot of nickels and dimes and quarters. They work those slots ten, twenty hours a day without going to the rest room. You don't believe me? You know why they wear those gloves? To keep their hands from bleeding.''

Bond grunted noncommittally.

"All right, all right," agreed Leiter. "Sure these people collapse. Hysteria, heart attacks, apoplexy. The cherries and plums and bells climb through their eyes and into their brains. But all the casinos have house physicians on twenty-four-hour call. Every now and then a woman gets carried out screaming 'Jackpot! Jackpot!' as if it was the name of a dead lover. And take a look at the bingo parlours, and the Wheels of Fortune, and the banks of slots downtown in the Golden Nugget and the Horseshoe. But don't you go and get the fever yourself and forget your job and your girl and your kidneys. I happen to know the basic odds at all the games and I know how you like to gamble, so do me a big favour and get them into your thick head. Now take them down.''

Bond was interested. He took out a pencil and tore a strip off the menu card.

Leiter squinted at the ceiling. "It's 1.4 per cent in favour of the House at craps, 5 per cent at blackjack"—he looked down at Bond—"except at your game, you crook! 5½ per cent at roulette. Up to 17 per cent at bingo and the Wheel of Fortune, and 15 to 20 per cent at the slots. Not bad for the House, huh? Every year 11,000,000 customers play Mr. Spang and his friends at those sucker odds. Take $200 as an average sucker's capital, and you can work out for yourself how much stays in Vegas over a year's play.''

Bond put the pencil and the piece of paper back in his pocket. "Thanks for the documentation, Felix. But you seem to forget I'm not going to this place for a holiday.''

"Okay, damn you," said Leiter resignedly, "but don't get cocky while you're there, chum. It's a big operation they've got and they won't stand for any monkey business.'' Leiter leaned across the table. "Let me tell you. The other day there was one of these dealers—blackjack, I think it was—decided to go into business for himself. Slipped a few bills into his pocket one evening during the play. Well, they spotted him. Next day some innocent guy is driving into town from Boulder City and he spots something pink sticking up out of the desert. Couldn't be a cactus. He stops and has himself a look." Leiter prodded Bond's chest with a finger. "My friend, that pink thing sticking up was an arm. And the hand at the top of the arm was holding a full deck of cards, fanned out. The cops came with spades and dug and found the rest of the dealer under the ground at the other end of the arm. They'd just blown the back of his head off and buried him. The fancy work with the arm was just an artistic warning to others. Pretty?"

"Charming," said Bond.

The broiled lobsters arrived and they went to work with their nutcrackers.

"Of course," said Leiter between mouthfuls, "the dealer should have known better than get caught with his duke in the tambourine. They've got a good trick in these Vegas casinos. Take a look at the overhead lighting. Very modern. Just holes in the ceiling with the light beamed through onto the tables. Very bright illumination and no sideways glare to distract the customers. But you'll notice that there's no light coming from the alternate holes. They just seem to be there to make a pattern." Leiter slowly shook his head from side to side. "Not so, my friend. Up on the floor above there's a television camera on a dolly that moves around the floor taking an occasional peek through those empty holes. Kind of spot-check on the play. If they're wondering about one of the dealers, or about one of the players, they'll take a picture of the whole of one session at that particular table, and every damn' card or throw will be monitored by the guys sitting quietly upstairs. Smart, huh? These dumps are wired for everything except smell. But the dealers know it, and this guy just hoped the camera wasn't looking at the time. Fatal error."

Bond smiled at Leiter. "I'll watch out," he promised. "But don't forget, I've somehow got to get another step down the pipe line. To the tap at the end of it. In fact, I've got to get right up close to your friend Mr. Seraffimo Spang. I can't do that by just sending up my card. And I'll tell you something else, Felix.'' Bond's voice was deliberate. ''I've suddenly taken a strong dislike to the brothers Spang. I didn't like those two men in hoods. The way the man hit that fat Negro. The way he poured boiling mud over that jockey. I wouldn't have minded so much if he'd just beaten him up—ordinary cops-and-robbers stuff. It was the calculated brutality of it. And I don't like Pissaro and Budd. I don't know what it is, but I've just taken against all of them.'' Bond's voice was apologetic. ''Thought I ought to tell you.''

''Okay,'' sighed Leiter, pushing away his plate. ''I'll be around to try and pick up the pieces. And I'll tell Ernie to keep an eye on you. But don't think you can ask for a lawyer or the British consul if you get in dutch with the Mob. Only law firm out there's called Smith and Wesson.'' He rapped on the table with his hook. ''Better have one last bourbon and branch water. It's desert where you're going. Dry as a bone and hotter'n hell this time of year. No rivers, so no branches to get the water out of. You'll be drinking it with soda and then mopping it off your forehead. It'll be 120 in the shade out there. Only, there isn't any shade.''

The whiskey came. ''I shall miss you out there, Felix,'' said Bond, glad to get away from his thoughts. ''No one to teach me the American way of life. And by the way, I thought you did a hell of a fine job over Shy Smile. Wish you could come along and tackle Spang Senior with me. Together, I believe we could take him.''

Leiter looked affectionately at his friend. ''That sort of rough stuff's no good if you're working for Pinkertons,'' he said. ''I'm after the guy too, but I've got to get him legitimate. If I can find out where the remains of that horse are buried, that crook's going to have a rough time of it. It's all right for you to come over here and tangle with him on a one-shot basis and get away back to England. The gang has no idea who you are.

From what you tell me, they won't ever find out. But I've got to live here. If I had a shooting match or anything like that with Spang, his pals would be after me and after my family and after my friends. And they wouldn't rest until they'd hurt me more than I ever hurt their boss. Even if I killed him. It's not so funny to come home and find your sister's house burned down with her inside it. And I'm afraid that can still happen in this country. The gangs didn't go out with Capone or Luciano. Look at the Kefauver Report. Now the criminals don't run liquor. They run state governments if they can, and some can and do. Articles get written about it. And books and speeches. Sermons. But what the hell.'' Leiter laughed abruptly. ''Maybe you can strike a blow for Freedom, Home and Beauty with that rusty old equalizer of yours. Is it still the Beretta?''

''Yes,'' said Bond, ''still the Beretta.''

''You still got that double-0 number that licenses you to kill?''

''Yes,'' said Bond drily. ''I have.''

''Well, then,'' said Leiter, getting up, ''let's go home to bed and give your shooting eye a rest. My guess is you're going to need it.''

CHAPTER 15

Rue De La Pay

The plane made a big curve out over the sparkling blue Pacific and then swept over Hollywood and gained height so as to make the Cajon Pass through the great golden cliff of the High Sierras.

Bond caught a glimpse of endless miles of palm-lined avenues, of sprinklers whirling over emerald lawns in front of palatial homes, of sprawling aircraft factories, of the outside lots of film studios with their jumble of gimcrack sets—city streets, Western ranches, racing tracks, a full size four-masted schooner planted in the ground—and then they were in the mountains and through them over the interminable red desert that is the back yard of Southern California.

They flew over Barstow, the junction from which the single track of the Santa Fe strikes off into the desert on its long run across the Colorado Plateau, skirting on their right the Calico Mountains and leaving far behind to the left the bone-strewn wastes of Death Valley. Then came more mountains streaked with red, like gums bleeding over rotten teeth, and then a glimpse of green

in the midst of the blasted, Martian landscape, and then
a slow descent and "Please fasten your seat belts and ex-
tinguish your cigarettes."

The heat hit Bond's face like a fist, and he began to
sweat before he had crossed the fifty yards between his
cool plane and the blessed relief of the air-conditioned
terminal building. The glass doors, operated by seeing-
eye photoelectric cells, hissed open as he approached
and slowly closed behind him. The slot-machines, four
banks of them, were right in his path. It was only
natural to bring out the small change and jerk the
handles and watch the lemons and the oranges and the
cherries and the bell fruits whirl round to their final
click-pause-*ting,* followed by a soft mechanical sigh.
Five cents, ten cents, a quarter. Bond gave them all a
try, and only once did two cherries and a bell fruit
cough back three coins for the one he had played.

As he moved away, waiting for his baggage to appear
on the ramp near the exit, his eye caught a notice over a
big machine that might have been for ice water. It said
"OXYGEN BAR." He strolled over to it and read the
rest: "BREATHE PURE OXYGEN," it said. "HEALTHFUL
AND HARMLESS. FOR A QUICK LIFT. EASES DISTRESS OF
OVER-INDULGENCE, DROWSINESS, FATIGUE, NER-
VOUSNESS AND MANY OTHER SYMPTOMS."

Bond obediently put a quarter into the slot, and bent
over so that his nose and mouth were enclosed in a wide
black rubber mouthpiece. He pressed a button and, as
instructed, breathed in and out slowly for a full minute.
It was like breathing very cold air—no taste, no smell.
At the end of the minute there was a click from the
machine and Bond straightened himself. He felt nothing
but a slight dizziness, but later he recognised that there
had been carelessness in the ironic grin he gave to a man
with a leather shaving kit under his arm who had been
standing watching him.

The man smiled briefly back and turned away.

The loudspeaker asked passengers to collect their
luggage, and Bond picked up his case and pushed

through the swing doors of the exit into the red-hot arms of noon.

"You for the Tiara?" said a voice. A chunky, barrel-chested man with a dynamic jaw and large, very direct brown eyes under a peaked chauffeur's cap shot the question at him from the corner of a wide, humorous mouth. From the other corner a wooden toothpick protruded jauntily.

"Yes."

"Okay. Let's go." The man didn't offer to carry Bond's suitcase for him. Bond followed him over to a smart-looking Chevrolet with a lucky beaver tail tied to its chrome naked-lady mascot. He threw his suitcase into the back and climbed in after it.

The car moved off out of the airport onto the parkway. It turned right. Other cars hissed by. Bond's driver kept to the outside lane, driving slowly. Bond felt himself being examined in the driving mirror. He looked up at the driver's identification tag. "ERNEST CUREO. No. 2584."

The cab smelled of old cigar smoke, and Bond rolled down the window. A furnace-blast of air made him close it again.

The driver half turned in his seat. "Don't want to do that, Mr. Bond," he said in a friendly voice. "Cab's conditioned. May not seem so, but it's better'n outside."

"Thanks," said Bond, and then: "I believe you're a friend of Felix Leiter's."

"Yeah," said the driver, over his shoulder. "Nice guy. Told me to watch out for you. Be glad if I can do anything while you're here. Staying long?"

"Can't say," said Bond. "Few days, anyways."

"Tell you what," said the driver. "Don't think I'm trying to sell you anything, but if we're going to do some work together and you got the dough, maybe you better hire the cab by the day. Fifty bucks, but I got to make a living. It'll make sense to the front boys at the hotels and so on. Don't see how I can keep tabs on you otherwise. But you hire the heap full-time and they'll understand me hanging about waiting for you half the day. They're a suspicious lot of bastards on the Strip.''

''Couldn't be better.'' Bond at once liked and trusted the man. ''It's a deal.''

''Okay.'' The driver expanded a little. ''See, Mr. Bond, the folks round here don't like anything out of the ord'nary. Like I say. They're suspicious. I mean. You don't look much like a tourist who's come to lose his wad. Anyone can see you're a Limey even before you start talking. Clothes, and so forth. Well, what's a Limey doing here? And what sort of a Limey is this? He looks like he knows what the score is. So let's just take a good look at him.'' He half turned. ''You see a guy hangin' around the terminal with a leather shaving kit under his arm?''

Bond remembered the man who had watched him at the Oxygen Bar. ''Yes, I did,'' he said, and it was then he realised that the oxygen had made him careless.

''Bet he's looking at your picture right now,'' said the driver. ''Sixteen-millimetre camera in that kit. Just pull down the zip and press y'arm against it and off it goes. He'll have taken fifty feet. Straight and profile. And that'll be with 'Mug Identification' at Headquarters this afternoon with a list of what you got in your bag. You don't look as if you're carryin' a gun. Maybe it's a flat holster job. But if you are, there'll be another guy with a gun, watching you all the time you're in the rooms. Word'll be sent down the line by sunset. Better watch out for anybody with a coat on. Nobody wears 'em here except to house the artillery.''

''Well, thanks,'' said Bond, annoyed with himself. ''I can see I'll have to keep a bit wider awake. Pretty good machine they seem to have here.''

The driver grunted affirmatively and drove on in silence.

They were just entering the famous ''Strip.'' The desert on both sides of the road which had been empty except for occasional billboards advertising the hotels was beginning to sprout gas stations and motels. They passed a motel with a swimming pool which had transparent glass sides. As they drove by a girl dove into the bright green water and her body sliced through the tank, trailing a banner of bubbles. Then came a gas station with an elegant drive-in restaurant attached. "GASETERIA," it said. "FRESH UP HERE! HOT DOGS! JUMBOBURGERS! ICE-COOL DRINKS!!! DRIVE IN." There were two or three cars being served by waitresses in high-heeled shoes and two-piece bathing suits.

The magnificent six-lane highway stretched on through a forest of multi-coloured signs and frontages until it lost itself downtown in a dancing lake of heat waves. The day was as hot and sultry as a fire opal. The swollen sun burned straight down the middle of the frying concrete, and there was no shade anywhere except under the few scattered palms in the forecourts of the motels. A glittering spray of light-splinters pierced Bond's eyes from the windshields and chrome of oncoming cars, and he felt his shirt clinging stickily to his skin.

"Coming into the Strip now," said Cureo. "Otherwise known as the 'Rue de la Pay.' *P-a-y.* Joke. Get it?"

Bond smiled dutifully. "Got it," he said.

"On your right, the Flamingo," said Cureo as they passed a long, low, modernistic hotel with a huge tower of neon, now dead, outside it. "Buggsy Siegel built that back in '46. He came over to Vegas from the coast one day and took a look around. Had a lot of hot money that wanted investing. Vegas was goin' great guns. Town wide open. Gambling. Legalised catshops. Nice setup. It didn't take long for Buggsy to catch on. He saw the possibilities."

Bond laughed at the understatement.

"Yes, sir," continued the driver, "Buggsy saw the possibilities and moved right in. Stayed with it until 1947 when they blew some of his head off with so many bullets the cops never got around to finding them all. And here's the Sands. Plenty of lettuce behind that one too. Don't rightly know whose. Built a couple of years ago. Front guy's a nice feller name of Jack Entratter.

Used to be at the Copa in New York. Maybe you heard of him?''

Bond shook his head.

''Here's the Desert Inn. Wilbur Clarke's place. The money came from the old Cleveland-Cincinnati combination. And that pile with the flatiron sign is the Sahara. Latest thing. Listed owners are a bunch of small-time gamblers from Oregon. Funny thing, they lost $50,000 on their opening night. Would ya believe it! All the big shots come along with their pockets full of dough to make some courtesy play, make the first night a success, see. It's the custom here for the rival outfits to help celebrate an opening. But the cards just wouldn't co-operate and the opposition walked off with fifty G's. Town's still laughing about it. Then''—he jerked a thumb to the left where the neon was wrought into a twenty-foot covered wagon bowling along at full tilt—''you get the Last Frontier. That's a dummy Western town on the left. Worth seein'. And over there's the Thunderbird and across the road's the Tiara. Snazziest joint in Vegas. Guess you know about Mister Spang and all that?'' He slowed down and stopped opposite the Spang hotel, which was topped by a ducal coronet of brilliant lights that winked on and off in a lost battle with the glaring sun and the reflections from the highway.

''Yes, I know the outlines,'' said Bond. ''But I'd be glad for you to fill them in for me later. And now what?''

''Whatever you say, Pal.''

Bond suddenly felt he had had enough of the Strip. He only wanted to get indoors and out of the heat, have some lunch and perhaps a swim and take things easy until nightfall. He said as much.

''Suits me,'' said Cureo. ''Guess you won't get into much trouble your first night. Take it easy, though. Act natural. If you got work to do in Vegas you better wait till you know your way around. And watch the gambling, friend.'' He chuckled. ''Y'ever hear of those Silence Towers they have in India? They say it only takes those vultures twenty minutes to strip a guy to the bones. Takes just a little longer at the Tiara. Guess the Unions slow 'em down.''

The car swung across the traffic and under the pillared portico in front of the wide glass doors of the sprawling pink stucco building. The bell captain, imposing in a sky-blue uniform, opened the cab door and reached for Bond's bag. Bond stepped out into the heat.

As he shouldered his way through the glass doors he heard Ernie Cureo say to the bell captain: "Some crazy Limey. Hired me for fifty bucks a day! How about that?''

And then the door swung to behind him and the beautiful cold air welcomed him with a chill kiss into the glittering palace of the man called Seraffimo Spang.

CHAPTER 16

The Tiara

Bond had lunch in the air-conditioned Sunburst Room beside the big kidney-shaped swimming pool (LIFESAVER: BOBBY BILBO—POOL SCOURED DAILY BY HYDRO-JET said a sign), and having decided that only about one percent of the customers should be allowed to wear bathing suits, he walked very slowly through the heat across the twenty yards of baked lawn that separated his building from the central establishment, took off his clothes and threw himself naked on his bed.

There were six buildings containing the bedrooms of the Tiara and they were all named after jewels. Bond was on the ground floor of the Turquoise. Its motif was eggshell blue with furnishings materials of dark blue and white. His room was extremely comfortable and equipped with expensive and well designed modern furniture of a silvery wood that might have been birch. There was a radio beside his bed and a television set with a twenty-one-inch screen beside the broad window. Outside the French windows was a small enclosed breakfast patio. It was very quiet. The air-conditioning was soundless, and Bond was almost instantly asleep.

He slept for four hours, and during this time the wire-recorder concealed in the base of the radio beside him wasted several hundred feet of wire on dead silence.

When he awoke it was seven. The wire-recorder then noted that he picked up the telephone and asked for Miss Tiffany Case and after a pause said, "Would you please tell her that Mr. James Bond called," and put back the receiver. It then picked up the noise of Bond moving about the room, the hiss of the shower and, at 7:30, the click of his key in the lock as he went out and shut the door.

Half an hour later the recorder registered a knock on his door and then, after a pause, the noise of the door opening. A man dressed like a waiter, with a basket of fruit bearing a note saying "With the Compliments of the Management," came into the room and walked quickly over to the radio. He undid two screws, removed the reel of fine wire on the recorder's turn-table, replaced it with a fresh spool, put the basket of fruit on the dressing table and went out and closed the door.

And then for several hours the recorder whirred silently on, recording nothing.

Bond sat at the long bar and sipped a vodka Martini and examined the gambling room with a professional eye.

The first thing he noticed was that Las Vegas seemed to have invented a new school of functional architecture which he dubbed the Gilded Mousetrap School, its main purpose being to channel the customer-mouse into the central gambling trap whether he wanted the cheese or not.

There were only two entrances, one from the street outside and one from the bedroom wings and the swimming pool. Once you had come in through either of these, whether you wanted to buy a paper or cigarettes at the newsstand, have a drink or a meal in one of the two restaurants, get your hair cut or have a massage in the "Health Club," or just visit the lavatories, there was no way of reaching your objective without passing between the banks of slot machines and gambling tables. And when you were trapped in the vortex of the whirring machines, from which there sounded always, from somewhere, the intoxicating silvery cascade of coins into a metal cup, or occasionally the golden cry of "Jackpot!" from one of the change-girls, you were lost. Besieged by the excited back-chat from the three big crap tables, the seductive whirl of the two roulette wheels, and the clank of silver dollars across the green pools of the blackjack tables, it would have to be a mouse of steel who could pass by without a tentative nibble at this provocative chunk of cheese.

But, reflected Bond, it could only be a trap for willing and unwary mice—mice who would be tempted by cheese. It was, essentially, an inelegant trap, obvious and vulgar, and the noise of the machines had a horrible mechanical ugliness which beat at the brain. It was like the steady clanking of the engines of some old iron freighter on its way to the knacker's yard, unoiled, uncared for, condemned.

And the gamblers stood and clawed at the handles of the machines as if they hated what they were doing. And once they had seen their fate in the small glass window, they didn't wait for the wheels to stop spinning but rammed in another coin and reached up a right hand that knew exactly what to do. *Crank-clatter-ting. Crank-clatter-ting.*

With an occasional silvery waterfall the metal cup would overflow and the gambler would have to go down on his knees to scrabble for a rolling coin. Or, strictly speaking, her knees, for they were mostly women, as Leiter had said—elderly women of the prosperous housewife class. Droves of them stood at the banks of machines like hens in an egg battery, conditioned by the delicious coolness of the room and the hypnosis of the spinning wheels to go on laying it on the line until their roll was gone.

Then, as Bond watched, a change-girl's voice cried

"Jackpot!" and some of the women raised their heads and the picture changed. Now they reminded Bond of Dr. Pavlov's dogs, saliva drooling at the treacherous bell that brought no dinner, and he shuddered at the empty eyes and the flaccid skin and the half open mouths and the thoughtless minds.

Bond turned his back on the scene and sipped his Martini, listening with half an ear to the music from the famous name-band at the end of the room next to the half-dozen shops. Over one of them was a pale blue neon sign which said "The House of Diamonds." Bond beckoned to the barman. "Mr. Spang been around tonight?"

"Ain't seen him," said the barman. "Mostly comes in after the first show. Around eleven. You know him?"

"Not personally."

Bond paid his check and drifted over to the blackjack tables. He stopped at the centre one. This one would be his. At exactly five minutes past ten. He glanced at his watch. 8:30.

The table was a small, flat kidney of green baize. Eight players sat on high stools facing the dealer, who stood with his stomach against the edge of the table and dealt two cards into the eight numbered spaces on the cloth in front of the stakes. The stakes were mostly five or ten silver dollars, or counters worth twenty. The dealer was a man of about forty. He had a pleasant half-smile on his face. He wore the dealer's uniform—white shirt buttoned at the wrists, a thin black Western gambler's tie, a green eyeshade and black trousers. The front of the trousers was protected from rubbing against the table by a green baize apron. "Jake" was embroidered in one corner.

The dealer dealt and handled the stakes with unruffled smoothness. There was no talk at the table except when a player ordered a "courtesy" drink or cigarettes from one of the waitresses in black silk pajamas who circulated in the central space inside the ring of tables. From this central space the run of the play was watched over by two tough, lynx-eyed pit-bosses.

The game was fast and efficient and dull, as dull and mechanical as the slot machines. Bond watched for a while, and then moved away towards the doors marked "The Diamond Ring." On his way he passed four "Sheriffs" in smart grey Western uniform. The legs of their trousers were tucked into half-Wellingtons. These men were standing about unobtrusively, looking at nothing but seeing everything. At each hip they carried a gun in an open holster and the polished brass of fifty cartridges shone at their belts.

Plenty of protection around, thought Bond as he walked back through the tables.

The low circular restaurant in pink and white and grey was half full. The hostess swept over and piloted him to a corner table. She bent over to arrange the flowers in the middle of the table and to show him that her fine bosom was at least half real, gave him a gracious smile and went away. After ten minutes, a waitress with a tray appeared and put a roll on his plate and a square of butter. She also set down a dish containing olives and some celery lined with orange cheese. Then a second and older waitress bustled over and gave him the menu and said "Be right with you."

Twenty minutes after he had sat down, Bond was able to order a dozen cherrystone clams and a steak, and, since he expected a further long pause, a second vodka dry Martini. "The wine waiter will be right over," said the waitress primly, and disappeared in the direction of the kitchen.

Long on courtesy and short on service, reflected Bond.

During the excellent dinner that finally materialised Bond wondered about the evening ahead and about how he could force the pace of his assignment. He was thoroughly bored with his role of probationary crook who might, if he found favour in the eyes of Mr. Spang, be given regular work with the rest of the permanent adolescents who made up the gang. It irked him not to have the initiative. He resented having been ordered to Saratoga and then to this hideous sucker-trap at the say-so of a handful of bigtime hoodlums. Here he was, eating their dinner and sleeping in their bed, while they watched *him,* James Bond, and sized him up and debated whether his hand was steady enough, his appearance trustworthy enough and his health adequate to some sleazy job in one of their rackets.

Bond swallowed his steak without tasting it and cursed the day he had taken on this idiotic role. But then he checked himself and went on eating more calmly. What was he worrying about? This was a big assignment. So far it had gone well. And now he had penetrated right to the end of the pipe line, right into the parlour of Mr. Seraffimo Spang who, with his brother in London and with the mysterious A B C, ran the biggest smuggling operation in the world. What did Bond's personal feelings matter? It was only a moment of self-disgust, a touch of nausea brought on by being a stranger who had spent too many days too close to these sordidly powerful American criminals, too close to the gunpowder-scented "gracious living" of gangland aristocracy.

The truth of the matter, Bond decided over coffee, was that he felt homesick for his real identity. He shrugged. To hell with the Spangs. He looked at his watch. It was just ten o'clock. He lit a cigarette, signed his check, got to his feet and walked slowly across the room and out into the Casino.

There were two ways of playing the rest of the game: by lying low and waiting for something to happen—or by forcing the pace so that something *had* to happen.

Bond had decided to force the pace.

CHAPTER 17

Thanks for the Ride

The atmosphere in the big gambling room had changed. It was now much quieter. The orchestra had gone, and so had the droves of women, and there were only a few players at the tables. There were two or three shills at the roulette wheels, smart girls in evening dresses who had been given $50 with which to warm up the dead tables, and there was a very drunk man clinging to the high surrounding wall of one of the crap tables and shouting exhortations to the dice.

And something else had changed. The dealer at the centre blackjack table nearest the bar was Tiffany Case.

So that was her job at the Tiara.

And then Bond saw that all the blackjack dealers were pretty women and that they were all dressed in the same smart Western outfit in grey and black—short grey skirt with a wide black metal-studded belt, grey blouse with a black handkerchief around the neck, a grey sombrero hanging down the back by a black cord, black half-Wellingtons over flesh-coloured nylons.

Bond looked at his watch again and moved slowly

into the room. So Tiffany was going to false-deal him to win $5,000. And of course they had chosen the moment when she had just come on duty and the first show of the big-name revue was still running in the Platinum Room. He would be alone with her at the table. No witnesses among the customers in case she muffed a deal from the bottom of the deck.

At exactly 10.05 Bond strolled easily up to the table and sat down facing her.

"Good evening."

"Hi." She gave him a thin, correct smile.

"What's the maximum?"

"A grand."

As Bond slapped the ten one hundred dollar notes down across the betting line, the pit-boss strolled over and stood beside Tiffany Case. He barely glanced at Bond. "Mebbe the gent would like a new deck, Miss Tiffany," he said. He handed her a fresh pack.

The girl stripped the cover off it and handed him the used cards.

The pit-boss stood back a few paces and appeared to lose interest.

The girl snapped the pack with a fluid motion of the hands, broke it and put the two halves flat on the table and executed what appeared to be a faultless Scarne shuffle. But Bond saw that the two halves did not quite marry and that when she lifted the pack off the table and carried out an innocent reshuffle she would be getting the two halves of the pack back into their original order. She repeated the manoeuvre again and put the pack down in front of Bond in an invitation to cut. Bond cut the cards and watched with approval as she carried out the difficult single-handed Annulment, one of the most difficult gambits in card-sharping.

So the "new" deck was fixed, and the only result of all this fair-play routine was to get all the cards back into the order in which they were arranged when they left the wrappers. But it was brilliant manipulation, and Bond was full of admiration for the assurance of the girl's hands.

He looked up into her grey eyes. Was there a hint of complicity in them, a hint of amusement at the odd game they were playing across the narrow green board?

She dealt him two cards and then gave two to herself. Suddenly Bond realised that he would have to be careful. He must be scrupulously careful to play the conventional game or he might upset the whole sequence in which the cards had been prepared.

Printed across the table were the words, "The Dealer Must Draw on Sixteen and Stand on Seventeen." They would presumably have given him fool-proof winning cards, but just in case there were another player or a kibitzer, they would have to make his winning seem a natural run of luck and not, for instance, just deal him twenty-one each time and a seventeen to the girl.

He glanced at his two cards. A jack and a ten. He looked up at the girl and shook his head. She turned up sixteen and drew a card, busting herself with a King. She had a rack beside her which contained only silver dollars and counters for twenty, but the pit-boss was quickly at her side with a thousand-dollar plaque. She took it and tossed it over to Bond. He put it over the line and pocketed his notes. She flipped out two more cards to him and two to herself. Bond had seventeen and again shook his head. She had twelve and drew a three and then a nine—twenty-four and bust again. The pit-boss stepped up once more with a plaque. Bond slipped it into his pocket and left his original stake. This time he had nineteen and she turned up a ten and a seven on which, by the rule, she had to stand. Another plaque went into Bond's pocket.

The wide doors at the far end of the room had opened and a stream of people were milling into the gambling room from the dinner revue. Soon they would be around the tables. This was his last play. After this he must get up from the table and leave her. She was watching him impatiently. He picked up the two cards that she had given him. Twenty. She also turned up two tens. No play. Bond smiled at the refinement. She quickly dealt him two more cards just as three more players came up to the table and hitched themselves up on the stools. He had nineteen and she had sixteen.

And that was that. The pit-boss didn't even bother to hand the girl the fourth plaque, but tossed it across the table to Bond with an expression on his face that was very like a sneer.

"Jee-sus," said one of the new players as Bond pocketed the plaque and stood up.

Bond gazed deliberately across the table at the girl. "Thank you," he said. "You deal beautifully."

"I'll say!" said the player who had spoken.

Tiffany Case looked hard at Bond. "You're welcome," she said. She held his eyes for a fraction of a second and then looked down at her cards, shuffled them thoroughly and handed them to one of the new players for a cut.

Bond turned his back to the table and moved off round the room, thinking of her and occasionally glancing across at the straight, imperious little figure in the exciting Western uniform. Others obviously found her as attractive as Bond did, for soon there were eight men sitting at her table and others standing about, just watching her.

Bond felt a pang of jealousy. He walked over to the bar and ordered himself a bourbon and branch water to celebrate the $5,000 in his pocket.

The barman produced a corked bottle of water and put it beside the shot of Kentucky.

"Where does this come from?" asked Bond, remembering what Felix Leiter had said.

"Over by Boulder Dam," said the barman seriously. "Comes in by truck every day. Don't worry," he added. "It's the real stuff."

Bond threw two silver dollars on the bar. "I'm sure it is," he said with equal seriousness. "Keep the change."

He stood with his back to the bar, rolling the glass between his hands, deciding on his next move. So now he had been paid off. And he had been told on no account to go back to the tables.

All right, then.

Bond finished his drink and walked straight across the room to the nearest roulette table. There was only a sprinkling of gamblers at it, playing small.

"What's the maximum here?" he said to the stick-man, an elderly balding individual with dead eyes who was just picking the ivory ball out of the wheel.

"Five grand," said the man indifferently.

Bond took the four plaques and the ten one-hundred dollar bills out of his pocket and put them beside the croupier. "On Red."

The croupier sat up straighter in his chair and squinted sideways at Bond. He tossed the four plaques one by one down on to red, catching them there with his stick. He counted out Bond's bills, pushed them through a slot in the table, took a fifth plaque from the rack of counters beside him and tossed this down to join the others. Bond saw his knee go up under the table. The pit-boss heard the buzzer and strolled over to the table just as the croupier spun the wheel.

Bond took out a cigarette and lit it. His hand was steady. He felt a wonderful sense of freedom at having at last taken the initiative away from these people. He knew he was going to win. He hardly glanced at the wheel as it slowed down and the little ivory ball rattled into its slot.

"Thirty-six. Red. High and Even."

The stick-man raked in a few losing counters and silver dollars and tossed some money down the table to the winners. Then he took a thin plaque as big as a prayer-book out of his rack and put it softly down beside Bond.

"Black," said Bond. The man threw a single plaque for $5,000 down on Black and raked in Bond's stake from the Red.

There was a buzz of conversation around the table and several more people drifted over and stood watching. Bond felt the curious eyes on him, but he only looked across the table into the eyes of the pit-boss. They were hostile as an adder's, and yet somehow scared.

Bond smiled blandly at him as the wheel whirred and there was the whizz of the little ball as it set off on its journey.

"Seventeen. Black. Low and Odd," said the stick-man. There was a sigh from the crowd, and hungry eyes watched the big plaque being slipped out of the rack and placed in front of Bond.

Once more, thought Bond. But not this turn.

"I'll stay away," he said to the croupier. The man glanced up at Bond and then reached out with his rake and pulled in Bond's stake and handed it to him.

And then there was another man inside the pit, standing beside the pit-boss, and he was looking at Bond with bright, hard eyes like camera lenses and the fat cigar exactly in the centre of his red lips was pointing straight at Bond like a gun. Though the big square body in the midnight-blue tuxedo was motionless, a sort of steel-spring tension exuded from it. It was a tiger watching the tethered donkey, voracious yet sensing danger. The face was ivory pale, but there was a likeness to the brother in London in the very straight, angry black brows, the short cliff of wiry hair cut *en brosse* and in the ruthless jut of the jaw.

The wheel whirred again and the two pairs of eyes bent to watch it.

It fell into one of the two green slots in the wheel, and Bond's heart lifted at the escape he had had.

"Double Zero," said the stick-man, raking in all the money on the table.

Now for the last throw, thought Bond—and then out of here with $20,000 of Spang money. He looked across at his employer. The two camera lenses and the cigar were still trained on him, but the pale face was expressionless.

"Red." He handed a $5,000 plaque to the croupier and watched it slither down the table.

Would the last coup be asking too much of the wheel? No, decided Bond with certitude. It would not.

"Five. Red. Low and Odd," said the croupier tonelessly.

"I'll take the stake," said Bond. "And thanks for the ride."

"Come again," said the stick-man unemotionally.

Bond put his hand over the four fat plaques in his coat pocket, eased his way through the crowd behind him, and walked straight across the long room to the cashier's desk. "Three bills of five thousand and five of ones," he said to the man with the green eyeshade behind the bars. The man took the four plaques and counted out the bills and Bond put them in his pocket and walked over to the reception desk. "Airmail envelope, please," he said. He moved to a writing desk beside the wall and sat down and put the three big bills in the envelope and wrote on the front: "Personal. The Managing Director, Universal Export, Regent's Park, London, N.W. 1, England." Then he bought stamps at the desk and slipped the envelope down the slot marked "U.S. Mail" and hoped that there, in the most sacrosanct repository in America, it would be safe.

Bond glanced at his watch. Five minutes to midnight. He surveyed the big room for the last time, noted that a new dealer had taken over at Tiffany Case's table and that there was now no sign of Mr. Spang, and then he walked out through the glass door into the hot stuffy night and across the lawn to the Turquoise building and let himself into his room and locked the door behind him.

CHAPTER 18

Night Falls in the Passion Pit

"How'd you make out?"

It was the next evening and Ernie Cureo's cab was rolling slowly along the Strip towards downtown Las Vegas. Bond had got tired of waiting for something to happen and he had called up the Pinkerton man and suggested they get together for a talk.

"Not bad," said Bond. "Took some money off them at roulette, but I don't suppose that'll worry our friend. They tell me he's got plenty to spare."

Ernie Cureo snorted. "I'll say," he said. "That guy's so loaded he don't wear glasses when he drives. Has the windshields of his Cadillacs ground to his prescription."

Bond laughed. "What's he spend it on besides that?" he asked.

"He's nuts," said the driver. "He's crazy about the Old West. Bought himself a whole ghost town way out on Highway 95. Shored the place up, wooden sidewalks, a fancy saloon, clapboard hotel where he rooms the boys, even the old railway station. Way back in '05 or thereabouts this dump—Spectreville, it's called, seeing how it's right alongside the Spectre range—was a riproarin' silver camp. For three years they dug millions out of those mountains, and a spur line took the stuff into Rhyolite, fifty miles away. That's another famous ghost town. Tourist centre now. Got a house made out of whiskey bottles. Used to be the railhead where the stuff got shipped to the coast. Well, Spang bought himself one of the old locos, one of the old 'Highland Lights' if y'ever heard of the engine, and one of the first Pullman state coaches, and he keeps them there in the station at Spectreville and weekends he takes his pals for a run into Rhyolite and back. Drives the train himself. Champagne and caviar, orchestra, girls—the works. Must be something, but I never seen it. You can't get near the place. Yessir''—the driver let down the side window and spat emphatically into the road—''that's how Mr. Spang spends his money. Nuts, like I said.''

So that explained it, thought Bond. That was why he had heard nothing from Mr. Spang or his friends all day. It was Friday, and they would all be out at the boss's place playing trains. While he had swum and slept and hung about the Tiara all day waiting for something to happen. It was true that he had caught an occasional eye shifting away from his, and there had always been a servant of some sort, or one of the uniformed sheriffs, hanging about in his vicinity rather elaborately doing nothing in particular, but otherwise Bond might have been just any one of the hotel guests.

He had caught a single glimpse of the big man, however, and the circumstances had given him a perverse pleasure. At about ten o'clock in the morning, after a swim and breakfast, Bond had decided to get a haircut. There were still very few people about, and the only other customer in the barbershop was a large figure in a purple terrycloth bathwrap whose face, as the man lay tilted back in the chair, was hidden beneath hot towels. His right hand, dangling down over the arm of the chair, was being attended to by a pretty manicurist.

She had a pink-and-white doll's face and a short mop of butter-coloured hair and she squatted beside him on a low stool with a bowl full of instruments balanced on her knees.

Bond, gazing into the mirror in front of his own chair, had watched with interest as the head barber carefully lifted up first one corner of the hot towels and then the other and with infinite delicacy snipped the hair out of the customer's ears with small, thin scissors. Before he replaced the edge of the towel over the second ear he bent down and said deferentially into it, "And the nostrils, sir?"

There was an affirmative grunt, and the barber proceeded to open a window through the towels in the neighbourhood of the man's nose. Then he again went cautiously to work with the thin scissors.

After this ceremony there was dead silence in the small white-tiled room except for the soft clacking of the scissors around Bond's head and the occasional ting as the manicurist dropped an instrument into her enamel bowl. And then there was a soft creaking as the head barber gently tilted the customer's chair upright.

"How's that, sir?" said Bond's barber, holding a hand-mirror behind his head. It was as Bond was inspecting the back of his head that it happened.

Perhaps with the elevation of the chair the girl's hand slipped, but there was suddenly a muffled roar and the man in the purple dressing gown sprang out of his chair, tore the towels off his face and plunged a finger into his mouth. Then he took it out and bent quickly down and slapped the girl hard across the cheek. She was knocked off her stool, and the enamel bowl of instruments went flying across the room. The man straightened himself and turned a furious face on the barber.

"Fire that bitch," he snarled. He put the wounded finger back in his mouth and his slippers crunched amongst the scattered instruments as he strode blindly out of the door and disappeared.

"Yes, sir, Mr. Spang," said the barber in a stunned voice. He started to dress down the sobbing girl.

Bond turned his head and said quietly, "Stop that." He got up from his chair and unwrapped the towel from around his neck.

The barber gave him a surprised glance. Then he said quickly, "Yes, sir, mister," and bent to help the girl gather up her instruments.

While Bond paid for his haircut he heard the kneeling girl say plaintively: "It weren't my fault, Mr. Lucian. He was nervous today. His hands were jerky. Honest, they were. Ain't never seen him like that before. Tense, sort of."

And Bond had had a moment of pleasure at the thought of Mr. Spang's tension.

Ernie Cureo's voice broke sharply in on his thoughts. "We got ourselves a tail, mister," he said out of the corner of his mouth. "Two of 'em. Fore an' aft. Don't look back. See that black Chevy sedan in front? With the two guys. They got two driving mirrors and they been watching us and keeping pace for quite a while. Back of us there's a little red sex-ship. Old sports-model Jag with a rumble seat. Two more guys. With golf clubs in the back. But it just happens I know them guys. Detroit Purple Mob. Coupla lavender boys. You know, pansies. Golf ain't their game. The only irons they can handle are in their pockets. Just swivel around as if you was admiring the scenery. Watch their gunhands while I try 'em out. Ready?"

Bond did as he was told. The driver put his foot on the accelerator and simultaneously turned off the ignition switch. The exhaust let go like an .88 millimetre, and Bond saw the two right hands dive into the two brightly coloured sports jackets. Bond turned his head back. "You're right," he said. He paused. "Better let me out, Ernie. I don't want to get you into trouble."

"Hell," said the driver disgustedly. "They can't do nothin' to me. You pay for any damage to the cab, and I'll try and shake 'em. Okay?"

Bond took a thousand-dollar bill out of his wallet and leaned over and stuffed it into the pocket of the driver's shirt. "There's a grand to start with," he said. "And thanks, Ernie. Let's see what you can do."

Bond slipped his Beretta out of the holster and cradled it in his hand. This, he thought to himself, was just what he had been waiting for.

"Okay, Jack," said the driver cheerfully. "I been looking for a chance to take a poke at the gang. I don't like being leaned on, and they been leaning on me and some of my friends for too long. Hold tight. Here we go!"

It was a straight stretch of road with little traffic. The tops of the distant mountains were yellow in the setting sun and the street was beginning to turn blue with those few minutes of dusk when you can't make up your mind whether or not to switch on your lights.

They were cruising easily at forty with the lowslung Jaguar right on their tail and the black sedan a block ahead of them. Suddenly, so that Bond pitched forward, Ernie Cureo put his brakes full on and dry-skidded to a stop with a scream of tires. There was a shattering splinter of metal and glass as the Jaguar hit their fenders. The cab lurched forward against its brakes, and then the driver jammed it into gear and with a horrible tearing of metal freed himself from the smashed radiator of the car behind and accelerated away down the road.

"That fixed 'em proper," said Ernie Cureo with satisfaction. "How they making out?"

"Busted radiator grille," said Bond, peering out of the rear window. "Both front mudguards flattened. Fender hanging off. Windshield starred, maybe broken." He lost the car in the dusk and turned around. "They're out on the road trying to pull the front mudguard off the tires. They may be able to go before long, but it was a good start. Got any more like that?"

"Not so easy now," grunted the driver. "War's been declared. Watch it. Better get down. The Chevy's pulled up at the side of the road. They may try some shootin'. We're off."

There was a clang and two sharp cracks as they

flashed past the Chevrolet, and a handful of glass showered around Bond. Ernie Cureo swore, and the car gave a swerve and then got back on its course.

Bond knelt on the back seat and knocked out the glass of the rear window with the butt of his gun. The Chevrolet was coming after them, its headlights blazing.

"Hold it," said Cureo with an odd, muffled voice. "Goin' to do a sharp turn and stop under cover of the next block. Give y' a clear shot as they come round after us."

Bond braced himself as the tires screamed again and the cab lurched on two wheels and then righted itself and stopped. Then he was out of the door and crouching with his gun up. The lights of the Chevrolet tore into the side road and there was a squeal of tortured rubber as it made the turn on the wrong side. Now, thought Bond, before they can straighten up.

Crack. A pause. *Crack. Crack. Crack.* Four bullets, at twenty yards, dead on the target.

The Chevrolet didn't straighten up. It went over the curb on the other side of the road, hit a tree broadside, bounced off it and smashed into a streetlight, turned completely around and slowly toppled over on its side.

As Bond watched it, waiting for the echoes of the smashing metal to stop ringing in his ears, flames began to bleed slowly from the chromium mouth of the car. Someone was scrabbling at a window, trying to get out. At any moment the flames would find the vacuum pump and run the whole length of the chassis to the tank. And then it would be too late for whoever was inside.

Bond had started across the road when there was a groan from the front seat of the cab. He turned around to see Ernie Cureo slip from under the wheel to the floor. Bond forgot the burning car as he tore open the door of the cab and bent over the driver. Blood was everywhere. The whole of Cureo's left arm was soaked in it. Bond somehow hauled him into a sitting position on the seat, and the driver's eyes opened. "Oh, brother," he said through clenched teeth. "Get me out

of here, mister, and drive like hell! Next thing that
Jag'll be after us. Then get me to a medic.''

"Okay, Ernie," said Bond, slipping behind the
wheel. "I'll take care of it." He rammed the car into
gear and moved fast off down the road and away from
the blazing pyre and the frightened people who had
materialised out of the dusk and were standing watching
the flames, their hands up to their mouths.

"Keep goin'," muttered Cureo. "This'll get y'out
near the Boulder Dam road. See anything in the
mirror?''

''There's a low-slung car with a spotlight coming
after us fast," said Bond. "Could be the Jag. About
two blocks away now." He stamped on the accelerator
and the cab rocketed through the deserted side street.

"Keep goin'," said Ernie Cureo. "We gotta hide up
someplace and let them lose us. Tell you what. There's a
passion pit just where this comes out onto 95. Drive-in
movie. Here we come. . . . Slow. . . . Sharp right. . . .
See those lights? Get in there quick. . . . Right. . . .
Straight over the sand and between those cars. . . .
Douse the lights. . . . Easy. . . . Stop.''

The cab came to rest in the back row of half a dozen
ranks of cars lined up to face the concrete screen that
soared up into the sky and on which a huge man was
murmuring something to a huge girl.

Bond turned and looked back down the lanes of
metal standards, like parking meters, from which
speakers could be connected with your car to pick up the
sound. As he watched, one or two cars drove in and
ranged themselves in the rear rank. Nothing low enough
for a Jaguar. But it was dark now, and hard to see, and
he stayed slewed round in his seat, his eyes on the
entrance.

An attendant came up, a pretty girl dressed as a page
boy, with a tray slung around her neck. "That'll be a
dollar each," she said, glancing into the car to make
sure there were only two in the cab. She had pick-ups
coiled over her right arm and she took one off, plugged
it into the nearest standard and hung the small speaker

through the window on Bond's side. The huge man and woman on the screen started talking heatedly.

"Coca-Cola, cigarettes, candy?" asked the girl, taking the bill Bond handed her.

"No, thanks," said Bond.

"You're welcome," said the girl, and sauntered off towards the other late arrivals.

"Mister, for Chris'sake willya switch off that crap?" pleaded Ernie Cureo through his teeth. "And keep an eye peeled. We'll give 'em a while longer and then you gotta get me to a doc. Gotta dig out the slug." His voice was weak, and now that the girl had gone he was half lying with his head against the door.

"Won't be long, Ernie. Try and stick it." Bond fiddled with the speaker, found the switch and silenced the wrangling voices. The huge man on the screen looked as if he was going to hit the woman, and her mouth gaped in a noiseless scream.

Bond turned and strained his eyes across the dark expanse behind them. Still nothing. He glanced at the neighbouring cars. Two faces glued together. A shapeless huddle on a back seat. Two prim, rapt, elderly faces staring upwards. The glint of light on an upturned bottle.

And then a wave of musky after-shave lotion came up to his nose and a dark figure rose up from the ground and a gun was in his face and a voice on the other side of the car beside Ernie Cureo whispered softly, "Okay, boys. Take it easy."

Bond looked into the suety face beside him. The eyes were smiling and cold, and the wet lips parted and whispered: "Out, Limey, or your pal's cold turkey. My friend has a silencer. You and us're goin' for a little drive."

Bond turned his head and saw the black sausage of metal against the back of Ernie Cureo's neck. He made up his mind. "Okay, Ernie," he said, "better one than two. I'll go with them. After we've gone, call for help. There may be a doctor in the house. Good luck."

"Shake it," said Suet Face, opening the door but

keeping his gun trained on Bond's face.

"Sorry, friend," said Ernie Cureo in a tired voice. "I guess—" but then there was a sharp thud as the gun hit him behind the ear and he slumped forward and was silent.

Bond gritted his teeth, and his muscles lumped under his coat. He wondered if he could reach the Beretta. He glanced from one gun to the other, measuring, adding up the odds. The four eyes above the two guns were greedy, longing for an excuse to kill him. The two mouths were smiling thinly; they wanted him to try something. He felt his blood cooling. He gave it another few seconds and then, with his hands in sight, he stepped slowly out of the car . . . with murder tucked away in the back of his mind.

"Go ahead to the gate," said Suet Face softly. "Look natural! I got you covered." His gun had disappeared but his hand was in his pocket. The other man joined them and his right hand was at the waistband of his trousers. He ranged himself on Bond's other side.

The three men walked swiftly towards the entrance. The moon rising over the rim of the mountains perambulated their long shadows in front of them across the white sandy lot.

CHAPTER 19

Spectreville

The red Jag was outside the entrance and up
against the wall of the enclosure. Bond let them take his
gun and climbed in beside the driver.

"No funny business if you want to keep your head on
straight," said Suet Face, climbing into the rumble seat
with the golf clubs. "There's a gun on you."

"Nice little car you had here," said Bond. The shat-
tered windshield had been lowered flat and a piece of
chrome from the radiator stuck up like a pennant between the two front tires. "Where are we going in the
remains?"

"You'll see," said the driver, a bony man with a hard
mouth and long sideburns. He swung the car out onto
the road and accelerated towards town, and they were
soon back in the jungle of neon and then through it and
going fast down a two-lane highway that ribboned away
towards the mountains across the moonlit desert.

There was a big sign which said "95," and Bond
remembered what Ernie Cureo had told him. He was on
the way to Spectreville. He hoped that somebody would

find Ernie quickly and get him off to a doctor. He hunched down in his seat to protect his eyes from the dust and insects and thought about the immediate future and how he might be able to revenge his friend.

So these men and the other two in the Chevrolet had been sent by Spang to bring him in. Why had four men been necessary? Surely that was a rather heavyweight answer to Bond's defiance of orders in the Casino?

The car sped on down the dead straight road with the needle of the speedometer wavering around eighty. The telegraph poles streamed by like the click of a metronome. Bond suddenly felt that he didn't know quite enough of the answers.

Was he completely exposed as an enemy of the Spangled Mob? He could argue himself out of the game of roulette on the grounds that he hadn't understood his orders, and if he had been a bit troublesome when the four men came for him he could at least pretend that he had thought they were from a rival mob. "If you wanted me, why didn't you just call me in my room?" Bond could hear himself saying that in an injured tone of voice.

At least he had shown that he was tough enough for any job Mr. Spang might offer him. And in any case, Bond reassured himself, he was just about to achieve his main objective—to get to the end of the pipe line and somehow link Seraffimo Spang with his brother in London.

Bond crouched, his eyes on the luminous dials in front of him, concentrating on the interview ahead and wondering how much useful evidence about the pipe line he could possibly extract from it.

It was not in his make-up to worry about how he was going to get away again once he had achieved his objective. He still had no respect for these people. Only contempt and dislike.

Bond was still rehearsing imaginary conversations with Mr. Spang when, after two hours of driving, he felt the speed of the car coming down. He lifted his head above the dashboard. They were coasting up to a section of high wire fence with a gate in it and a big notice lit up by their single headlight. It said, "Spectreville. City limits. Do not enter. Dangerous Dogs." The car drew up below the notice and beside an iron post embedded in concrete. On the post were a bellpush and a small iron grille and a message written in red: "Ring and State Your Business."

Without leaving the wheel, Sideburns reached out and pressed the button. There was a pause and then a metallic voice said, "Yes?"

"Frasso and McGonigle," said the driver loudly.

"Okay," said the voice. There was a sharp click. The high wire gate slowly opened. They drove through and over an iron strip in the narrow dirt road beyond. Bond looked back over his shoulder and saw the gate close behind them. He also noticed with pleasure that the face of—presumably—McGonigle was plastered with dust and the blood of dead insects.

The dirt road continued for about a mile across the brutal, stony surface of the desert in which an occasional clump of gesticulating cactus was the only vegetation. Then there was a glow ahead and they rounded a spur of mountain and went down a hill and into a brightly lit, straggling assembly of about twenty buildings. Beyond, the moon glinted on a single railway track which lanced off, straight as a die, towards the distant horizon.

They drew up among the grey clapboard houses and shops marked "Drugs," "Barber," "Farmers Bank" and "Wells Fargo," under a hissing gaslight outside a two-storey building bearing the legend in faded gold, "Pink Garter Saloon," and underneath, "Beers and Wines."

From behind the traditional sawn-off swing-doors, yellow light streamed out onto the street and onto the sleek black and silver of a 1920 Stutz Bearcat roadster at the curb. There was the sweet nasal twang of a honky-tonk piano playing "I Wonder Who's Kissing Her Now," slightly flat. The music was reminiscent of sawdust floors, straight drinks and girls' legs in the widest mesh stockings, and the whole scene was like something out of an exceptionally well mounted Western.

"Out, Limey," said the driver. The three men climbed stiffly out of the car and onto the raised wooden sidewalk. Bond bent to massage a leg that had gone to sleep, watching the feet of the two men.

"Come on, Limey," said McGonigle, giving him a shove with his loosely held gun. Bond slowly straightened himself, measuring inches. He limped heavily as he followed the first man to the door of the saloon. He paused as the swing doors flapped back into his face. He felt the prod of Frasso's gun from behind.

Now! Bond straightened himself and leaped through the still swinging door. McGonigle's back was just in front of him and, beyond, a brightly lit, empty barroom in which an automatic piano was playing to itself.

Bond's hands shot out and caught the man above the elbows. He lifted him off his feet and swung him round and back through the swing doors and into Frasso, who was just coming in. The whole clapboard house trembled as the two bodies collided violently, Frasso staggered back through the doors and crashed onto the sidewalk.

McGonigle catapulted back and twisted to face Bond. There was a rising gun in his hand. Bond's left caught him on the shoulder. At the same time his open right hand slapped down hard on the gun. McGonigle went back on his heels against the door jamb. The gun clattered to the floor.

The snout of Frasso's revolver appeared through the swing doors. It weaved quickly around towards Bond, like an aiming snake. As its blue-and-yellow tongue licked out, Bond, his blood singing, dove for the ground and the gun at McGonigle's feet. He got his hand on it and fired two quick shots upwards from the floor before McGonigle stamped on his firing hand and landed on top of him. As Bond went down he caught a glimpse of Frasso's gun arced up between the swing doors, pumping bullets into the ceiling. And this time the crash of the body on the planking outside sounded final.

Then McGonigle's hands were at him, and Bond was kneeling on the ground with his head down trying to protect his eyes. The gun was still on the floor within reach of the first free hand.

For seconds they fought silently, like animals, and then Bond got to one knee and gave a great heave and lashed upwards and the weight came off him and he rose to a crouch. As he did so, McGonigle's knee came up like a piston under his chin and knocked him to his feet with a snap of the teeth that shook his skull.

Bond had no time to clear his head before the gangster gave a thick grunt and came for him head downwards with both arms flailing.

Bond twisted to protect his stomach, and the gangster's head hit him in the ribs and the two fists crashed into his body. His breath whistled through his teeth with the pain; but he kept focus on McGonigle's head below him and, with a twist of the body that put all of his shoulder behind the movement, he whipped in a hard left and, as the gangster's head came up, a crossing right to the chin.

The impact of the two blows straightened McGonigle and rocked him back on his feet. Bond was on him immediately, crowding him and raining blows to the body until the gangster began to sag. Bond grabbed at one weaving wrist and dove for an ankle and yanked it away from the floor. With all his strength he made almost a full turn to gather momentum and slung the body sideways into the room.

There was a twanging crash as the flying figure hit the upright pianola; and then with an explosion of metallic discords and breaking wood the whole contraption toppled over, with McGonigle spreadeagled across it, and thundered to the floor.

Amidst the dying crescendo of echoes Bond stood in the centre of the room, his legs braced with the last effort and the breath rasping painfully in his throat. Slowly he lifted one bruised hand and ran it through his hair.

"Cut."

It was a girl's voice coming from the direction of the bar.

Bond shook himself and turned slowly around.

Four people were standing in line with their backs to the mahogany and brass bar behind which ranks of gleaming bottles rose to the ceiling. Bond had no idea how long they had been there.

A step in front of the other three stood the leading citizen of Spectreville, resplendent, motionless, dominant.

Mr. Spang was dressed in full Western costume down to the long silver spurs on his polished black boots. The costume, and the broad leather chaps that covered his legs, were in black picked out and embellished with silver. The big quiet hands rested on the ivory butts of two long-barrelled revolvers which protruded from a holster down each thigh, and the broad black belt from which they hung was ribbed with ammunition.

Mr. Spang should have looked ridiculous but he didn't. His big pale head was thrust slightly forward and his eyes were cold slits.

On Spang's right, her hands on her hips, stood Tiffany Case. In a Western dress of white and gold, she looked like something out of *Annie Get Your Gun*. She stood and watched Bond. Her eyes were shining. Her full red lips were slightly parted, and she was breathing as if she had just been kissed.

The other half of the quartet was composed of two men in black hoods—the same two he had last seen in Saratoga. Each of them held a .38 Police Positive trained on Bond's heaving chest.

Bond slowly took out a handkerchief and wiped his face with it. He was feeling lightheaded, and the scene in the brilliantly lit saloon, with its brass fittings and its homely advertisements for long-vanished beers and whiskeys, was suddenly macabre.

Mr. Spang broke the silence. "Bring him over." The hard jaws that operated the sharp thin lips separated and cut off each word as cleanly as a meat-slicer. "And tell someone to call Detroit and tell the boys they're suffering from delusions of adequacy up there. And tell 'em to send down two more. And tell 'em they got to be better than the last lot. And tell someone else to clean up this mess. 'Kay?''

There was a faint jingle of spurs on the wooden floor as Mr. Spang left the room. With a last look at Bond, a look that held some message that was more than the obvious warning, the girl followed him.

The two men came up to Bond and the big one said, "You heard him." Bond walked after the girl, and the two men lined up behind him.

There was a door behind the bar. Bond pushed through it and found himself in a station waiting-room with benches and old-fashioned notices about trains and admonitions not to spit on the floor. "Right," said one of the men, and Bond turned through a swing-door and onto a plank station platform.

And then Bond stopped in his tracks and hardly noticed a sharp prod in the ribs from a gun barrel.

It was probably the most beautiful toy in the world. The engine was one of the old locomotives of the "Highland Light" 4-4-0 class of around 1870 which Bond had heard called the handsomest steam locomotive ever built. Its polished brass handrails and the fluted sand-dome and heavy warning bell above the long gleaming barrel of the boiler glittered under the hissing gaslights of the station. A wisp of steam came from the towering balloon smokestack of the old woodburner. The great sweeping cowcatcher was topped by three massive brass lights—a bulging pilot beam at the base of the smokestack and two storm lanterns below. Above the tall driving wheels, in fine early Victorian gold capitals, was written *The Cannonball,* and the name was repeated along the side of the black-and-gold painted tender, piled with birch logs, behind the tall square driver's cabin.

Coupled to the tender was the maroon-coloured state Pullman. Its arched windows above the narrow mahogany panels were picked out in cream. An oval plaque amidships said *The Sierra Belle*. Above the windows and below the slightly jutting barrel roof, *Tonopah and Tidewater R.R.* was inscribed in cream capitals on dark blue.

"Guess you never seen nothin' like that, Limey," said one of the guards proudly. "Now get goin'." His voice was muffled by the black silk hood.

Bond walked slowly across and stepped up onto the brass-railed observation platform with the shining brakeman's wheel in the centre. For the first time in his life he saw the point of being a millionaire, and suddenly and also for the first time, he thought that there might be more to this man Spang than he had reckoned on.

The interior of the Pullman glittered with Victorian luxury. The light from small crystal chandeliers in the roof gleamed on the polished mahogany walls and winked off silver fittings and cut-glass vases and lampstands. The carpets and swagged curtains were wine red, and the domed ceiling, broken at intervals by oval framed paintings of garlanded cherubs and wreathed flowers against a background of sky and clouds, was cream, as were the slats of the dawn venetian blinds.

First came a small dining room with the remains of a supper for two—a basket of fruit and an open bottle of champagne in a silver bucket—and then a narrow corridor from which three doors led, Bond assumed, to the bedrooms and lavatory. Bond was still thinking about this arrangement as, with the guards at his heels, he pushed open the door into the stateroom. At the far end of this, with his back to a small open fireplace flanked by bookshelves gleaming richly with gold-tooled leather bindings, stood Mr. Spang. In a red leather armchair near a small writing desk halfway down the car Tiffany Case sat bolt upright. Bond didn't care for the way she was holding her cigarette. It was nervous and artificial. It looked frightened.

Bond took a few steps down the car to a comfortable chair. He turned it around to face them both and sat down and crossed his legs negligently. He took out his cigarette case and lit a cigarette and inhaled a deep lungful of smoke and let it come out from between his teeth with a long relaxed hiss.

Mr. Spang had an unlighted cigar jutting from the exact centre of his mouth. He took it out. "Stay here, Wint. Kidd, get along and do what I said. Now you." His eyes glittered angrily at Bond. "Who are you and what's going on?"

"I'll need a drink if we're going to chat," said Bond.

Mr. Spang eyed him coldly. "Get him a drink, Wint."

Bond half turned his head. "Bourbon and branch water," he said. "Half and half."

There was an angry grunt and Bond heard the floorboards creak as the heavy man walked back down the Pullman.

Bond was suspicious of Mr. Spang's question. He went back over his story. It still seemed all right. He sat and smoked and regarded Mr. Spang levelly, weighing him up.

The drink came and the guard thrust it into his hand so that some of it slopped onto the carpet, "Thanks, Wint," said Bond. He took a healthy swallow. It was strong and good. He took another. Then he put the glass down on the floor beside him.

He looked up again into the tense, hard face. "I just don't like being pushed around," he said easily. "I did my job and got paid. If I chose to gamble with my own money, that was my affair. I could have lost. And then a lot of your men started breathing down my neck and I got impatient. If you wanted to talk to me, why didn't you just call me up on the telephone? Putting that tail on me was unfriendly. And when they got rude and started shooting, I thought it was time to do some pushing of my own."

The pale, frozen face against the coloured books expressed nothing. "You don't get the message, chum," Mr. Spang said softly. "Maybe I better bring you up to date. Gotta signal yesterday from London." His hand went to the breast pocket of his black Western shirt, and he slowly pulled out a piece of paper, holding Bond's eyes with his.

Bond knew the piece of paper was bad news, really bad news, just as surely as you do when you read the word "Deeply" at the beginning of a telegram.

"This is from a good friend of mine in London," said Mr. Spang. He released Bond's eyes and looked down at the piece of paper. "It says: 'Reliably informed Peter Franks held by police on unspecified charge. Endeavour at all costs hold substitute carrier. Ascertain if operations endangered. Eliminate him and report.'"

There was silence in the car. Mr. Spang's eyes rose from the paper and glittered into Bond's. "Well, mister, this looks like you're down for a little elimination."

Bond swallowed, wondering how it was going to be done. But at the same time he had discovered what he wanted to know, what he had come to America to find out. The two Spangs did represent the beginning and the end of the diamond pipe line. At this moment he had completed the job he had set out to do. He knew most of the answers. Now, somehow he must get them back to M. He reached down for his drink. The ice rattled hollowly as he took the last deep swallow and put the glass down.

He looked candidly up at Mr. Spang. "I took the job from Peter Franks. He didn't like the looks of it and I needed the money."

"Don't give me that crap," said Mr. Spang flatly. "You're a cop or a private eye of some kind, and I'm going to find out who you are and who you work for and what you know—what you were doing in the Acme Baths alongside that crooked jock; why you carry a gun and where you learned to handle it; how come you're tied in with Pinkertons in the shape of that phoney cab driver. Things like that. You look like an eye and you act like one and"—he turned with sudden anger on Tiffany Case—"how in hell you fell for him, you silly bitch, I just can't figure."

"Cut it out," flared Tiffany Case. "I get handed the guy by A B C and he acts okay. You think maybe I should have told A B C to try again? Not me, brother. And don't think you can push *me* around. Anyway, for all you know this guy may be telling the truth." Her angry eyes swept over Bond, and he caught the glint of fear, fear for him, behind them.

"Well, we're going to find out," said Mr. Spang gently. "And go on finding out until the guy croaks. If he thinks he can hold out on us he's got another thing coming." He looked over Bond's head at the guard. "Wint, get Kidd and come back here with the boots."

The boots?

Bond sat silent, gathering his strength and his courage. It would be a waste of time to argue with Spang or to try to escape, fifty miles out in the desert. He had got out of worse jams. Just so long as they didn't intend to kill him outright. So long as he gave nothing away. There was Ernie Cureo and there was Felix Leiter. There might just possibly be Tiffany Case. He looked across at her. Her head was bent. She was carefully studying her fingernails.

Bond heard the two guards come up behind him.

"Take him out on the platform," said Spang. Bond saw the tip of his tongue come out and lightly touch the thin lips. "Brooklyn stomping. Eighty per center. Okay?"

"Okay, Boss." That was Wint's voice. It sounded greedy.

The two hooded men came up and sat down side by side on a dark red chaise longue that ran down the car opposite Bond. They put down football boots beside them and started to unlace their shoes.

Flames Coming Out of the Top

The black frogman's suit fitted tightly. It hurt everywhere. Why the hell hadn't Strangways made certain the Admiralty got his measurements right? And it was very dark under the sea and the currents were strong, pulling him against the coral. He would have to swim hard against them. But now something had got him by the arm. What the hell . . .

"James. James!" She shook him again, then pinched the naked blood-stained arm as hard as she could, and at last Bond's eyes opened between their puffed lids and he looked vacantly up at her from the wooden floor and gave a shuddering sigh.

She tugged at him, terrified that he would slip away from her again. He seemed to understand and he rolled over and struggled onto hands and knees, his head hanging down towards the ground like that of a stricken animal.

"Can you walk?"

"Wait." The thick whisper coming through the cracked lips sounded strange to him. Perhaps she hadn't understood. "Wait," he said again, and his mind started exploring his body to see what was left of it. He could feel his feet and his hands. He could move his head from side to side. He could see the bars of moonlight on the floor. He had been able to hear her. It ought to be all right, but he just didn't want to move. His will power had gone. He just wanted to sleep. Or even to die. Anything to lessen the pain that was in him and all over him, stabbing, hammering, grinding him, and to kill the memory of the four boots thudding into him, and the grunts coming from the two hooded figures.

As he thought of the two thugs and of Mr. Spang, the will to live flooded back into him and he muttered, "Okay." And then again, "Okay," so that she would be sure to understand.

"We're in the waiting room," she whispered. "We must get to the end of the station. Left outside the door. Do you hear me?" She reached out and brushed the damp, sticky hair away from his forehead.

"Have to crawl," said Bond. "Follow you."

The girl got to her feet and pushed open the door. Bond gritted his teeth and crawled out onto the moonlit platform, and when he saw the dark patch on the ground, rage gave him strength and he got clumsily to his feet, shaking his head to keep the red-black waves from drowning him and, with Tiffany's arm around him, he limped along the wooden boards to where they sloped down towards the ground beside the gleaming rails.

And there, in the single-line siding, was a railroad handcar.

Bond stopped and gazed at it. "Gas?" he said vaguely.

Tiffany Case gestured towards a row of cans against the station wall. "Just filled her up," she whispered back. "It's what they use for inspecting the line. I can work it. And I shifted the points. Hurry. Get aboard." She giggled excitedly. "Next stop Rhyolite."

"My God, you're quite a girl," whispered Bond.

"But hell of a noise when we start that thing. Wait. Got an idea. Got matches?" Half his pain had fallen away from him. His breath came fast as he turned away from her and focussed on the silent, tinder-dry buildings.

She was wearing slacks and a tailored shirt. She dug into the pocket of the slacks and handed him her lighter. "What's the idea?" she said. "We ought to get going."

But Bond lurched over to the row of gas cans and started opening them and sloshing the contents over the wooden walls and platform. When he had emptied half a dozen cans he went back to her. "Get her going." He bent agonisingly down and picked up a crumpled newspaper from beside the rails. There was the angry whine of the self-starter, and then the little two-stroke engine caught and started hammering busily.

Bond flicked the lighter. The piece of paper flared and he flung it away from him amongst the empty gas cans. The whoosh of flame almost caught him as he threw himself backwards onto the little platform of the car. Tiffany let in the clutch and the handcar started down the line.

After a rattle and a sickening lurch at the switch, they were out on the main line and the speedometer was trembling at thirty and the girl's hair was flowing back like a golden banner towards him.

Bond turned and looked back at the great bloom of flame they had left behind them. He could almost hear the dry boards crackling and the shouts of the sleepers as they were awakened by the glare. If only it would get Wint and Kidd and catch the paint on the Pullman and fire the wood in the tender of *The Cannonball*—finish off the gangster's box of toys.

But he and Tiffany had their own problems. What time was it? Bond gulped down the cool night air and tried to get his mind to function smoothly again. The moon was low. Four o'clock? Bond hunched his way painfully up the platform to the two bucket seats and somehow scrambled over and got down beside the girl.

He put an arm around her shoulders, and she turned and smiled into his eyes. She raised her voice above the noise of the engine and the hammer of the iron wheels on the rails. "That was quite an exit. Like something out of an old Buster Keaton movie. How d'you feel?" She surveyed the battered face. "You look terrible."

"Nothing broken," said Bond. "Suppose that's what's meant by an 80 per center." He grinned painfully. "It's better being kicked than being shot."

Tiffany winced. "I just had to sit there and pretend I didn't care. Spang stayed and listened and watched me. Then they trussed you up and slung you into the waiting room and locked it and everyone went happily to bed. I waited an hour in my room and then I got busy. The worst part was trying to wake you up."

Bond tightened his arm around her shoulders. "I'll tell you what I think of you when it doesn't hurt so much. But what about you, Tiffany? You'll be in a jam if they catch up with us. And how about those two in the hoods, Wint and Kidd? What are they going to do about all this? I wouldn't mind seeing a little more of them."

The girl glanced sideways at the grim set of the bruised mouth. "I've never seen them without those hoods on." she said. "They're supposed to be from Detroit. Strictly bad news. They do the strong-arm work and special undercover jobs. They'll all be after us now. But don't you worry about him." She looked up at him again and her eyes were shining and confident. "First thing is to get this crate to Rhyolite. Then we'll have to find a car somewhere and get over the border into California. I've got plenty of money. Then we'll get you to a doctor and buy you a bath and a shirt and we'll think again. I've got your gun. One of the help brought it over when they'd finished picking up the pieces of those two guys you argued with in the Pink Garter. I collected it after Spang had gone to bed, along with the key to the waiting room." She unbuttoned her shirt and dug into the waistband of her slacks.

Bond took the Beretta, feeling the warmth of her on the metal. He flicked out the magazine. Three rounds left. And one in the chamber. He replaced the magazine, put the gun on safety and tucked it into the top of his trousers. For the first time he realised that his coat was gone. One of his shirt sleeves hung in tatters. He tore it off and threw it away. He felt for the cigarette case in his right-hand hip pocket. It was gone. But in the left-hand pocket his passport and wallet were safe. He pulled them out. By the light of the moon he could see that they were cracked and dented. He felt for his money in the wallet. It was still there. He put the things back in his pocket.

For a while they drove on with only the purr of the little engine and the *clickety-click* of the wheels to break the looming silence of the night. For as far as they could see the thin silver line of the rails spun on towards the horizon with only an occasional break, marked by a points lever, where a rusty branch line curved off into the dark mass of the Spectre Mountains on their right. To their left was nothing except the endless floor of the desert on which the hint of dawn was beginning to edge the writhing cactus clumps with blue and, two miles away, the gunmetal shimmer of the moon on Highway 95.

The handcar sang happily on down the rails. There were no controls to bother with except a brake lever and a kind of joystick with a twist-grip accelerator which the girl held full open with the speedometer steady at thirty. The miles and the minutes ticked by, and every now and then Bond turned painfully in his seat and inspected the red glow in the sky behind them.

They had been going nearly an hour when a thin humming undertone in the air or in the rails made Bond stiffen. Again he looked back over his shoulder. Was there a tiny glowworm glimmer between them and the false red dawn of the burning ghost town?

Bond's scalp tingled. "D'you see anything back there?"

She turned her head. Then, without replying, she cut the engine. They coasted quietly.

They both listened. Yes. It was in the rails. A soft quivering, not more than a distant sigh.

"The *Cannonball,*" said Tiffany flatly. She gave a

sharp twist to the ignition and accelerated. The handcar sped on again.

"What can she do?" asked Bond.

"Maybe fifty."

"How far to Rhyolite?"

"Around thirty."

Bond worked on the figures for a few seconds in silence. "It's going to be a near thing. Can't tell how far away he is. Can you get anything more out of this?"

"Not a scrap," she said grimly. "Even if my name was Casey Jones instead of Case."

"We'll be all right," said Bond. "You keep her rolling. Maybe he'll blow his stack or something."

"Oh, sure," she said. "Or maybe the spring'll run down and he's left the wind-up key at home in his pants pocket."

For fifteen minutes they sped along in silence, and now Bond could clearly see the great pilot-light of the engine cutting through the night not more than five miles away and an angry fountain of woodsparks showering out of the huge dome of the smokestack. The rails were trembling beneath them, and what had been a distant sigh was now a low threatening murmur.

Perhaps he'll run out of wood, thought Bond. On an impulse he said casually to the girl, "I suppose we're all right for gas?"

"Guess so," said Tiffany. "Put in a whole can. There's no indicator, but these things'll run for ever on a gallon of gas."

Almost before the words were out of her mouth, and as if to comment on them, the little engine gave a deprecating cough. *Put. Put-put.* Then it ran merrily on.

"Christ!" said Tiffany. "Did you hear that?"

Bond said nothing. He felt the palms of his hands go wet.

And again: *Put. Put-put.*

Tiffany Case gingerly nursed the accelerator. "Oh, dear little engine," she said coaxingly. "Beautiful, clever little engine. Please be good."

Put-put. Put-put. Hiss. Put. Hiss-s . . . and they were freewheeling along in silence. Twenty-five, said the speedometer. Twenty . . . fifteen . . . ten . . . five. A last savage twist at the accelerator and a kick from Tiffany Case at the engine-housing and they had stopped.

Bond swore savagely, once. He got painfully out onto the side of the track and limped to the gas tank at the rear, pulling his bloodstained handkerchief out of his trouser pocket. He unscrewed the filler cap and lowered the handkerchief down far enough to reach the bottom of the tank. Then he pulled it out and felt it and sniffed it. Dry as a bone.

"That's that," he said to the girl. "Now just let's think hard." He looked all around. No cover to the left and two miles at least to the road. On the right, the mountains, perhaps a quarter of a mile away. They might get there and hide up. But for how long? It seemed the best chance. The ground beneath his feet was shaking. He looked down the line at the distant, im-placable eye. How far? Two miles? Would Spang see the handcar in time? Would he be able to stop? Could he be derailed? But then Bond remembered the great jutting cow-catcher that would sweep the light car out of the way like a bale of straw.

"Come on, Tiffany," he called. "We've got to take to the hills."

Where was she? He limped around the car. She was running back down the track in front. She came up panting. "There's a branch line just ahead," she gasped. "If we can push this thing there and you can work the old points, he might miss us."

"My God," said Bond slowly. Then, with awe in his voice, "We can do something better than that. Give me a hand," and he bent down and gritted his teeth against the pain and started pushing.

Once started, the car moved easily and they only had to follow behind it and keep it rolling. They came to the points and Bond went on pushing until they were twenty yards past.

"What the hell?" panted Tiffany.

"Come on," said Bond, half stumbling, half running back to where the rusty switch stuck up beside the rails. "We're going to put *The Cannonball* onto the branch line."

Tiffany nodded slowly, wide-eyed. And then they were both at the switch and Bond's bruised muscles were cracking as he heaved.

The rusty metal shifted by millimetres in the bed where it had lain unmoved for fifty years, and little by little the rails showed a crack and then a widening gap as Bond strained and hauled at the lever.

And then it was done and Bond knelt on the ground with his head down, fighting dizziness and nausea.

But then there was a glare of light on the ground, and Tiffany tugged at him and he was on his feet again, stumbling back to the car. The air was full of thunder and the doleful clanging of the warning bell as the great flaming iron beast came roaring towards them.

"Get down and don't move!" shouted Bond above the noise, and he thrust her to the ground behind the flimsy shelter of the handcar. Then he limped quickly to the side of the track and drew his gun and stood sideways with his pistol arm up like a duellist and squinted down the track into the blinding, onrushing eye below the volcano of swirling fire and smoke.

God, what a monster! Could it possibly take the curve? Wouldn't it just hurtle on into them and smash them to pulp?

On it came.

Phut. Something whipped into the ground beside him, and there was a pinpoint flash from the cabin.

There was another flash, and the bullet hit a rail and whined off into the night.

Crack. Crack. Crack. Now he could hear the gun above the roar of the engine. Something sang sharply in his ear.

Bond held his fire. Only four bullets, and he knew when he would use them.

Then, twenty yards away, the flying engine thundered into the curve and took the siding with a lurch that sent logs hurtling towards Bond off the top of the tender.

There was a shrill scream of metal as the flanges on the six-foot tall driving wheels ground into the bend, a swift impression of smoke and flame and pounding machinery, and then a glimpse into the cabin and of the black-and-silver figure of Spang, spreadeagled, clinging to the side of the cabin with one hand and with the other outflung to the long iron handle of the throttle lever.

Bond's gun spat its four words. There was a lightning impression of a white face jerked up towards the sky, and the great black-and-gold engine was past and hurtling towards the shadowy wall of the Spectre Mountains, the beam of its pilot-light scything the darkness ahead and its automatic warning bell clanging sadly on, *ding-dong, ding-dong.* . . .

Bond slowly returned the Beretta into his belt and stood looking after the coffin of Mr. Spang. A trail of thick smoke drifted over his head and for a moment put out the moon.

Tiffany Case came running to him and they stood side by side watching the flaming banner from the tall smokestack and listening to the mountains throw back the echo of the charging locomotive. The girl clutched his arm as the engine gave a sudden swerve and vanished behind a spur of rock. And now there were only a faraway drumming in the mountains and a red glow that flickered off the crags as *The Cannonball* tore on down the cutting into the belly of the rock.

Suddenly there was a great tongue of fire, followed a few breathless seconds later by a terrible iron crash as if a battleship had run hard onto rocks. And then a muffled clanging that seemed to come from under their feet. And finally a deep distant boom from the bowels of the earth and a barrage of miscellaneous echoes.

And then, with all noise gone, a steady, singing silence.

Bond heaved a deep sigh as if he were just waking up. So that was the end of one of the Spangs, of one of the brutal, theatrical, overblown dead-end adults who headed the Spangled Mob. He had been a stage-gangster surrounded with stage properties, but that didn't alter the fact that he had intended to kill Bond.

"Let's get out of here," Tiffany said urgently. "I've had enough."

Bond felt the pain creeping back into his body as his tension relaxed. "Yes," he said shortly. He was glad to turn his back on the memory of the upturned white face in the beautiful, black, charging engine. He felt lightheaded. He wondered if he would make it. "We'll have to get to the road. It'll be hard going. Come on."

It took them an hour and a half to cover the two miles, and by the time he collapsed in the dirt beside the cement highway, Bond was delirious. It was the girl who had got him there. But for her he would never have kept a straight course. He would have stumbled about amongst the cactus and rock and mica until his strength was exhausted and the broiling sun came to finish the job.

And now she was cradling his head against her and talking softly to him and wiping the sweat off his face with the corner of her unbuttoned shirt.

Every now and then she paused to look up and down the concrete road whose horizons were already shimmering in the heat waves of early morning.

An hour later she jumped to her feet and tucked in her shirt and ran into the middle of the road. A low black car was coming out of the dancing haze which hid the distant valley of Las Vegas.

It rolled to a stop just in front of her, and a hawk-like face under an untidy mop of straw-coloured hair poked out of the window. Keen grey eyes briefly looked her over. They glanced once at the sagging figure of the man in the dust beside the road and came back to her and then, in a friendly Texan drawl, the driver said, "My name's Leiter, ma'm. Anything I can do for you this beautiful morning?"

"Nothing Propinks Like Propinquity"

". . . and when I get into town I call my friend Ernie Cureo. His wife is having hysterics and Ernie's in the hospital. So I go right over and he tells me the score and I figure that James may need reinforcements. So I jump on my coal-black charger and gallop through the night and when I get near to Spectreville I see the light in the sky. Mr. Spang's having himself a barbecue, I figure. The gate in the fence is open so I decide to join the feast. Well, believe me or believe me not, there's not a soul in the place except a guy with a busted leg and multiple contusions who's crawling down the road trying to get away. And he looks to me mighty like a young hood called Frasso from Detroit. Ernie Cureo tells me he was one of the guys who carted James away. The greaser's in no state to deny this and I more or less get the picture and figure that Rhyolite's my next stop. So I tell the kid he'll soon be having plenty of company from the Fire Department and I take him to the gate and leave him there and then after a while there's a girl standing in the middle of the desert looking as if she's been fired out of a cannon and here we all are. Now you tell.''

So it's not all part of a dream and I really am lying in the back of the Studillac and this is Tiffany's lap under my head and that is Felix and we are going hell for leather down the road to safety, a doctor, a bath, some food and drink and an endless amount of sleep. Bond moved and he felt Tiffany's hand in his hair, telling him it was all real just as he hoped, and he lay still again and said nothing, but held each moment to him and listened to their voices and the zip of the tires on the road.

At the end of Tiffany's story, Felix Leiter gave a reverent whistle. ''Je-sus, ma'm,'' he said. ''The two of you sure seem to have busted a hole in the Spangled Mob. What in hell's going to happen now? There are plenty of other hornets in the nest and just sittin' around buzzin' isn't going to be their way. They'll want some action.''

''Check,'' said Tiffany. ''Spang was a member of the Syndicate at Vegas, and these guys stick pretty much together. Then there's Shady Tree and those two torpedoes Wint and Kidd. The sooner we cross the state line, the better. Then what?''

''We're doing all right so far,'' said Leiter. ''Be at Beatty in ten minutes, then we'll get on to 58 and be over the line in half an hour. Then there's a long ride across Death Valley and through the mountains down to Olancha where we hit No. 6. We could stop there and get James to a doc and do some eating and cleaning up. Then just stay on 6 until we get to L.A. It'll be a hell of a drive, but we should make L.A. by lunchtime. Then we can relax a bit. My guess is that we ought to get you and James out of the country pretty quick. The boys'll try to fix all kinds of phoney raps on you both, and once you're located I wouldn't give a nickel for either one of you. Best chance would be to get you both on a 'plane to New York tonight and off to England tomorrow. James can take it from there.''

''I guess that makes sense,'' said the girl. ''But who is

this Bond guy, anyway? What's his racket? Is he an eye?"

"You better ask him yourself, ma'm," Bond heard Leiter say carefully. "But I wouldn't let that worry you too much. He'll take care of you."

Bond smiled to himself, and in the long silence that followed he dropped off into a heavy sleep which lasted until they were halfway across California and had pulled up outside a white wicket gate and a mailbox reading "Otis Fairplay, M.D."

And then, a mass of surgical tape and streaked with merthiolate, washed and shaved and with a huge breakfast inside him, he was back in the car and back in the world and Tiffany Case had withdrawn into her old ironical and uncompromising manner and Bond was making himself useful by watching for State troopers as Leiter kept the needle in the eighties down the endless dazzling road towards the distant cloudline that hid the High Sierras.

Then they were rolling easily along Sunset Boulevard between the palm trees and the emerald lawns, the dust-streaked Studillac looking incongruous among the glistening Corvettes and Jaguars. And finally, towards evening, they were sitting in the dark, cool bar of the Beverly Hills Hotel and their new suitcases were in the lobby and they wore brand-new Hollywood clothes and even Bond's battle-scarred face drew no attention: he might have been a stunt man with a heavy work load.

There was a telephone on the table beside their Martinis. Felix Leiter finished talking to New York for the fourth time since their arrival.

"Well, that's fixed," he said, putting back the receiver. "My pals at the office have got you aboard the *Elizabeth*. Been delayed by a strike at the docks. Sails tomorrow night at eight. They'll meet you in the morning at La Guardia with the tickets and you'll go aboard any time in the afternoon. They picked up the rest of your things at the Astor, James. One small case and your famous golf clubs. And Washington's obliged with a passport for Tiffany. There'll be a man from the State Department at the airport. You'll both have some forms to sign. Got one of my old pals at the C.I.A. to fiddle it. The afternoon papers have made a big splash with the story—'Ghost Town Goes West,' and so on—but they don't seem to have found our friend Spang yet and your names don't figure. My boys say there's no call out for you with the cops, but one of our undercover men says the gangs are looking for you and your description's been circulated. Ten grand attached. So it's as well you're skipping quick. Better go aboard separately. Cover up as much as you can and go down to your cabins and stay there. All hell's going to bust loose when they get to the bottom of that old mine. That'll make any way three corpses to nothing and they don't like that kind of score.''

"Pinkertons seem to have quite a machine," said Bond with admiration. "But I'll be glad when we're both out of here. I used to think your gangsters were just a bunch of Italian greaseballs who filled themselves up with pizza pie and beer all week and on Saturdays knocked off a garage or a drugstore so as to pay their way at the races. But they've certainly got plenty of violence on the payroll.''

Tiffany Case laughed derisively. "You ought to have your head examined," she said flatly. "If we make the *Elizabeth* in one piece it'll be a miracle. That's how good they are. Thanks to Captain Hook here we've got a chance, but it's not more than that. Greaseballs!''

Leiter chuckled. "Come on, lovebirds," he said, looking at his watch. "We ought to get going. I've got to get back to Vegas tonight and start looking for the skeleton of our dear dumb friend Shy Smile. And you've got your 'plane to catch. You can go on quarrelling at twenty thousand feet. Get a better perspective from there. May even decide to make up and be friends. You know what they say"—he beckoned to the waiter—"nothing propinks like propinquity.''

Leiter drove them out to the airport and dropped them there. Bond felt a lump in his throat as he watched the lanky figure limp off to his car after being warmly embraced by Tiffany Case. "You've got yourself a good friend there," said the girl. Leiter slammed the door and they heard the deep boom of the exhaust as he accelerated away on his long drive back into the desert.

"Yes," said Bond. "Felix is all of that."

There was the glint of moonlight on the steel hook as Leiter waved a last goodbye, and then the dust was settling on the road and the iron voice of the loud-speakers came: "Trans-World Airlines, Flight 93, now loading at Gate No. 5 for Chicago and New York. All aboard, please," and they pushed their way through the glass doors and took the first steps of their long journey halfway across the world to London.

The new Super-G-Constellation roared over the darkened continent and Bond lay in his comfortable bunk waiting for sleep to carry away his aching body. He thought of Tiffany, asleep in the bunk below. And he thought of his assignment.

Bond knew that he was very near to being in love with this girl. And what about her? How strong was the obsession that had been born on that night in San Francisco when the men had broken into her room and taken her? Would the child and the woman ever come out from behind the barricade she had started to build that night between herself and all the men in the world.

Bond remembered moments in the last twenty-four hours when he thought he had known the answer, moments when a warm, passionate girl looked out happily from behind the mask of the toughie from the gangs, the smuggler, the shill, the blackjack dealer.

Yes, he had thought. It will be all right. That side of it. But was he prepared for the consequences? Once he committed himself to her it would be forever. His would be the role of the healer, the analyst, to whom the patient had transferred all her love and trust. There could be no cruelty equal to dropping her hand once he had taken it in his. Was he ready for all that that meant in his life and his career?

Bond stirred in his bunk and put the problem away. It

was too early for that. He was going too fast. Wait and
see. One thing at a time. And he obstinately shelved the
issue and shifted his thoughts to M and to the job which
still had to be finished before he could spend time
worrying about his private life.

Well, part of the snake had been smashed. Was it the
head or the tail? Difficult to say, but Bond was inclined
to think that Jack Spang and the mysterious A B C were
the real operators of the smuggling racket and that
Seraffimo had only handled the receiving end. Seraffimo could be replaced. Tiffany could be discarded.
Shady Tree, whom she could implicate in the diamond
smuggling, would have to be got under cover until the
storm, if Bond was indeed a storm signal, had blown
over. But there was nothing to implicate Jack Spang or
the House of Diamonds, and the only clue to A B C was
the London telephone number which Bond reminded
himself to extract from Tiffany as soon as possible.
That, and the machinery of contacts connected with it,
would be changed as soon as the full facts of Tiffany's
defection and Bond's escape had been communicated to
London, presumably by Shady Tree. So all this, reflected Bond, made Jack Spang his next target and,
through him, A B C. Then there only remained the
beginning of the pipe line in Africa, and that could only
be reached through A B C. Bond's immediate concern,
he concluded before letting sleep take him, was to report
the whole situation to M as soon as possible after
boarding the *Queen Elizabeth,* and let London take
over. Vallance's men would get working. There
wouldn't be much for Bond to do when he got back. A
lot of reports to write. The same old routine at the office. And in the evenings there would be Tiffany in the
spare room of his flat off the King's Road. He would
have to send a cable to May to get things fixed. Let's
see—flowers, bath essence from Floris, air the sheets . . .

Just ten hours after leaving Los Angeles they roared
over La Guardia and looped out over the sea for the
long run in.

It was eight o'clock on Sunday morning and there

were few people about at the airport, but an official stopped them as they were walking in off the tarmac and led them to a side entrance where there were two young men waiting, one from Pinkertons and one from the State Department. While they chatted about the flight their luggage was brought around and they were taken to a side door and out to where a smart maroon Pontiac was waiting, its engine purring and the special blinds in the rear pulled down.

And then there were some empty hours in the apartment belonging to the Pinkerton man. At around four in the afternoon, but with a quarter of an hour between them, they were climbing up the covered gangway into the great safe black belly of the *Queen Elizabeth* and were at last in their cabins on M deck with their doors locked against the world.

But, as first Tiffany Case and then James Bond went into the mouth of the gangway, a dockhand had walked swiftly to a phone booth in the customs shed.

Three hours later two American businessmen were dropped at the dockside by a black sedan and were just in time to get through immigration and customs and up the gangway before the loudspeakers began calling for all visitors to leave the ship, please.

One of the businessmen was youngish, with a pretty face and a glimpse of prematurely white hair under the Stetson with the waterproof cover, and the name on the brief case he was carrying was B. Kitteridge.

The other was a big fattish man with a nervous glare in the small eyes behind the bifocals. He was sweating profusely, and constantly mopped at his face with a big handkerchief. The name on the label of his grip was W. Winter, and below it in red ink was written, "My Blood Group is F."

Love and Sauce Béarnaise

Punctually at eight the great reverberating *efflatus* of the *Queen Elizabeth's* siren made the glass tremble in the skyscrapers and the tugs fussed the big ship out into midstream and nosed her around and at a cautious five knots she moved slowly downriver on the slack tide.

There would be a pause to drop the pilot at Ambrose Light and then the quadruple screws would whip the sea into cream and the *Elizabeth* would give a shudder of release and lance off on the long flat arc up from the 45th to the 50th parallel and the dot on it that was Southampton.

Sitting in his cabin, listening to the quiet creak of the woodwork and watching his pencil on the dressing table roll slowly between his hairbrush and the edge of his passport, Bond remembered the days when her course had been different, when en route for the flames of Europe she had zigzagged deep into the South Atlantic as she played her game of hide-and-seek with the U-boat wolfpacks. It was still an adventure, but now the *Queen,* in her cocoon of protective radio impulses—her radar, her Loran, her echo-sounder—moved with the precautions of an Oriental empress among her bodyguards and outriders, and, so far as Bond was concerned, boredom and indigestion would be the only hazards of the voyage.

He picked up the telephone and asked for Miss Case. When she heard his voice she gave a theatrical groan. "The sailor hates the sea," she said. "I'm feeling sick already and we're still in the river."

"Just as well," said Bond. "Stay in your cabin and live on Dramamine and champagne. I'll be no good for two or three days myself. I'm going to get the doctor and the masseur from the Turkish bath and try and stick the bits together again. And anyway, it won't do any harm to stay out of sight for most of the voyage. It's just conceivable they picked us up in New York."

"Well, if you promise to call me up every day," said Tiffany, "and promise to take me to the Veranda Grill as soon as I feel I can swallow a little caviar. Okay?"

Bond laughed. "If you absolutely insist," he said. "And now listen, in exchange I want you to try and remember anything you can about A B C and the London end of this business. That telephone number. And anything else. I'll tell you what it's all about and why I'm interested as soon as I can, but in the meantime you've just got to trust me. Is it a deal?"

"Oh, sure," said the girl indifferently, as if all that side of her life had lost its importance, and for ten minutes Bond questioned her minutely, but, except for small details, fruitlessly, about the A B C routine.

Then he put down the receiver and rang for the steward and ordered some dinner and sat down to write the long report which he would have to transpose into code and send off that night.

The "Metal Mike" took the ship quietly on into the darkness, and the small township of 3,500 souls settled down to the five days of its life in which there would be all the happenings natural to any other sizeable community—burglaries, fights, seductions, drunkenness, cheating; perhaps a birth or two, the chance of a suicide and, in a hundred crossings, perhaps even a murder.

As the iron town swept easily along the broad Atlantic swell and the soft night wind thrummed and moaned in the masthead, the radio aerials were already transmitting the Morse of the operator on duty to the listening ear of Portishead.

And what the duty operator was sending at exactly 10:00 P.M. Eastern Standard Time was a cable addressed "ABC, Care House of Diamonds, Hatton Garden, London," which said: "Parties located stop. If matter requires drastic solution essential you state price payable in dollars." The signature was "Winter."

An hour later, while the *Queen Elizabeth's* operator was sighing at the thought of having to transmit five hundred five-letter groups addressed to "The Managing Director, Universal Export, Regent's Park, London," Portishead radio was sending a short cable addressed "Winter, First Class Passenger, *Queen Elizabeth*," which said, "Desire tidy speedy conclusion of case stop Will pay twenty grand stop Will personally handle other subject on arrival London stop Confirm ABC."

And the operator looked up Winter in the passenger list and put the message in an envelope and sent it down to a cabin on A deck, the deck below Bond and the girl, where two men were playing gin-rummy in their shirtsleeves. As the page left the cabin he heard the fat man say cryptically to the man with white hair: "Whaddya know, Kid! It's twenty G's for a rub these days. Boy, oh, boy!"

It was not until the third day out that Bond and Tiffany agreed to meet for cocktails in the Observation Lounge and later to have dinner in the Veranda Grill. At midday weather was dead calm, and after lunch in his cabin Bond had got a peremptory message in a round girlish hand on a sheet of the ship's writing paper. It said, "Fix a rendex-mo, today. Fail not," and Bond's hand had gone at once to the telephone.

They were thirsty for each other's company after three days' separation, but Tiffany's defences were up when she joined him at the obscure corner table he had chosen in the gleaming semi-circular cocktail bar in the bows.

"What kind of table's this?" she enquired sarcastically. "You ashamed of me or something? Here I put on the best those Hollywood pansies can dream up and you hide me away as if I was Miss Rheingold of 1914. I want to have myself some fun on this old paddleboat and you stash me in a corner. What's the matter. Am I catching?"

"That's about it," said Bond. "I don't want you raising the temperature of every man in the room."

"What d'you expect a girl to do on the *Queen Elizabeth?* Fish?"

Bond smiled and signalled to the waiter and ordered vodka dry Martinis with lemon peel. "I could give you one alternative."

"Dear Diary," said the girl, "having wonderful time with handsome Englishman. Trouble is, he's after my family jewels. What do I do? Yours truly, Puzzled." Then suddenly she leaned over and put her hand on his. "Listen, you," she said. "I'm as happy as a cricket. I love being here. I love being with you. And I love this nice dark table where no one can see me holding your hand. Don't mind my line of chatter. I just can't get over being so happy."

She was wearing a heavy cream Shantung silk shirt and a charcoal skirt in a cotton and wool mixture, and the neutral colours showed off her café-au-lait suntan. The small square Cartier watch with the black strap was her only jewellery, and the short fingernails on the small brown hand that lay over his were unpainted. The reflected sunlight from outside shone on the pale gold heavy falling swerve of her hair, in the depths of the chatoyant grey eyes and on the glint of white teeth between half parted lips.

"I'm glad," said Bond.

She looked into his eyes and was satisfied. The drinks came and she withdrew her hand and observed him quizzically over the rim of her glass.

"Now tell me a few things," she said. "First of all, what do you do and who are you working for? At the beginning, in the hotel, I thought you were a crook. But somehow, as soon as you had gone out of the door I knew you weren't. Guess I should have warned A B C and we'd have avoided a lot of fuss. But I didn't. Come on, now. Give."

"I work for the Government," said Bond. "They want to stop this diamond smuggling."

"Sort of a secret agent?"

"Just a civil servant."

"Okay. So what are you going to do with me when we get to London? Lock me up?"

"Yes. In the spare room of my flat."

"That's better. Shall I become a subject of the Queen like you? I'd rather like to be a subject person."

"I expect we could fix that."

"Are you married?" She paused. "Or anything?"

"No. I occasionally have affairs."

"So you're one of those old-fashioned men who like sleeping with women. Why haven't you ever married?"

"I expect because I think I can handle life better on my own. Most marriages don't add two people together. They subtract one from the other."

Tiffany thought this over. "Maybe there's something in that," she said finally. "But it depends what you want to add up to. Something human or something inhuman. You can't be complete by yourself."

"What about you?"

The girl hadn't wanted the question. "Maybe I just settled for the inhuman," she said shortly. "And who in hell do you think I should have married? Shady Tree?"

"There must have been lots of others."

"Well, there weren't," she said angrily. "Maybe you think I shouldn't have got mixed up with those people. Well, I guess I just got off on the wrong foot." The flare of anger died and she looked at him defensively. "It does happen to people, James. It really does. And sometimes it's really not their fault."

Bond took her hand and held it tightly. "I know, Tiffany," he said. "Felix told me a little about it. That's why I haven't asked any questions. Just don't think about it. It's here and today now. Not yesterday." He changed the subject. "Now you give me some facts. For instance, why are you called Tiffany and what's it like being a dealer at the Tiara? How the hell did you come to be so good? It was brilliant the way you handled those cards. If you can do that you can do anything."

"Thanks, pal," said the girl ironically. "Like what? Playing the boats? And the reason I got called Tiffany is because when I was born dear father Case was so sore I wasn't a boy he gave my mother a thousand bucks and a compact from Tiffany's and walked out. Joined the Marines. In the end he got killed at Iwo Jima. So my mother dubbed me Tiffany Case and set about earning a living for us both. Started with a string of call-girls and then got more ambitious. Maybe that doesn't sound so good to you?" She looked at him half defiantly and half pleadingly.

"Doesn't worry me," said Bond drily. "You weren't one of the girls."

She shrugged. "Then the place got busted by the gangs." She paused and drank the rest of her Martini. "And I lit out on my own. The usual jobs a girl takes. I found myself in Reno. They've got a School of Dealing there, and I signed on and worked like hell at it. Took the full course. Majored in craps, roulette, and blackjack. You can earn good money dealing. Two hundred a week. The men like to have girls dealing and it gives the women confidence. They think you'll be kind to them. Sisters under the skin, kind of. The men dealers frighten them. But don't get the idea it's fun. It reads better than it lives."

She paused and smiled up at him. "Now it's your turn again," she said. "Buy me another drink and then tell me what sort of woman you think would add to you."

Bond gave his order to the steward. He lit a cigarette thoughtfully. "Somebody who can make Sauce

Béarnaise as well as love," he said.

"Holy mackerel! Just any old dumb hag who can cook and lie on her back?"

"Oh, no. She's got to have all the usual things—" Bond examined her. "Gold hair. Grey eyes. A sinful mouth. Perfect figure. And of course she's got to be witty and poised and know how to dress and play cards and so forth. The usual things."

"And you'd marry this person if you found her?"

"Not necessarily," said Bond. "Matter of fact, I'm almost married already. To a man. Name begins with M. I'd have to divorce him before I tried marrying a woman. And I'm not sure I'd want to do that. She'd get me handing round canapés in an L-shaped drawing-room. And there'd be all those ghastly 'Yes you did No I didn't' rows that seem to go with marriage. It wouldn't last. I'd get claustrophobia and run out on her. Get myself sent to Japan or somewhere."

"What about children?"

"Like to have some," said Bond shortly. "But only when I retire. Not fair to the children otherwise. My job's not all that secure." He looked into his drink and swallowed it down. "Now then. Over to you."

"I guess every girl would like to come home and find a hat on the hall table," said Tiffany moodily. "Trouble is, I've never found the right sort of thing growing under the hat. Maybe I haven't looked hard enough or in the right places. You know how it is when you get in a groove. You get so that you're quite glad not to peer over the edges. In that way I've had it good with the Spangs. Always knew where the next meal was coming from. Put some money by. But a girl can't have friends in that company. You either put up a notice saying 'No Trespassing' or you're apt to pick up a bad case of round heels. But I guess I'm fed up with being on my own. You know what the chorus girls say on Broadway? 'It's a lonesome wash without a man's shirt in it.' "

Bond laughed. "Well, you're out of the groove now," he said. He looked at her quizzically. "But what about Seraffimo? Those two bedrooms on the Pullman and the champagne supper laid for two . . .''

Before he could finish, her eyes blazed briefly and she got up from the table and walked straight out of the bar.

Bond cursed himself. He put some money down on the check and hurried after her. He caught up with her halfway down the Promenade Deck. "Now listen, Tiffany,'' he began.

She turned brusquely round and faced him. "How mean can you be?'' she said, and angry tears glistened on her lashes. "Why did you have to spoil everything with an abrasive remark like that? Oh, *hell*—'' Forlornly she turned to the windows, searching for a handkerchief in her bag. She dabbed at her eyes.

Bond put an arm around her and held her to him. "I didn't mean to hurt you. I just wanted to know. That was a bad night on the train, and that supper-table hurt me much more than what happened later. I had to ask.''

She looked up at him doubtfully. "You mean that?'' she said, searching his face. "You liked me then?''

"Don't be a goose,'' said Bond impatiently. "Don't you know anything about anything?''

She turned away from him and looked out of the window at the endless blue sea and the handful of dipping gulls that were keeping company with their wonderfully prodigal ship. After a while she said, "You ever read *Alice in Wonderland*?''

"Years ago,'' said Bond, surprised. "Why?''

"There's a line in it I often think of,'' she said. "About the pool of tears. It says: 'O Mouse, do you know the way out of this pool? I am very tired of swimming about here, O Mouse!' Remember? Well, I thought you were going to tell me the way out. Instead of that you pushed me under. That's why I got upset.'' She glanced up at him. "But I guess you didn't mean to hurt.''

Bond kissed her hard on the lips.

She didn't respond, but broke away and her eyes were laughing again. She linked her arm in his and turned towards the open doors that led to the lift. "Take me down," she said. "I must go and rewrite my face and I want to spend a long time at it." She paused and then put her mouth close up to his ear. "In case you're interested," she said softly, "I've never what you'd call 'slept with a man' in my life." She tugged at his arm. "And now come on," she said impetuously. "And anyway it's time you went and had a 'Hot Domestic' before dinner. I suppose that's part of the subject-language you'll be wanting me to pick up. You subject-people have the craziest things in your bathrooms."

Bond took her to her cabin and then went on to his and had a "Hot Salt" bath followed by a "Cold Domestic" shower. Then he lay on his bed and smiled to himself over some of the things she had said, and thought of her lying in her bath and thinking, perhaps, of him.

There was a knock on the door and his steward came in with a small tray which he placed on the table.

"What's that?" said Bond.

"Just come up from the chef, sir," said the steward, and went out and closed the cabin door.

Bond eased off the bed and went over and examined the contents of the tray. He smiled to himself. There was a quarter-bottle of Bollinger, a chafing dish containing four small slivers of steak on toast canapés, and a small bowl of sauce. Beside this was a pencilled note which said, "This Sauce Béarnaise has just been created by Miss T. Case without any assistance from me." *Signed* "The Chef."

Bond filled a glass with champagne and spread a lot of the Béarnaise on a piece of the steak and munched it judicially. Then he went to the telephone.

"Tiffany?"

He heard the low delighted laugh at the other end.

"Well, you can certainly make wonderful Sauce Béarnaise. . . ."

He let the sentence hang unfinished in the air and softly returned the receiver to its cradle.

CHAPTER 23

The Job Comes Second

It is a wonderful moment in a love affair when for the first time a man puts his hand under the table at a restaurant and lays it on a girl's thigh and she slips her own hand over his and presses it against her. The two gestures say everything that need be said. All is agreed. All the pacts are signed. And there is a long minute of silence during which the blood sings.

It was eleven o'clock and there was only a scattering of people left in their corner of the Veranda Grill. There was a soft sighing from the moonlit sea outside as the great liner scythed the black meadow of the Atlantic and, in the stern, only the slightest lope in her stride indicated a long soft swell, the slow heartbeat of a sleeping ocean. In the grill, Tiffany and Bond sat close together behind the pink-shaded light.

The waiter came with the check and their hands rose and parted. But now there was all the time in the world and no need for reassurance from words or further contact.

They got into the lift for the Promenade Deck. "Now what, James?" said Tiffany. "I'd like some more coffee and a stinger while we listen to the Auction Pool. I've heard so much about it, and we might make a fortune."

"All right," said Bond. "Anything you say." He held her arm close to him as they sauntered through the big lounge where Bingo was still being played and through the waiting ballroom where the musicians were limbering up. "But don't make me buy a number. It's a pure gamble. Nearly as bad as Las Vegas odds. But it's fun if there's a good auctioneer, and they tell me there's plenty of money on board this trip."

The Smoking Room was almost empty and they chose a small table away from the platform where the Chief Steward was laying out the auctioneer's paraphernalia, the box for the numbered slips, the hammer, the carafe of water.

"In the theatre this is what's known as dressing a thin house," said Tiffany as they sat down amidst the forest of empty chairs and tables. But as Bond gave his order to the steward, the doors leading to the cinema opened and soon there were nearly a hundred people in the Smoking Room.

The auctioneer, a paunchy, jovial Midlands businessman with a red carnation in the buttonhole of his dinner jacket, rapped on his table for silence and announced that the Captain's estimate of the next day's run lay between 720 and 739 miles, that any distance shorter than 720 was the Low Field and anything longer the High Field. "And now, ladies and gentlemen, let's see if we can't break the record for this trip which stands at the impressive figure of £2,400 in the Pool." Applause.

A steward offered the box of folded numbers to the richest-looking woman in the room and then handed up the piece of paper she had drawn to the auctioneer.

"Well, ladies and gentlemen, here we have an exceptionally good number to start with: 738. Right in the top range and since I see a lot of new faces here tonight [laughter] I think we can all agree that the sea is exceptionally calm. Ladies and gentlemen, what am I bid for 738? May I say £50? Will anybody bid me £50 for this admirable number? Was it £20 you said, sir? Well, we've got to start somewhere. Any increase? Twenty-five. Thank you, madam. And thirty. Forty over there, Steward. And forty-five from my friend Mr. Rothblatt. Thank you, Charlie. Any increase on £45 for Number 738? Fifty. Thank you, madam, and now we're all back where we started [laughter]. Any increase on £50? Nobody tempted? High number. Calm sea. Fifty pounds. Will anybody say fifty-five? Going at £50. Going once. Going twice.'' And the raised hammer fell with a bang.

''Well, thank heavens he's a good auctioneer,'' said Bond. ''That was a good number and cheap if this weather goes on and nobody falls overboard. The High Field'll cost a packet this evening. Everyone will expect us to do more than 739 miles in this weather.''

''What do you mean by a packet?'' asked Tiffany.

''Two hundred pounds. Perhaps more. I expect the ordinary numbers will sell for around a hundred. The first number's always cheaper than the others. People haven't warmed up. The only smart thing you can do at this game is buy the first number.''

As Bond finished speaking, the next number was knocked down for £90 to a pretty, excited girl who was obviously being staked by her companion, a grey-haired fresh-complexioned man who was a caricature of an *Esquire* sugar-daddy.

''Go on. Buy me a number, James,'' said Tiffany. ''You really don't treat a girl right. Look at the way that nice man treats his girl.''

''He's past the age of consent,'' said Bond. ''He must be sixty. Up to forty, girls cost nothing. After that you have to pay money, or tell a story. Of the two it's the story that hurts most.'' He smiled into her eyes. ''Anyway, I'm not forty yet.''

''Don't be conceited,'' said the girl. She looked at his mouth. ''They say that older men make much the best lovers. And yet you're not naturally a tightwad. I bet it's because gambling's illegal in subject-ships or something.''

"It's all right outside the three-mile limit," said Bond. "But even so, Cunard has been damn' careful not to involve the Company in it. Listen to this." He picked up the orange card that lay on their table. " 'Auction Sweepstake on Ship's Daily Run,' " he read. " 'In view of enquiries it is considered desirable to re-state the Company's position in connection with the above. It is not the Company's wish that the Smoke-Room Steward or other members of the ship's personnel should play an active part in organising sweepstakes on the daily run.' " Bond looked up. "You see," he said. "Playing it pretty close to the chest. And then they go on, 'The Company suggests that the passengers should elect a Committee from amongst themselves to formulate and control the details. The Smoke-Room Steward may, if requested and if his duties permit, render such assistance as the Committee require for auctioning of numbers.' Pretty cagey. It's the Committee that holds the baby if there's any trouble. And listen to this. This is where the trouble comes in." He read on: " 'The Company draws special attention to the provisions of the United Kingdom Finance Regulations as affecting the negotiability of sterling cheques and the limitation on the importation of sterling bank notes into the United Kingdom.' "

Bond put down the card. "And so forth," he said. He smiled at Tiffany. "So I buy you the number that's just being auctioned and you win £2,000. That'll be a pile of dollars and pound notes and checks. The only way of spending all that sterling, even supposing that those checks are all good, which is doubtful, would be by smuggling them through under your garter belt. And there we'd be, back in the same old racket, but now with me on the side of the devil."

The girl was not impressed. "There used to be a guy in the gangs called Abadaba," she said. "He was a crooked egghead who knew all the answers. Worked out the track odds, fixed the percentage on the numbers racket, did all the brain work. They called him the Wizard of Odds. Got rubbed out quite by accident in

the Dutch Schultz killing," she added parenthetically.
"I guess you're just another Abadaba the way you talk
yourself out of having to spend some money on a girl.
Oh, well." She shrugged her shoulders resignedly.
"Will you stake your girl to at least another stinger?'

Bond beckoned to the steward. When he had gone she
leaned over so that her hair brushed his ear and said
softly: "I don't really want it. You have it. I want to
stay sober as Sunday tonight." She sat up straight.
"And now what's going on around here?" she said impatiently. "I want to see some action."

"Here it comes," siad Bond. The auctioneer raised
his voice and there was a hush in the room. "And now,
ladies and gentlemen," he said impressively, "we come
to the $64,000 question. Who is going to bid me £100
for the choice of High or Low Field? We all know what
that means, the option to choose the High Field, which I
seem to feel may be the popular choice this evening
[laughter] in view of the wonderful weather outside. So
who will open the bidding with £100 for the choice of
High or Low Field? Thank you, sir! And one hundred
and ten. One hundred and twenty and one hundred and
thirty. Thank you, madam."

"Hundred and fifty," said a man's voice not far from
their table.

"A hundred and sixty." This time it was a woman.

Monotonously the man's voice called the one hundred and seventy.

"Eighty," said someone.

"Two hundred pounds."

Something made Bond turn round and look at the
man who had spoken.

It was a biggish man. His face had the glistening,
pasty appearance of a spat-out bull's-eye. Small, cold,
dark eyes were looking towards the auctioneer's platform through motionless bifocals. All of the man's neck
seemed to be at the back of his head. Sweat matted the
curly black algae of his hair, and now he took off his
glasses and picked up a napkin and mopped the sweat
off his face with a circular motion that started with the

left cheek and swirled round to the back of his head where his right hand took over and completed the circuit as far as the dripping nose. "Two hundred and ten," said someone. The big man's chin wobbled and he opened his tight-buttoned mouth and said, "Two hundred and twenty," in a level American voice.

What was there about the man that struck a chord in Bond's memory? He watched the big face, running his mind's eye over the filing system of his brain, pulling out drawer after drawer, hunting for the clue. The face? The voice? England? America?

He gave it up and turned his attention to the other man at the table. Again, the same urgent sense of recognition. The curiously delicate young features under the slicked-back white hair. The soft brown eyes and the long lashes. The general effect of prettiness spoiled by the fleshy nose over the wide thin mouth, now open in a square empty smile like the grin of a letter-box.

"Two hundred and fifty," said the big man mechanically.

Bond turned to Tiffany. "Ever see those two before?" he said, and she noticed the line of worry between his eyes.

"Nope," she said definitely. "Never did. Look like a couple of cloak-and-suiters from the garment district. Why? Do they mean anything to you?"

Bond gave them another glance. "No," he said doubtfully. "No, I guess not."

There was a burst of clapping in the room and the auctioneer beamed and rapped on the table. "Ladies and gentlemen," he said triumphantly, "this is really splendid. Three hundred pounds I am bid by the charming lady in the beautiful pink evening dress." (Heads turned and craned and Bond could see the mouths saying, "Who is she?") "And now, sir"—he turned towards the fat man's table—"May I say £325?"

"Three hundred and fifty," said the fat man.

"Four hundred," squealed the pink woman.

"Five hundred." The voice was toneless, indifferent.

The pink girl chattered angrily at her escort, who suddenly looked bored, caught the auctioneer's eye, and shook his head.

"Any increase on £500?" said the auctioneer. He now knew that he had squeezed all he would get out of the room. "Going once. Going twice." *Bang!* "Sold to the gentlemen over there, and I really think he deserves a hand." He clapped and the crowd dutifully followed suit, although they would have preferred the pink girl to win.

The fat man lifted himself a few inches off his chair and then sat down again. There was no acknowledgement of the applause in his glistening face, and he kept his eyes fixed on the auctioneer.

"And now we must go through the formality of asking this gentleman which Field he prefers [laughter]. Sir, do you choose the High Field or the Low Field?" The auctioneer's voice was ironical. The question was a waste of time.

"Low Field."

There was a moment of dead silence in the crowded Smoking Room. It was quickly followed by a buzz of comment. There had been no question. It was obvious that the man would take the High Field. The weather was perfect. The *Queen* must be doing at least thirty knots. Did he know something? Had he bribed someone on the bridge? Was there a storm coming up? Was a bearing running hot?

The auctioneer rapped for silence. "I beg your pardon, sir," he said, "but did you say the Low Field?"

"Yes."

The auctioneer rapped again. "In that case, ladies and gentlemen, we shall now proceed to auction the High Field. Madam"—he turned with a bow towards the girl in pink—"would you care to open the bidding?"

Bond turned to Tiffany. "That was a queer business," he said. "Extraordinary thing to do. Sea's as calm as glass." He shrugged his shoulders. "The only answer is that they know something." The matter was of no interest, anyway. "Someone's told them something." He turned and looked carelessly at the two men and then let his eyes swing past and away from them. "They seem to be quite interested in us."

Tiffany glanced past his shoulder. "They're not looking at us now," she said. "I figure they're just a couple of dopes. The white-haired guy's looking stupid and the fat man's sucking his thumb. They're screwy. Doubt if they know what they've bought. They just got their signals crossed."

"Sucking his thumb?" said Bond. He ran his hand distractedly through his hair, a vague memory nagging at him.

Perhaps if she had allowed him to follow the train of thought another few seconds he would have remembered. As it was, she put her hand over his and leaned towards him so that her hair brushed against his face again. Her eyes were suddenly ardent and demanding. "I've had enough of this place. Take me somewhere else."

Without saying anything more they got up and left the table and walked out of the noisy room to the staircase. As they went down the stairs to the deck below, Bond's arm went around the girl's waist and her head fell against his shoulder.

They came to the door of Tiffany's cabin, but she pulled him away and on down the long softly creaking corridor.

"I want it to be in your house," she said.

Bond said nothing until he had kicked the door of his cabin shut behind them and they had twisted round and stood locked together in the middle of the wonderfully private, wonderfully anonymous little room. And then he just said, softly, "My darling," and put one hand in her hair so that he could hold her mouth where he wanted it.

And after a while his other hand went to the fastener at the back of her dress, and without moving away from him she took off her clothes. "I want it all, darling. Now. Quickly."

And Bond bent down and put an arm around her thighs and picked her up and gently lowered her to the floor.

Death Is So Permanent

The last thing Bond remembered before the telephone rang was Tiffany bending over him in bed and kissing him and saying: "You shouldn't sleep on your left side, my treasure. It's bad for the heart. Turn over." And obediently he had turned and as the door clicked he was at once asleep again with her voice and the sigh of the Atlantic and the soft roll of the ship all jumbled together in gentle blackness.

And then a bell rang stridently in the dark cabin and went on ringing and Bond cursed and reached for it and a voice said: "Sorry to disturb you, sir. This is the wireless operator. There's a cypher signal just come in for you and it's got an *en clair* prefix of 'Most Immediate.' Shall I read it to you or send it down?"

"Send it down, would you?" said Bond. "And thanks."

Now what the hell? All the beauty and heat and excitement of passionate love were pushed roughly away as he turned on the lights, slipped out of bed and, shaking his head to clear it, took the two steps into the shower.

For a full minute he let the water hit him and then he rubbed himself down and picked up his trousers and shirt from the floor and climbed into them.

There was a knock on the door and he took the cable and sat down at the desk and lit a cigarette and set grimly to work. And as the groups gradually dissolved into words his eyes grew narrower and his scalp began to tighten and prickle.

The cable was from the Chief of Staff. It said:

FIRSTLY CLANDESTINE SEARCH OF SAYES OFFICE REVEALED SIGNAL FROM QE ADDRESSED ABC SIGNED WINTER ADVISING OF YOUR AND CASES PRESENCE ABOARD REQUESTING INSTRUCTIONS STOP REPLY ADDRESSED WINTER SIGNED ABC ORDERS ELIMINATION OF CASE COMMA PRICE TWENTY THOUSAND DOLLARS STOP SECONDLY WE CONSIDER RUFUS B SAYE IS ABC WHICH IS PARTLY EQUIVALENT OF HIS INITIALS IN FRENCH THUS AH DASH BAY DASH SAYE STOP THIRDLY POSSIBLY ALERTED BY SIGNS OF SEARCH SAYE FLEW PARIS YESTERDAY AND NOW REPORTED BY INTERPOL BE IN DAKAR STOP THIS TENDS CONFIRM OUR SUSPICION THAT DIAMONDS ORIGINATE SIERRA LEONE MINES THENCE SMUGGLED OVER FRONTIER INTO FRENCH GUINEA STOP WE STRONGLY SUSPECT MEMBER OF SIERRA INTERNATIONAL DENTAL SURGERY STAFF WHO BEING WATCHED STOP FOURTHLY RAF CANBERRA AWAITS YOU BOSCOMBE DOWN FOR IMMEDIATE ONWARD FLIGHT TOMORROW NIGHT TO SIERRA LEONE SIGNED COS

Bond sat for a moment frozen to his chair. Suddenly there flashed unwanted into his mind that most sinister line in all poetry, "They reckon ill who leave me out, when me they fly, I am the wings."

So somebody from the Spangled Mob was on board and travelling with them. Someone named Winter.

His hand leaped to the telephone.

"Miss Case, please."

He could hear the telephone beside her bed click and

then give its first ring. The second. The third. Just one more. He crashed the receiver back onto its cradle and ran out of his room and up the corridor to her cabin. Nothing. Empty. The bed unslept in. The lights burning. But her evening bag lay on the carpet by the door and its contents were scattered around it. She had come in. The man had been behind the door. Perhaps she had been clubbed. And then what?

The portholes were closed. He looked into the bathroom. Nothing.

Bond stood in the middle of the cabin and his mind was cold and smouldering as dry ice. What would he have done in her assailant's place? Before he killed her he would have questioned her. Found out what she knew, what she had told, who this man Bond was. Got her to his cabin where he could work on her undisturbed. If somebody met him carrying her there, it would only have needed a wink and a shake of the head. "Bit too much champagne tonight. No thanks, I can manage." But which cabin? How long did he have?

Bond looked at his watch as he ran back down the silent corridor. Three o'clock. She must have left him some time after two. Should he call the bridge? Give the alarm? A ghastly vista of explanations, suspicions, delays. "My dear sir, that hardly seems possible. . . ." Attempts to calm him. "Of course, sir, we'll do our best. . . ." The polite eyes of the Sergeant-at-Arms who would be thinking in terms of drunkenness and lovers' quarrels. Or perhaps he would be suspected of trying to delay the ship so as to win the Low Field in the ship's auction.

The Low Field! Man overboard! The ship delayed!

Bond slammed the door of his cabin and dived for the Passenger List. Of course. Winter. Here he was. A49. The deck below. And then suddenly his mind clicked like a comptometer. Winter. Wint and Kidd. The two torpedoes. The men in the hoods. Back to the passenger list. Kitteridge. In A49 too. The white-haired man and the fat man in the BOAC plane from London. "My blood group is F." The secret escort for Tiffany. And

Leiter's description. "He's called 'Windy' because he hates travelling. One day that wart on his thumb will catch him out." The red wart on the first joint holding back the hammer of the gun over Tingaling Bell. And Tiffany saying, "The fat man's sucking his thumb!" And the two men in the Smoking Room cashing in on the death that had been arranged. The woman overboard. The alarm given anonymously in case the stern watch missed her. The ship stopped, turning, searching. And £3,000 extra to the killers.

Wint and Kidd. The killers from Detroit.

The whole reel of jumbled pictures whirred through Bond's mind, and even while he was scanning them he was opening his small attaché case and extracting the squat silencer from its hidden pocket. Automatically, as he took the Beretta from under his shirts at the back of a drawer, checked the magazine and screwed the silencer into the muzzle, he was weighing the odds and working out his moves.

He hunted for the ship's plan that had come with his ticket. He examined it while he pulled on his socks. A49 was directly below him. Would there be any chance of shooting the lock off the door and getting both of them before they got him? Damn' little. And they would have bolted the door as well as locked it. Should he take some of the staff with him, if he could persuade them of the danger to Tiffany? During the palaver of "Excuse me, sirs," through the door they would get her out of the porthole and be innocently reading books or playing cribbage and, "What's all the fuss about?"

Bond shoved the gun into his waistband and wrenched one of his two portholes wide open. He thrust his shoulders through, relieved to find that there was at least an inch to spare. He craned down. Two dimly lit circles directly below him. How far? Eight, nine feet. The night was still calm. No wind, and he was on the dark side of the ship. Would he be spotted from the flying bridge? Would one of their portholes be open?

Bond dropped back into his cabin and tore the sheets off his bed. The Blood Knot. That would be safest. But he would have to rip the sheets in half to get enough length. If he won, he would have to get some sheets from A49 and leave their steward to puzzle out the loss. If he lost, nothing would matter.

Bond put all his strength on the rope. Should hold. As he tied one end around the hinge of the porthole he glanced at his watch. Only twelve minutes since he had read the cable. Had it been too long? He set his teeth and threw the rope out down the side of the ship and climbed out head foremost.

Don't think. Don't look down. Don't look up. Never mind the knots. They'll hold. Slowly, firmly, hand over hand.

The night wind tugged softly at him and swayed him against the black iron rivets, and from far below sounded the deep boom and whoosh of the sea. From somewhere above came the ropey twang of the wind in the rigging and far above that the stars would be swinging slowly around the twin masts.

Don't think about it. Don't think of the huge ship, the hungry sea, the great quadruple screws waiting to slash his body. You are a boy climbing down an apple tree. It's so easy and so safe there in the orchard with the grass to fall on.

Bond shut his mind and watched his hands and felt the roughness of the paint against his knuckles, and his feet were as sensitive as antennae as they groped below him for the first contact with the porthole.

There. The toes of his right foot had touched the protruding rim. He must stop. He *must* be patient and let his foot explore further—the wide-open porthole, held by its big brass latch; the feel of cloth against his foot; the curtains closed. Now he could go on. It was nearly over.

And then two more handholds and his face was level and he could get a hand to the metal rim of the frame and take some of the weight off the taut white rope and give one arm a blessed rest, and then the other, shifting the burden from the cracking muscles and gathering himself for the slow heave up and through and then the final dive with one hand clutching for his gun.

He listened, gazing at the circle of slowly swaying curtain, trying to forget that he was clinging like a fly halfway down the side of the *Queen Elizabeth,* trying not to hear the sea far below him, trying to still his own heavy breath and the hammering of his heart. There was a mumble from inside the cabin. A few words in a masculine voice. And then a girl's voice, thin and frightened.

There was a moment's silence and then a slap. It was as loud as a pistol shot and it jerked Bond's body up and through the porthole as if he had been wrenched inwards by a huge hook.

Even as he dived cleanly through the three-foot circle he was wondering what he would hit, and his left arm protected his head as his right went to his gun.

Crash onto a suitcase under the porthole, a ragged somersault that took him halfway across the room, and he was somehow on his feet and backing, crouched low, towards the porthole, and the knuckles were white with tension on his gun hand and there was a thin white line around his clenched lips.

Through the slitted lids the ice-grey eyes flickered from side to side; the blunt black gun stood at dead center between the two men.

"All right," said Bond, coming slowly to his full height.

It was a statement of fact. He was in control, and the mouth of his gun had said he would keep it.

"Who sent for you?" said the fat man. "You're not in the act."

There were hidden reserves in the voice. No panic. Not even enough surprise. "Come to make a fourth at gin?"

He was sitting in buttoned shirt sleeves sideways at the dressing table, and the small eyes glittered in the moist face. In front of him, with her back to Bond, Tiffany Case sat on an upholstered stool. She was naked except for brief flesh-coloured pants, and her knees were gripped between the big man's thighs. Her face, with red marks across its paleness, was turned towards Bond. Her eyes were wild, like a trapped animal's, and her mouth was open with disbelief.

The white-haired man had been lying relaxed on one of the beds. Now he was up on one elbow, and his other hand was at his shirt, halfway up to the gun in the black holster at his armpit. He looked incuriously at Bond, and his mouth was square with the empty letter-box smile. From the middle of it a wooden toothpick protruded from between closed teeth like the tongue of a snake.

Bond's gun held the neutral space between the two men. When he spoke his voice was low and taut.

"Tiffany," he said slowly and distinctly, "get down on your knees. Edge away from that man. Keep your head down. Get into the middle of the room."

He didn't watch her; his eyes continued to flicker between the man on the chair and the man on the bed.

Now she was clear of the two targets.

"I'm there, James." Her voice thrilled with relief and excitement.

"Get up and walk straight into the bathroom. Shut the door. Get into the tub and lie down."

His eyes slid towards her to see that he was being obeyed. She had stood up and was facing him. His eyes registered the red splays of a whole hand on the white skin of her body. Then she had obeyed him and there was the click of the bathroom door shutting.

Now she was safe from flying bullets. And she would not witness what had to be done.

There were five yards between the two men, and Bond reflected that if they could draw fast enough they had him bracketed. With men like these, even in the split second it took to kill one of them, the other would have drawn and fired. While his own gun was silent, its threat was infinite. But with his first bullet, for a flash the threat would be lifted from the other man.

"Forty-eight, sixty-five, eighty-six . . ."

The variation on the American football signal, one of fifty other combinations which they must have practised together a thousand times, spat out of the fat man's mouth. Simultaneously he hurled himself on the floor and his hand flashed to his waistband.

In a swirl of motion the man on the bed swung his legs sideways and away from Bond so that his body was now only a narrow head-on target. The hand at his chest flickered up.

Bond's gun gave a single muffled grunt. A blue keyhole opened just beneath the peak of the white hair.

The dead man's pistol answered, fired by the last convulsive twitch of the finger, and the bullet buried itself into the bed beneath his corpse.

The fat man on the floor let out a strangled scream. He was staring up into the single empty eye of Bond's gun. His own gun had only achieved the elevation of Bond's knees and was pointing futilely between Bond's braced legs at the white painted ironwork behind him.

"Drop it."

There was a small thud as the gun fell to the carpet.

"Get up."

The fat man scrambled to his feet and stood looking into Bond's eyes, fearfully, as a tubercular looks into his handkerchief.

"Sit down."

Was there a glint of relief in the surrendered eyes? Bond stayed tense as a stalking cat.

The fat man turned slowly. He stretched his hands above his head, although Bond had not told him to do so. He took the two steps back to his chair and slowly turned around as if to sit down.

He stood facing Bond, and quite naturally let his hands fall down to his side. And the two hands, relaxed, swung naturally back, the right hand a trifle more than the left. And suddenly, at the top of the back-swing, the right arm flashed forward and the throwing-knife bloomed from the tips of the fingers like a white flame.

The quiet bullet and the quiet knife crossed in mid-air, and the eyes of the two men flinched simultaneously.

But the flicker in the eyes of the fat man turned into an

upward roll of the eyeballs as he stumbled and fell, clawing at his heart, while Bond's eyes only looked incuriously down at the spreading stain on his shirt and at the flat handle of the knife hanging loosely from its folds.

There was a crash as the chair splintered under the fat man and a rasping sound, and then a rhythmic drumming on the floor.

Bond looked once and then turned away towards the porthole.

For a moment he stood with his back to the room, staring at the softly swaying curtains. He took a shuddering lungful of air and listened to the liquid sea-sounds from the world outside that still belonged to him and to Tiffany, but not to the two others. Very slowly his cramped muscles and strung nerves relaxed.

After a time he pulled the knife out of his shirt with a sharp jerk. He didn't look at it, but reached up and drew the curtain aside and threw the knife far out into the blackness beyond. Then, still gazing out into the quiet night, he put up the safety of the Beretta and, with a hand that suddenly seemed sheathed in lead, thrust the gun back into place.

Almost reluctantly he turned back and faced the shambles of the cabin. He looked it over thoughtfully and with an unconscious gesture wiped his hands down the sides of his trousers. Then he carefully picked his way across the floor to the bathroom and said, "It's me, Tiffany," in a low, tired voice and opened the door.

She hadn't heard him. She was lying face down in the empty tub, with her hands over her ears; and when he had half lifted her out and had taken her into his arms she still couldn't believe it but clung to him and then slowly explored his face and his chest with her hands to make sure it was true.

He flinched as her hand touched his cut rib, and she broke away from him and looked at his face and then at the blood on her fingers and then at his scarlet shirt.

"Oh, God! You're hurt," she said, and her nightmares were forgotten as she took off his shirt and washed the gashed rib with warm water and bound it with strips of towel cut with one of the dead men's razor blades.

She asked no questions. Bond collected her clothes from the floor of the cabin and gave them to her and told her not to come out until he was ready, but to clean up everything and wipe every object she had touched, to get rid of the fingerprints.

She just stood and looked at him with her eyes shining. When Bond kissed her on the lips she still said nothing.

He gave her a reassuring smile and walked out and shut the door of the bathroom behind him and went about his business, doing everything with great deliberation and pausing before each move so as to examine its effect on the eyes and minds of the detectives who would come on board at Southampton.

First he tied an ash tray in his blood-stained shirt to weight it and went to the porthole and threw it as far out as he could. The men's tuxedos were hanging behind the door. He took the handkerchiefs out of the breast pockets and wrapped them around his hands and searched through the cupboards and the chest of drawers until he found the white-haired man's evening shirts. He put one on and stood for a moment in the center of the cabin, thinking. Then he gritted his teeth and heaved the fat man into a sitting position and took off the corpse's shirt and went to the porthole and took out his Beretta, held it against the small hole over the heart of the shirt and fired another bullet through the hole. Now there was a smoke smudge around the hole to give evidence of suicide. He dressed the corpse again in its shirt, wiped his Beretta thoroughly, pressed the fingers of the dead man's right hand all over it and finally fitted the gun into his hand with the index finger on the trigger.

After another pause in the middle of the room, he took Kidd's tuxedo down from its hook and dressed Kidd's body in it. Then he dragged the man across the floor to the porthole and, sweating with the effort, heaved him up and pushed him through.

He wiped the porthole for prints and paused again,

the hell was the damn' plane? He picked up a handful of dirt and threw it into the middle of the flowing column of ants. They hesitated and spilled over the walls of their road as the hurrying rear ranks behind crowded into them. Then the soldiers started frantically digging and carrying, and in a few minutes the highway was clear. The man took off his shoe and slapped it down hard across the moving column. There was another brief moment of confusion. The ants set upon the dead bodies and devoured them and the road was open again and the black river flowed on.

The man swore briefly in Afrikaans and pulled on his shoe. Black bastards. He would show them. Crouching and holding up an arm against the thorns, he stamped along the column of ants and out into the moonlight. That would give them something to think about.

And then he forgot the hatred he had for all black things and cocked his head towards the north. Thank God! He moved around the bush to get the flashlights and the packet of diamonds out of the toolboxes.

A mile away in the low bush the big iron ear of the sound-detector had already stopped searching, and the operator who had been softly calling the range to the group of three men beside the Army truck now said: "Thirty miles. Speed one twenty. Height nine hundred."

Bond glanced at his watch. "Looks as if midnight at full moon is the rendezvous," he said. "He'll be about ten minutes late."

"Looks like it, sir," said the officer from the Freetown Garrison Force who was standing next to him. He turned to the third man. "Corporal, make certain there's no metal showing through the camouflage net. This moon'll pick up anything."

The truck was standing under cover of the low bush on a dirt track that ran across the plain in the direction of the village of Telebadou in French Guinea. That night they had started off from the hills as soon as the locator had picked up the sound of the dentist's motor-cycle on the parallel track. They had driven without

lights and they had stopped as soon as the motorcycle
had stopped and there was no longer protection from
the noise of its engine. They had put a camouflage net
over the truck and over the locator and the bulge of the
Bofors mounted beside it. Then they had waited, not
knowing what to expect—another motorcycle, a rider
on a horse, a jeep, an aeroplane?

Now they could hear the distant clatter in the sky.
Bond gave a short laugh. "Helicopter," he said.
"Nothing else makes that racket. Get ready to take the
net down when he lands. We may have to give him a
warning shot. Is the loud-hailer switched on?"

"Yes, sir," said the corporal at the locator. "And
he's coming in fast. You should be able to see him in a
minute. See those lights just come on, sir? Must be the
landing ground."

Bond glanced at the four thin shafts of light and then
he looked up again into the great African sky.

So here came the last of them, the last of the gang,
and yet the first. The man he'd taken a look at in Hatton Garden. The first of the Spangled Mob, the gang
that had rated so high in Washington. The only one, except the harmless, rather pitiful Shady Tree, he had not
yet had to kill or—he thought of the Pink Garter Saloon
and the two men from Detroit—almost kill. Not that he
had wanted to kill these people. The job M had given
him had only been to find out about them. But, one by
one, they had tried to kill him and his friends. Violence
had been their first resort, not their last. Violence and
cruelty were their only weapons. The two men in the
Chevrolet in Las Vegas who had shot at him and hit
Ernie Cureo. The two men in the Jaguar who had
bludgeoned Ernie and had been the first to draw guns
when it came to a fight. Seraffimo Spang, who had
started to torture him to death and had then tried to
shoot or run them down on the railway track. Wint and
Kidd, who had given Tingaling Bell the treatment, and
then Bond, and then Tiffany Case. And of the seven, he
had killed five—not because he had wanted to but
because somebody had had to. And he had had luck and

three good friends—Felix and Ernie and Tiffany.

And now here came the last of the mob. The man who had ordered his death and Tiffany's. The man who, according to M, had built up the traffic in diamonds, organised the pipe line and run it ruthlessly and efficiently through the years.

On the telephone to Boscombe Down M had been brief and his voice had had an edge to it. He had reached Bond on the Air Ministry line a few minutes before the Canberra was to take off for Freetown. Bond had taken the call in the Station Commander's office with the scream of the Canberra testing her jets on the background.

"Glad you got back all right."

"Thank you, sir."

"What's this in the evening papers about a double killing on the *Queen Elizabeth*?" There was more than suspicion in M's voice.

"They were the two killers from the gang, sir. Travelling as Winter and Kitteridge. My steward told me they were supposed to have had a row over cards."

"Do you think your steward was right?"

"It sounds possible, sir."

There was a pause. "Do the police think so?"

"I haven't seen any of them, sir."

"I'll talk to Vallance."

"Yes, sir," said Bond. He knew that this was M's way of saying that if Bond had killed the men, M would make sure that neither Bond nor the Service was mentioned at the inquest.

"Anyway," said M, "they were small people. This man Jack Spang, or Rufus Saye, or A B C, or whatever he calls himself—I want you to get him. As far as I can make out he's going back down the pipe line. Sealing it off. Probably killing as he goes. The end of the line is this dentist. Try and get them both. I've had 2804 working alongside the dentist for the last week or so, and Freetown thinks they've got the local picture clear enough. But I want to close this case and get you back on your proper job. This has been a messy business. Never liked it from the first. More luck than good management that we've got as far as we have.''

"Yes, sir," said Bond.

"What about this Case girl?" said M. "I've talked to Vallance, and he doesn't want to prosecute unless you feel strongly about it."

Was M's voice a shade too indifferent?

Bond tried to prevent his answer being too hasty. "She's been a great help, sir," he said—casually, he hoped. "Perhaps we could decide when I've put in my final report."

"Where is she now?"

The black receiver was getting slippery in Bond's hand. "She's on her way to London in a Daimler hire, sir. I'm putting her up in my flat temporarily. In the spare room, that is. I've a very good housekeeper. She'll look after her until I get back. I'm sure she'll be all right, sir." Bond took out a handkerchief and wiped his face.

"I'm sure," said M. There was an absence of irony in his voice. "All right then. Well, best of luck." There was a pause. "Look after yourself. And"—the voice at the other end was suddenly gruff—"don't think I'm not pleased with the way things have gone so far. Exceeded your brief, of course, but you seem to have stood up to these people very well. Goodbye, James."

"Goodbye, sir."

Bond looked up into the spangled sky and thought of M, and of Tiffany, and hoped that this would really be the end, and that it would be quick and easy, and that he would soon be home again.

The smuggler from the mines stood and waited, holding the fourth flashlight in his hand. There it was. Coming right across the moon. Hell of a noise as usual. That was another risk he'd be glad to get away from.

Down it came, and now it was hovering twenty feet above his head. The hand came out and flashed A, and the man on the ground winked back the B and the C.

Then the rotor blades flattened, and softly the great iron insect sank to the ground.

The dust settled. The diamond smuggler took his hand away from his eyes and watched the pilot climb down his small ladder to the ground. He was wearing a flying helmet and goggles. Unusual. And he looked too tall to be the German. The dentist's spine tingled. Who was this? He walked slowly to meet him.

"Got the stuff?" Two cold eyes under straight black brows looked sharply out from behind the goggles. They were hidden as the man's head moved and the moon caught the glass. Now they were just two round blazing white circles in the middle of the shiny black leather helmet.

"Yes," said the man from the mines nervously. "But where's the German?"

"He won't be coming again." The two white circles stared blindly at the smuggler. "I am A B C. I am closing down the pipe line."

It was an American voice, hard and coarse and final.

"Oh."

Automatically the smuggler's hand went inside his shirt. He took out the moist packet and held it out as if it were some kind of peace offering. Like the scorpion, a month earlier, he sensed the raised stone above him.

"Give me a hand with the gas."

It was the voice of an overseer giving an order to a coolie, but the smuggler stepped quickly forward to obey it.

They worked in silence. Then it was finished and they were on the ground again. The dentist had been thinking desperately. He summoned up the voice of an equal partner, the voice of someone who knew what the score was and had equal control of the situation.

He peered into the patch of indigo blackness where the pilot stood with his hand on the ladder.

'I've been thinking things over and I'm afraid—'

And then the voice stopped and the lips drew back from the teeth in the slack mouth and the mouth began to make a noise between a snarl and a scream.

The gun in the pilot's hand stammered three times. The dentist said "Oh," in an obsequious voice. He pitched backwards into the dust, gave one heave and lay still.

"Don't move!" The clanging voice came over the plain with the screeching echo of the amplifier. "You're covered." There was the sound of an engine starting up.

The pilot didn't wait. He leaped for the ladder. The door of the cockpit slammed and there was the whirr of the self-starter. The engine roared and the rotor blades swung and slowly gathered speed until they were two whirlpools of silver. Then there was a jerk and the helicopter was in the air, climbing vertically into the sky.

Down among the low bush the truck stopped with a jerk, and Bond jumped for the iron saddle of the Bofors.

"Up, Corporal!" he snapped to the man at the elevation lever. He bent his eyes to the grid-sight as the muzzle rose towards the moon. He reached to pull the firing selector lever off "Safe" and put it on "Single Fire." "And left ten."

"I'll keep feeding you tracer." The officer beside Bond had two racks of five yellow-painted shells in his hand.

Bond's feet settled into the trigger pedals and now he had the helicopter in the centre of the grid. "Steady," he said quietly.

Boompa.

The tracer swung lazily up into the sky just below the speed of sound.

Low and left.

The corporal delicately twisted the two levers.

Boompa.

The tracer curved away high over the rising plane. Bond reached forward and pulled the selector lever to "Auto Fire." The movement of his hand was reluctant. Now it would be certain death. He was going to have to do it again.

Boompa—boompa—boompa.

The red fire sprayed across the sky. Still the helicopter went on rising towards the moon, and now it was veering away to the north.

Boompa—boompa.

There was a flash of yellow light near the tail rotor, and they heard the distant sound of an explosion.

"Got him," said the officer. He picked up a pair of nightglasses. "Tail rotor's gone," he said. And then, excitedly: "Christ! It looks as if the whole cabin's going round with the main rotor. Pilot must be getting hell."

"Any more?" said Bond, holding the whirring machine in his sights.

"No, sir," said the officer. "Like to get him alive if we can. But it looks as if—yes, he's out of control now. Coming down in great swoops. Must be something wrong with the main rotor blades. There he goes."

Bond raised his head from the grid sight and squinted his eyes against the blazing moon.

Yes. There he was. Only about a thousand feet up now, the engine roaring and the great blades whirling uselessly as the tangle of metal pitched and yawed down the sky in long drunken arcs.

Jack Spang. The man who had ordered Bond's death. Who had ordered Tiffany's death. The man Bond had only once seen for a few minutes in an overheated room in Hatton Garden. Mr. Rufus B. Saye of the House of Diamonds, Vice-President for Europe. The man who played golf at Sunningdale and visited Paris once a month. "Model citizen," M had called him. Mr. Spang of the Spangled Mob who had just killed a man—the last of how many?

Bond could imagine the scene in the narrow cockpit, the big man bracing himself with one hand and wrenching frantically at the controls with the other as he watched the needle of the altimeter dip down through the hundreds. And there would be the red glare of terror in the eyes, and the £100,000 pocketful of diamonds would be just so much deadweight and the gun which had been a strong right arm since boyhood would be no comfort.

"He's coming right back to the bush," shouted the corporal above the clatter in the sky.

"He's a goner now," said the captain, half to himself.

They watched the last bucketing lurches, and then they held their breath as the aircraft, seesawing wildly, gave a final dip and, as if the bush had been its enemy, made an angry dive through a twenty-yard curve and hurled itself and the threshing rotors into the bank of thorns.

Before the echoes of the crash had died, there came a hollow boom out of the heart of the bush followed by a jagged ball of flame that grew and billowed up into the air so that the moon was dimmed and the whole plain was bathed in an orange glow.

The captain was the first to speak.

"Ouch!" he said with feeling. He slowly lowered his nightglasses and turned to Bond. "Well, sir," he said resignedly, "that's just about that. 'Fraid it's going to be morning before we can get anywhere near that lot. And then it's going to be hours more before we can start raking about in it. And this is going to bring the French frontier guards along at the gallop. Luckily, we're on pretty good terms with them, but the Governor's going to have a fine time arguing the toss with Dakar." The officer saw a vista of excruciating paperwork ahead. The prospect made him more tired than he already was. He was matter of fact. He had had enough for one day. "Mind if we get a bit of shut-eye, sir?"

"Go ahead," said Bond. He looked at his watch. "Better get under the truck. Sun'll be coming up in about four hours. Not feeling tired myself. I'll keep an eye out in case the fire looks like spreading."

The officer gave a curious glance at this quiet, enigmatic man who had suddenly arrived in the Protectorate amidst a flurry of "Absolute Priority" signals. If ever a man needed sleep . . . But all this had nothing to do with Freetown. London stuff. "Thanks, sir," he said, and jumped down from the truck.

Bond slowly took his feet off the trigger-pedals and

sat back in the iron saddle. Automatically, with his eyes still on the leaping flames, his hands felt in the pockets of the faded khaki bush-shirt, borrowed from the Garrison C.O., for his lighter and cigarettes and he took out a cigarette and lit it.

So this was the end of the diamond pipe line. The last page in the file. He took a deep lungful of smoke and let it out in a long, quiet sigh. Six corpses to zero. Game, set, and match.

Bond put up a hand and drew it across his dripping forehead. He pushed back the damp comma of hair above the right eyebrow, and the red blaze lit up the hard lean face and flickered in the tired eyes.

So this great red full stop marked the end of the Spangled Mob and the end of their fabulous traffic in diamonds. But not the end of the diamonds that were baking at the heart of the fire. They would survive and move off again across the world, indestructible, as permanent as death.

And Bond suddenly remembered the eyes of the corpse which had once had a Blood Group F. They had been wrong. Death is forever. But so are diamonds.

Bond dropped down off the truck and started walking slowly towards the leaping fire. He smiled grimly to himself. All this business about death and diamonds was too solemn. For Bond it was just the end of another job. Another job for which the wry phrase of Tiffany Case might be the epitaph. He could see the passionate, ironic mouth saying the words:

"It reads better than it lives."